DAN FOUND
THE TWO STARLETS LUXURIATING
IN THE HEAT OF THE JACUZZI.

He refilled their champagne glasses and prayed Cici Connors would agree to star in his new series . . .

"It's really tempting, Danny." Cici leaned back against the lip of the tub and pouted a bit. "I might do it if I could bring myself to forgive you for being so nasty to me . . ."

Dan bit his tongue. He needed Cici to get the backing for the series and she knew it.

Dee Dee reached out and took her friend's arm. "Don't make the man suffer, darling. Tell him you'll do it."

"Well . . ." Cici wiggled a little and stretched. "I guess I might sign, Danny . . . but only if you do me a big favor in return."

He drew a great sigh of relief. "Sure, Cici. Anything."

"Take off your clothes and hop in here . . ."

Harold Robbins

Presents:

Station Break

A Novel by
John Fischer

PUBLISHED BY POCKET BOOKS NEW YORK

This novel is a work of fiction. Names, characters, places and incidents are either the product of the author's imagination or are used fictitiously. Any resemblance to actual events or locales or persons, living or dead, is entirely coincidental.

Another *Original* publication of POCKET BOOKS

POCKET BOOKS, a division of Simon & Schuster, Inc.
1230 Avenue of the Americas, New York, N.Y. 10020

Copyright © 1987 by Pocket Books,
a division of Simon & Schuster, Inc.
Cover photo copyright © 1987 Magic Image Studio, Ltd.

ISBN: 0-671-63196-9

First Pocket Books printing October 1987

10 9 8 7 6 5 4 3 2 1

POCKET and colophon are trademarks of
Simon & Schuster, Inc.

HAROLD ROBBINS PRESENTS is a trademark of
Harold Robbins.

Printed in the U.S.A.

FOR RUEL AND JOANNE

Sine qua non

_____ Prologue

Four Years Ago
Los Angeles, California

"Good morning, Mr. Courtney."

José Hernandez, the Global Radio Network security guard, raised his white-gloved hand as Dan Courtney pulled up to the studio's ornate wrought-iron gate. José had worked at the studio for the past eight years. He knew most of the producers in Los Angeles and Dan was one of his favorites.

Today Dan was wearing a designer sweatsuit in the exact shade of blue as his eyes. With his light blond hair and tanned complexion, he was as handsome as the young turks starring in GRN's afternoon soaps. Most men in Southern California worked at maintaining a young, athletic appearance. There were tanning salons for busy executives who didn't have time to court the actual rays of the sun, exercise programs especially formulated for the business tycoon who spent most of his time behind a desk. Many of Dan's show business colleagues had gone off for what they called a vacation and had come back looking ten years younger. Dan knew they'd spent the entire time in an exclusive resort-type hospital that specialized in plastic surgery for businessmen who needed to look young and fit. Luckily, Dan had no need for that sort of thing. He had inherited a well-muscled body that needed no help from the fitness experts, even though he was only four years short of the big four-o. The girl who came to relieve José for his lunch break claimed that Dan

Courtney was the spitting image of a younger Robert Redford, and it was common knowledge that every floater in the secretarial pool was dying to be assigned to him, even on a temporary basis.

Dan smiled as José reached out to slap a parking sticker on the corner of his windshield.

"Did you notice if Ned Richards came in yet, José?"

José nodded. He knew that Dan was doing another Big Green variety special and he'd heard all the gossip from his vantage point at the studio gates. Dan was concerned about his star, a not-so-reformed drunk who habitually arrived late.

"His limo drove through the gates at eight-seventeen and the driver said they were going directly to makeup. Mr. Richards looked just fine, if you know what I mean."

"That's good news, José." Dan smiled and José noticed that he looked relieved. There was big trouble on the set but Dan was known in the trade as a miracle worker.

"You're all set, Mr. Courtney."

José stepped to the side and patted the fender of Dan's 1973 Chevrolet Impala. At GRN, where even the studio grips owned prestige cars, Dan's old station wagon was a real oddity. Some people said it was reverse snobbery but José knew it was a protest against the show business life-style. Other GRN producers drove Jaguars and Ferraris in designer colors to match their wardrobes. Dan preferred to impress people with his talent, not with his car.

As José stepped clear and waved him on, Dan dropped the powerful V8 engine into neutral and leaned out the window. "Today's the big day, isn't it, José?"

"How's that, Mr. Courtney?" José was thoroughly puzzled.

"I'm talking about the science fair. At Hollywood High."

"That's right, Mr. Courtney!" José's polite smile turned into an earsplitting grin. He'd forgotten telling Dan about his son's science project. Roberto had earned the highest honors in science and math. When José and his wife had first become American citizens, nine years ago, both of them had insisted that the children avoid bilingual classes. Of course they still spoke Spanish occasionally at home but it was now their second language.

"Be sure to congratulate Roberto for me."

"Thank you, Mr. Courtney."

José waved the station wagon through the gate. Imagine a big producer like Mr. Courtney remembering something like that!

Dan turned left at the writers' building and slowed to let three women dash across the street. It was easy for an insider to tell the secretaries from the actresses. Secretaries arrived at the studio dressed in the height of fashion, with manicured nails, carefully styled hair, and perfect makeup. Actresses came through the gates in old jeans and sweatshirts, hair tucked up in a scarf on their way to wardrobe and makeup. It wasn't unusual for a visitor touring the studio to ask a secretary for an autograph and pass right by a famous actress, mistaking her for a member of the cleaning crew.

Dan pulled into the producers' lot and parked in his space between a red Ferrari and a silver Porsche with a monogrammed sun cover. Names were lettered in black on the concrete retainers that marked off the spaces. His space had read ANN CALLAWAY for the past eight months. As Dan got out of his station wagon, he saw that the studio maintenance department had finally gotten around to painting in DAN COURTNEY. It was not a good omen. Most Big Green employees believed that the day your name appeared on your parking spot, you were slated to be fired.

Even though it was only eight-thirty in the morning, the day promised to be a scorcher, and Dan kept to the shady side of the street as he headed for the commissary. His designer sweatsuit was too heavy for such a day, but Dan knew he'd be spending the entire day in the sound studio where the air conditioning was set on high to counteract the hot lights. Most Big Green employees kept a sweater or jacket in the office. There was often a forty-degree difference between the outside temperature and the frigid air on the set.

The takeout window at the commissary was open and Dan ordered a sweet roll and a cup of coffee to go. When he'd left his house in Brentwood, his wife had been sleeping. She had spent the entire night studying for her bar exam this afternoon. Dan felt a little guilty about not being with Joanna at this important time in her life but there was no way he could take the day off. Naturally he'd arranged for a celebration dinner tonight, and a huge bouquet of roses would be waiting for her at the house when she got back from her test. He'd also told his secretary to transfer Joanna's calls directly to the set, even if he was in the middle of shooting. That might very well get him into trouble with the big boys but he wanted Joanna to know that he was behind her, one hundred percent.

There were times when Dan was amazed at his wife's persistence. He'd watched her spend hours on her assignments until she was utterly exhausted. Passing the bar meant everything to Joanna. She was bound and determined to finish the law degree she'd started before their marriage. If she passed, and Dan was positive she would, it would be a great relief for both of them. Then there would be no more excuses about being too tired to socialize or not having the time to spend an evening with him. Dan knew he was being unfair but he'd begun to resent the sight of Joanna with her pretty nose buried in a thick book of legal statutes. He wanted his wife back.

Dan knew Joanna's sudden interest in a legal career stemmed from the fact they'd been unsuccessfully trying for a baby the past five years. After the first year, Joanna had consulted a fertility specialist and gone through the whole rigamarole with carefully kept temperature charts but nothing had happened. Then she'd checked into the hospital and gone through a three-day battery of tests. The results were positive. As far as the doctors were concerned, Joanna was fertile. They had told her to go home, relax, and keep trying.

There had been a series of frantic calls back and forth, from Joanna at home to Dan at the studio.

"I think I'm ovulating. Can you come home?"

"Now?"

"Yes, now!"

Dan had driven home at breakneck speeds at least four times a month to make love to his wife. It might have put a terrible strain on their marriage if both of them hadn't seen the inherent humor in the situation. Still, nothing had happened. Dan had even gone all out for the cause, refraining from touching Joanna for two long weeks at her doctor's advice, then taking her on a vacation to Hawaii where they had spent the entire weekend in bed making up for lost time.

Joanna had gone from expert to expert. One doctor had told her that spontaneity was the key, and she had seduced him in the kitchen on top of the counter, in the shower where both of them got thoroughly waterlogged, and once, in the backseat of the station wagon, like two guilty teenagers. The net result was the same.

Dan had tried to comfort his wife but Joanna's disappointment had run deep. Dan had wanted children, too, but he'd refused to keep the appointments with the specialist that Joanna had made for him, claiming he didn't have time for sperm tests and examinations. Perhaps, he now admitted to himself, he had been afraid of the results.

"Hey, Dan! How's it going?"

"Fine, Bill." Dan quickly put a smile on his face as he waved to Bill Bryant, a character actor he'd used in his last special. Bill was in full costume with a white powdered wig and colonial garb. He was sitting at a table with two extras in spacesuits and an actress with a parasol and a gay-nineties bustle.

Dan picked up his order in a paper bag and took a shortcut between sound stages nineteen and twenty-three to emerge on New York Street. The three-story brownstone false fronts had been refaced during the night to resemble bombed-out buildings in wartime London. Dan stepped over an electrical cable, turned the corner, and found himself in what resembled Saigon. The ordinary little street in Anytown, U.S.A., with its generic shops had been re-dressed for Big Green's newest war drama, all the signs relettered in Vietnamese. Another shortcut through the small-town park with its cannon and bandstand and he was at the door to sound stage nine.

Most tourists were disappointed when they toured GRN's facilities. They expected glamour and found that a working studio was more like a factory. The huge sound stages were heavily insulated warehouse-type buildings, large enough to hold dozens of sets. Dan's special required five standing sets.

Dan's garden set with its rolling lawn and blooming rose arbor required constant care from the greenmen. A large share of the greenery was artificial but the roses were real and had to be replaced frequently under the hot lights. The huge trees in massive tubs were sprayed with green dye for the numbers that took place in the summer, and re-dressed in autumn colors for the fall. The prop department brought in sacks of multicolored plastic leaves and scattered them over the lawn so Ned Richards could lean on a rake and look authentic.

The penthouse set had a large ornate balcony with two skyline backdrops, one for day and one for night. Next to it was the roadside diner set used in three of the sketches, and the Las Vegas casino set, complete with gambling tables, where two of the singers performed. The fifth set was a forties ballroom and Ned Richards used it to introduce the dance numbers.

His hand on the knob, Dan took a deep breath. He felt like his biblical predecessor, braving the lion's den. Naturally there had been problems with the other four specials he'd done for Big Green, but they'd been child's play compared to his current assignment.

Ned had been drinking between takes and it showed. His performance was sloppy and he fluffed his lines more often than not. This necessitated retake after retake and the budget couldn't handle it. One of Dan's responsibilities as executive producer was to keep his star in line.

Dan knew there was nothing to be gained by discussing the problem with the network again. After the second day of shooting, he'd gone straight to the tower, the thirty-story building in the center of the lot which housed GRN's high-powered executives, to request a more reliable star. The network officials had been sympathetic but unmoving. Dan would just have to do the best he could. Their hands were tied. Ned Richards had carved his niche into the GRN power structure last year by marrying the network president's sister. Ralph Barton, the president, had not only agreed to cast Ned in the starring role, he had personally assured his new brother-in-law that his position was secure.

As he stood there gathering the necessary energy, Dan ticked Ned's faults off on his fingers. He was late for his calls, found constant fault with his costumes, and objected to his lines. He demanded his own personal makeup man, insulting the woman assigned to him and sending her off in tears. He insisted on a two-hour lunch break and wouldn't work a minute past one o'clock even if they were in the middle of a scene. He refused to rehearse, claiming that good acting was a matter of being in the right mindset. He was constantly chasing the young women on the set and having them fired if they didn't cooperate. He had no respect for the talent that surrounded him and no regard for the show's budget. As Ralph Barton's golden boy, Ned knew that he could do no wrong. And to make matters even more difficult, he had started drinking again. Dan's job was to cajole Ned Richards into giving an acceptable performance.

Dan squared his shoulders; he'd run out of fingers. He opened the door to the usual bedlam. Stand-ins for the singers were positioned under the hot lights while the spots were set and the engineers checked out the readings. Telephones were ringing, carpenters were hammering, and various personnel carrying clipboards rushed about shouting orders. Dan stepped inside and shut the door quietly behind him. If he could find a deserted corner without being spotted, he might be able to grab five precious minutes for breakfast.

The first time Dan had seen the inside of a sound stage, at the age of sixteen, he'd been tremendously disappointed. His parents had toured a then-famous studio and Dan had been looking forward to the glamour and the excitement of watching a television program in the making. The studio guide, a pretty girl in a bright red uniform, had taken them to a sound stage at the back of the lot. Dan had half expected an immaculate modern building with wall-to-wall carpeting and crystal chandeliers but what he'd seen was a huge, barnlike building with corrugated metal sides and sliding doors big enough to accommodate trucks. Painted partitions were propped up to simulate the inside walls of a house. A circular staircase ended abruptly seven steps up and the second-story landing was really on the ground level, next to the fake-looking garden. All the rooms were a lot smaller than Dan had expected but the guide had told them that the camera would provide the perspective so everything would appear to be the proper scale on the screen.

Young Dan had been amazed when he walked through the shallow rooms and noticed that there were no ceilings. The guide had laughed and explained that it wouldn't show on the screen and the top of the set was always left open for lights. The kitchen had been another shock when Dan had discovered that the metal cupboards were really a solid sheet of wood. The guide had told him that since no one opened the cupboards over the sink in the script, there was no need for the real thing.

Dan had nodded and told her that he understood cost economy. But the whole set looked fake. Wouldn't people be able to tell? No, the lighting and the camera would make the set appear totally realistic. Dan would see when he watched the program at home. It was what they called studio magic.

The tour group had been scheduled to watch some actual filming of a scene and Dan and his parents had perched on folding chairs, watching what had seemed like bedlam.

Lights had been blinking on and off, bells had been ringing, and buzzers had been buzzing. People had rushed around shouting at each other and carrying things, stepping over the heavy black electrical cables and giving orders over walkie-talkies. Then the director had appeared, a klaxon horn had sounded, and suddenly it had been very quiet. The director had been dressed in blue jeans and a denim workshirt. No ascot. No pipe. He hadn't shown any of the dashing, artistic mannerisms that Dan had imagined.

As the cast had assembled, Dan had held his breath. His favorite television star, Melody Harmon, had the lead in this television drama. When Miss Harmon had taken her place, Dan had almost failed to recognize her. The object of his adolescent fantasies had been dressed in an old bathrobe with makeup stains around the collar. Even worse, her long blond hair had somehow turned into an ugly brown frizz. Dan had watched with a sinking heart as the hairdresser rushed onto the set carrying a long blond wig.

It hadn't helped when Miss Harmon had removed the grubby robe to reveal her lovely costume. Dan's illusions had been thoroughly shattered. He'd thought he'd never recover, but after a few moments of watching the director in action, an overwhelming interest overshadowed his disappointment.

Nothing seemed to be shot chronologically. Miss Harmon's wedding scene had been shot first, followed by the scene that showed her first meeting with her husband-to-be. After a whispered conversation with the guide, Dan had learned that the whole drama would be shot out of sequence. Scenes containing the same bit player, like the actor who played Miss Harmon's brother, were shot together to save money. That way the studio only had to pay the actor for one day's work.

After the two scenes had been shot, six times, the crew had broken for lunch. Dan had asked questions until the guide was worn to a frazzle. How did the director keep it all straight when he was shooting scenes out of sequence? Why had someone put up a card that read *HOT* and cordoned off the set with tape? How about the board Dan had seen, listing second-unit assignments? What were they? And then, before Dan had been able to ask any more questions, the guide had taken them back to the bus.

Many months later, when Dan had watched the

Melody Harmon drama, his future had been decided. The guide had been right. Everything had looked very real. Dan had gone through the next decade with a single purpose in mind. He was determined to be part of that studio magic.

Now Dan looked around him, comparing past and present. There had been tremendous technological advances but the basics hadn't changed at all. The sound stage was still a barn and the studio was a factory whose only product was illusion. Today his primary task was to create the illusion that Ned Richards was a competent actor instead of the no-talent, egomaniac drunk he really was.

Dan glanced at his watch and stepped out into the noise. Over fifty people were dashing here and there, shouting to each other, pushing dollies, and carrying things. It looked like total confusion but insiders like Dan knew that every move had been carefully planned. Everyone had a job to do and, on a good shoot, they did it with superb efficiency, carefully sidestepping anyone in the way. The Ned Richards special was a good shoot with the exception of Ned Richards.

For one brief moment, Dan went unnoticed. Then Paul Feldman spotted him. Paul was the best art director in the business, a short man, painfully thin, with so much nervous energy he always seemed on the verge of a massive breakdown.

"Jesus, Dan! I'm glad you're here!" Paul rushed up to him waving a memo. "This just came in from the tower. They want us to change the goddamn sike again!"

"Take it easy, Paul." Dan took the memo and scanned it quickly. Paul was clearly upset and Dan couldn't blame him. The color on the cycloramic backdrop had been changed three times in the past week. The first time Ned Richards had demanded a color more complimentary to his skin tone. The second complaint had come from the costume department. The color Richards had chosen meant that all the third-act costumes had to be redone. Just when Paul had found a color that pleased both Ned and the costume designer, the engineering department had objected: the new color values were impossible to balance. A third color was selected and the problem was solved . . . until this morning's urgent memo from administration.

Dan handed the memo back to Paul. "Okay, Paul. Make it the color they want it. I just wish I knew why they changed their minds."

Paul popped another antacid pill into his mouth and chewed as he scribbled a note. He looked up and shrugged. "I heard it was the sponsor this time. Something about the new color being too close to Pepsi blue . . ."

Dan shook his head and walked away. The sike color was the least of his problems. They were doing the chorus line segment today and Coral Connors, the net rep's girlfriend, was driving the dance director crazy with her demands. Cici, as she preferred to be called, was upset she wasn't a featured dancer. Both Dan and the dance director knew the only reason Cici had been cast in the first place was to keep the net rep happy.

"Dan? We have a little misunderstanding here!"

Lew Abrams, the line producer, hailed Dan from the partially completed garden set. It was in the farthest corner of the sound stage and, as Dan stepped over cables and made his way past several dancers who were using a wooden beam nailed against the back wall as a barre, he noticed that all sounds of construction had stopped. The huge sound stage was unnaturally silent without the constant hammering of the carpenters.

Dan found Lew leaning against the gazebo that had been erected in the center of the set. A bucket of paint, open and probably drying out in the heat from the lights, was at his feet. A paintbrush covered with paint was lying on the roof of the gazebo and it looked as if the painter had stopped in midstroke. Lew was surrounded by a crowd of hostile grips while Jerry Niehoff, the local union representative, thumbed through a book of union regulations. Everyone seemed to be looking at Phil Bachman, Dan's assistant director. Phil, who had been nicknamed "Sunny" because of his constant smile, was uncharacteristically solemn. There was definitely trouble on the garden set.

"We're filing a formal protest." Jerry Niehoff turned to glower at Dan as he approached. "Your AD committed a deliberate breach of union rules!"

Dan felt the beginnings of panic. A union walkout would be a disaster.

"Okay, what happened?" Dan nodded to Jerry. "You go first."

"Your AD moved a cable and that amounts to a direct violation. I'm authorized by the union to pull my grips until this matter is settled to our satisfaction. A fine now or arbitration later, it's up to you!"

Dan thought fast. Jerry was dead right. No one but a union man was allowed to touch an electrical cable.

"All right." Dan turned to his assistant director. "How did it happen, Sunny?"

"One of the greenmen had a cart with three potted trees and he was headed straight for a cable. I just reached down and pushed it out of the way before he cut it in two."

"There you have it . . . an admitted violation!" Jerry jumped in again.

"Could I talk to you for a second, Jerry?" Dan interrupted him. "Just the two of us?"

Dan led the shop steward over to the side of the sound stage, away from the crowd of people who had gathered. Both men sat down in canvas director's chairs and Jerry pulled out a cigarette.

"Let me get this straight." Dan handed Jerry a book of matches with the studio imprint on the cover. "If Sunny hadn't picked up that cable, it would have been cut. That makes it an emergency situation, doesn't it?"

Jerry nodded. "Sure it was an emergency, but that doesn't change anything. Your AD still moved a cable. It's like I said before, Dan. You can pay the fine or take it to arbitration."

"We'll win on arbitration."

"Sure you will"—Jerry shrugged—"but you'll be without grips for the time it takes to get a federal arbitrator out here. That means a total shutdown of production for at least three days. The fine's only two grand. Personally, I think you'd be smart to pay it."

Dan didn't need a calculator to figure it out. Production costs were running over eighty thousand dollars a day.

"We'll pay the fine. How soon can we get back to work?"

Jerry stood up and blew two short blasts on the silver whistle he wore on a chain around his neck. The crowd of grips hurried back to their stations and picked up their tools.

"Fast enough for you?" Jerry grinned as he headed back toward the set.

Dan looked down and realized that he was still holding the takeout sack from the commissary. There was no hope that the coffee was still hot but, at this point, he badly needed a jolt of caffeine. Dan had just raised the container to his lips when Maxine Berringer, his costume designer, barreled across the floor to grab his arm. Maxine had adopted black as her color this year and she wore it in an astonishing variety of textures and styles. Today she was dressed in a sweeping black jersey dress with high-heeled black patent leather boots. Her waist-length silver hair was caught up in a ponytail and secured with a long fluttering black silk scarf.

"Really, Daniel. I just can't cope with these continual memos." Maxine tapped one ebony-tipped nail against the note on her clipboard. "Standards and practices objects to our chorus line costumes. They want something more modest."

"Okay, Maxine. Do what you can to keep them off our backs. Stuff some lace in the necklines or something."

Maxine frowned.

"Then you want me to ignore this other memo from production? They want more tits'n'ass."

"Okay, okay." Dan massaged the back of his neck with his fingers and sighed deeply. "Tell you what, Maxine. Cover the girls from the neck down . . . in Saran Wrap!"

Maxine was laughing as she walked away but Dan felt a tension headache coming on. Problems, nothing but problems. And here came another one.

Dan looked around but there was no place to hide. Cici Connors was waving frantically from the makeup tables and it would be a mistake to ignore her. Her boyfriend, Herb Gelson, was top dog at the network.

"Dan, darling . . ." Cici sashayed across the floor in her gold high-heeled sandals. She was wearing a see-through silk dressing gown over her chorus line costume and a feather boa was draped around her neck. Dan hadn't seen an outfit like that since Gloria Swanson in *Sunset Boulevard* on the late-late show.

"I'm so glad we have this chance to talk, Dan." Cici inched up so close Dan had trouble breathing. She smelled as if she'd taken a bath in Chanel No. 5.

"I was talking to Herbie just last night and we both feel the part I have isn't utilizing my full talents. How do you feel about that, Dan?"

Dan put a carefully thoughtful expression on his face and took a full minute to consider it. Then he nodded.

"You're absolutely right, Cici. Your full talents are definitely not being utilized."

"I knew you'd see it our way!" Cici put her hand on Dan's arm and squeezed affectionately. "That's just what I told Herbie last night. I said, 'Dan Courtney's the best in the business. He knows my part isn't right for me.' And then Herbie said that if I approached you directly and explained our little problem, you'd find some way of solving it."

"Yes, indeed." Dan nodded emphatically. He'd had about all he could take of Cici's machinations to enlarge her part. It was time to beat her at her own game. "I really don't think we could utilize your . . . uh . . . full talents without a showcase number. Do you agree, Cici?"

"A showcase number?" Cici looked stunned. "Oh, yes! I'd definitely need a showcase number."

"And wouldn't you say that something smaller would be an insult to your . . . uh . . . considerable talents?"

"Oh, yes. Very definitely. I couldn't settle for anything less."

Dan managed to look crestfallen. "I was afraid you'd feel that way but it's your decision and I respect that. I'm just sorry that you're leaving the show. It's been a real pleasure working with you."

Cici grabbed him with both hands. There was near panic on her face. "Leaving the show? Who said anything about leaving the show?"

"It's like this, Cici. . . ." Dan patted her hand in a very fatherly way. "I'm sure Herbie's mentioned that we're already over budget. And that means the kind of showcase you deserve is out of the question. Quite truthfully, Cici, I wouldn't dream of insulting you by asking you to stay on in that chorus line number. It just wouldn't be right."

Cici blinked and her eyes narrowed. "I . . . uh . . . I'd better talk to Herbie about this. I'll get back to you, Dan."

"Of course, Cici. You run right along and call him. And be sure to tell him that I'm very impressed with your talents."

As Cici dashed off to use the telephone by the makeup tables, Dan heard Jay Ginsberg, the unit manager, calling him. Jay was a continual bearer of bad news about the budget but Dan hurried over anyway. At least he knew what to expect.

Jay shook his head dolefully and Dan was certain he'd been a funeral director in a former lifetime. "Bad news, Dan. We're running eleven and a half percent over budget."

"That's good news, Jay. We would have been fifteen percent over if Cici had insisted on that showcase."

"What showcase?"

"Never mind, Jay. Just a little humor."

"This is not the time for levity, Dan. You know Big Green's policy. Overruns are limited to a strict ten percent. We're going to have to cut back somewhere."

Dan glanced at his watch. They were shooting in less than an hour and he didn't have time for a long discussion about the budget. "Look, Jay, programming is screaming for more production values. They want to see glitz up there on the screen and that costs."

Jay nodded. "That's all very well and good, Dan, but we've got to shave off one and a half percent. The word came down this morning."

"Okay, Jay. We'll cut down to the bare bones on our animation budget. That'll give the tower their extra one and a half percent."

"Sounds good, Dan. I told them you'd listen to reason."

Dan grinned and turned away but Jay grabbed his arm again.

"Wait a second, Dan. Nothing in the script calls for animation. We don't *have* an animation budget!"

"I know that. And now you know that. The whole question is, does the tower know that? Go on up there and tell them we're ditching every scrap of animation to demonstrate our concerned effort to keep within our budget. Then show them some numbers on animation costs, point out all the money they'll save by cutting those numbers, and you'll be a hero."

Jay took a moment to think it over, then nodded. "You know, that might just work. I'll try it, Dan. Thanks a lot."

"Mr. Courtney?" One of the production assistants buttonholed Dan as he was about to dump his cold coffee in the green metal dumpster that sat inside the sound stage, next to the huge sliding door. "I sent a runner out to get Mr. Richards ten minutes ago, but he still hasn't shown. And I called his trailer but there's no answer."

"I'll take care of it, Sheila. Which runner did you send?"

"Alice. She hasn't come back either."

Dan took four aspirins from the giant thousand-count bottle that sat on the coffee cart and gulped them down with a swallow of cold coffee. He was doing a slow burn as he opened the door and stepped out into the bright sunlight. Ned Richards, that dipso has-been, was probably passed out cold. There was no way Alice Dolinski, who weighed less than ninety pounds dripping wet, could sober Ned up and drag him to the set.

The star's trailer was parked by the side of the sound stage in the shade of a temporary awning. Ned Richards had refused to accept one of the studio-owned Winnebagos, instead demanding the right to bring in his personal trailer so he could pocket an additional thousand a week in rental fees. The Winnebago stunt wasn't all that unusual and Dan might not have minded if Ned's performance had been up to par. As it was, Ned was earning eighty grand a week for sitting in his mobile living room, swilling studio booze.

As Dan approached the forty-foot land yacht, he heard the sounds of a scuffle inside. Alice's desperate voice carried clearly through the open window.

"Please, Mr. Richards . . . No!"

The door to the trailer flew open and Alice stumbled down the steps, clutching her torn blouse together. On her heels was Ned Richards, charging like a bull in heat. Alice was so panicked, she didn't even see Dan as she raced for the safety of the sound stage. Dan stepped neatly in front of Ned, blocking his attempt to follow her.

Ned glared at Dan and tried to push him out of the way. "I want her back here, Courtney. Now!"

Ned's breath was boozy and it was all Dan could do to keep the pleasant expression on his face. "Sorry, Ned. We need you on the set."

Ned drew himself up to his full height and gave a smug smile. "Get her back here, asshole."

As Dan stood his ground, he thought about all the concessions he'd been forced to make in the past five weeks. He'd shot around Ned when he was too drunk to work. He'd authorized the rental of Ned's damn trailer. He'd spent hours in the cutting room, trying to figure out ways to make Ned's lousy acting look good. He'd even changed the script countless times to satisfy Ned's crazy whims. Dan knew that if he didn't capitulate damned fast, he'd be committing professional suicide.

"Well?" Ned's smirk widened and Dan made up his mind.

It felt good to move, even though everything seemed to happen in slow motion. Dan's right arm drew back and then forward, connecting solidly with his star's front teeth. He watched three expensive porcelain caps drop out of Ned's bloodied mouth and saw the expression of disbelief on his star's face. Then Dan turned on his heel and walked toward the parking lot. His career at Big Green was over. There was no reason to stick around for the tower's inevitable memo.

1

Two Years Later
Minneapolis, Minnesota

TOM COURTNEY STEPPED onto the green and white city bus, dropped the fare he couldn't really afford into the hopper next to the driver, and made his way down the slushy aisle. A harassed-looking woman, wearing a maroon parka that made her look at least fifty pounds heavier than her actual weight, was blocking the way with a huge Dayton's shopping bag.

"Excuse me, ma'am. Why don't you sit down and I'll hand you your bag?"

The woman turned to look at Tom, obviously trying to decide if he was going to steal the Christmas presents she'd spent all afternoon buying. Tom gave her his best honest smile. Just then the bus lurched and the woman grabbed Tom's arm to keep from falling.

"Oh . . . yes. Thanks a lot." The woman handed Tom her bag, slid into the nearest seat, and smiled as he gave it back to her. "Christmas shopping's awful in weather like this but I won't have to put up with it next year. My husband's being transferred to California."

As soon as the woman was settled, Tom moved on to an unoccupied seat in the rear and sat down with a sigh. He knew he'd be more comfortable if he took off his bulky jacket but he didn't have far to go and it was a bother to put it back on again. He settled for loosening the zipper and stuffing his gloves in his pockets.

The window was covered with frost and Tom scraped a patch clear to watch the snow swirling outside. As the bus bumped along the icy streets, Tom found himself thinking of his older brother, who lived in Los Angeles.

Dan was probably swimming in his designer pool right now, relaxing in the ninety-degree heat.

People who saw Dan and Tom together had no idea that they were related. Dan looked like a native Californian. With his surfer-blond hair, tanned skin, and athletic physique, he belonged in Los Angeles. Tom had never been able to figure out where he belonged. Perhaps in a smoke-filled room dealing off the bottom of the deck in a high-stakes poker game. With his dark wiry hair, brown eyes, and prominent cheekbones, Tom's mother swore that he was a throwback to her great-grandfather's side of the family. And Tom's father had never tired of teasing her about her ancestors, that infamous branch of bearded horse thieves and riverboat gamblers that had surely gone into making up Tom's genes. From the tenth grade on, Tom had been plagued by a persistent five o'clock shadow. Rather than shave three times a day, he had let his beard grow in and he hadn't been clean-shaven since.

Although he was a handsome man, Tom sometimes looked as if he'd slept in a bus station overnight and the fact that he was naturally thin and had perpetual dark circles under his eyes, merely added to that illusion. Tom's girlfriends seemed to think that his slightly disreputable appearance was exciting. Though he'd been short on food and money on occasion, he'd never lacked female companionship. Dan hadn't either, but Tom was glad when his brother had settled down and married Joanna. He thoroughly approved of his sister-in-law.

Somehow, just thinking of his brother made Tom feel even colder. They'd had one of their classic shouting matches when they'd seen each other a little over two years ago, another rehash of their constant argument about artistic integrity. Tom had accused Dan of selling out to the establishment and prostituting his talent at

GRN. And Dan had called Tom a pigheaded fool for freezing his ass off in the icy north, existing at a ridiculously substandard level, and turning out "art for art's sake." The two brothers hadn't spoken since. It was only through Joanna's regular letters that Tom had learned of Dan's new business. And Tom thought that Dan had finally shown some sense when he'd walked out at GRN and started his own cable television company.

As the bus neared downtown and dusk approached, the Christmas decorations blinked on. There were huge red bells and garlands of lighted stars on wires over the city streets. It was the week before Christmas, the time of year when families made up their differences and celebrated the holidays together. The prospect of going out to California for Christmas was tempting, especially since this particular Minnesota winter had already set a new record for cold temperatures. Perhaps he should make the first gesture and call Dan.

The bus stopped at the corner and Tom pulled up the fur-lined hood on his war surplus army parka before he stepped out into the blowing snow. He was colder than he'd ever been before in his life. He'd landed a temporary job as a U.P.S. delivery man and he'd spent the entire day searching for addresses and trying to keep the old brown van from swerving on the icy streets. The driver's door had refused to close properly and the heater, turned up full blast, hadn't been able to cut the chill.

By the time Tom had walked to the downtown warehouse that had been converted into artists' lofts, his feet felt like blocks of ice. He clumped up the three flights of stairs and unlocked his door with numb fingers. As soon as he stepped inside, he stomped the snow off his old Red Wing boots and pulled them off, leaving them to drip slush on the rug by the door. Then he threw his parka over a rickety chair and hurried to the thermostat. The inside of his loft was almost as cold as the delivery van; he'd turned down the heat when he left at noon, to save on money.

There was no place like home. Tom lifted the cushions on his ratty, overstuffed couch to look for his slippers, a thrift-store bargain for only ten cents. Most of the loft was done in what Tom called Salvation Army chic.

Tom's loft covered an entire floor of a converted warehouse in downtown Minneapolis. It was little more than a bare rectangular room with high windows and plasterboard walls. Tom had rented it for the huge work space it provided. Scattered around the room were pieces of photographic and cinematic equipment, jury-rigged lights, a homemade animation stand, and an ancient Moviola that looked like the one Griffith had used to cut *Intolerance*. Tom had partitioned off a small sleeping alcove in the back by hanging six panels of hideous, orange-and-pink-flowered curtains, another thrift-store acquisition.

Tom got down on his knees to peer under the couch. There were a couple of empty film cans and a herd of dust balls but no slippers. Perhaps he'd left them in the bathroom?

Tom's bathroom was about the size of a voting booth and sported the smallest metal shower cubicle that Sears Roebuck manufactured. One of Tom's guests, an architectural student, claimed that Tom's bathroom was a perfect example of the term "water closet." The toilet, which the friend thought was salvaged from a kindergarten lavatory, sat up on a pedestal facing the door. Since Tom was over six feet tall, he had to open the door while seated on the john to keep from banging his knees.

Finding no slippers in the bathroom, Tom tried the kitchen, a long corridor running the length of the loft with a walk space barely three feet wide. The slippers were sitting on the drainboard. Tom had no idea how they had gotten there but he pulled them on and opened the 1951 model Norge refrigerator to see what he could salvage. There was no extra money for food this week and he wouldn't be paid for the U.P.S. job until Friday. Then he would have a little "snorkeling money," not enough to keep his head above water but at least he'd be able to breathe for a while longer.

Even though another small grant had come in from the National Endowment for the Arts, every cent had been spent on photographic supplies. Tom's rent was still overdue and he had received two threatening letters from the power company. Thanks to a Minnesota law, it was illegal for the power company to shut off service in the winter months, but the rent was another story. Tom had been avoiding his landlord since the beginning of November.

It was the wrong time of year to be evicted. The weatherman predicted a drop to thirty below tonight and the wind chill factor would bring that down to at least minus fifty. If he could magically squeeze inside the tiny freezer section of the Norge, which never got colder than zero, he'd be fifty degrees warmer than he'd be outside. The concept was mind-boggling.

The refrigerator was nearly full, not with food. Storing film in the Norge extended the "use before" date, and Tom was able to buy about-to-expire film at a considerable savings. In the summer the film stayed cool and in the winter the Norge kept that same film from freezing. Tom sighed as he moved the boxes and cans of film around to see if there was anything edible on the metal shelves.

A white bag on the center shelf looked promising. A sculptor who rented the floor below had brought him some leftover garlic bread and calamari alfredo from the Italian restaurant where she worked on the weekends. But after one look at the congealed mass, Tom returned it to the refrigerator, untouched. Perhaps he wasn't that hungry after all.

Tom grabbed an open box of stale Saltines on top of the refrigerator and hurried back to his editing station. His last film, an avant-garde study of snow and the people who moved it, had won critical acclaim from the artistic community, and last year the Walker Art Center had honored him by holding a premier screening of *Snow*. Unfortunately, rave reviews from the art world didn't pay the bills, and grants were few and far between. Tom relied on the "Employment Opportunities—Temporary" from the classified section of the *Minneapolis Tribune* for food and rent.

Tom had just begun to work when he felt a cold draft on his neck. It was coming from one of the high windows where the wind whistled through a crack between the frame and the glass. Tom got up on a stool to plug the crack, but gaffers tape, the multipurpose "fix-it" of his profession, refused to stick to the icy windowpane. Tom finally made do with a sheet of cardboard stapled to the window frame. It didn't stop the whistling sound but it cut off most of the draft.

A knock sounded at the door before Tom could sit down again. Should he or shouldn't he? Tom hesitated, his hand on the knob. It was either his landlord or Jim, from the first-floor loft, asking to use the bathroom again.

Tom decided to take a chance. The plumbing in Jim's place had been on the blink for the past three days and it would probably be at least another week before it was fixed. He unlocked the door and pulled it open.

"Hi, Tom."

"Jesus!"

Tom stepped back, much too surprised to greet his visitor properly. It was his brother, Dan. He gulped once and then remembered his manners. "Oh . . . Dan! Uh . . . would you like to come in?"

Tom stared at his brother's back as Dan walked over to the sofa and sat down. He didn't know what to expect.

Dan looked uncomfortable. "Let's clear the air, Tom. I've missed you."

Tom drew a deep breath of relief. He and Dan were alike in one way at least: both of them hated to apologize. But if Dan could do it, so could he.

"I was in the wrong. My reactions were all out of proportion."

"No, they weren't. The whole thing was my fault."

"You're wrong, Dan . . . It was mine!"

Dan started to laugh. "I think we'd better forget about apologizing. If we argue about whose fault it was, it could be another two years before I see you again."

"You've got a point." Tom laughed too. "So what brings you here, Dan? The balmy Minnesota weather?"

"Nope. I came to tell you what I've been doing the past two years. I finally got fed up with the establishment and quit Big Green."

"Joanna mentioned that. What happened?" Tom lit the last cigarette in his crumpled pack. He'd been saving it for later but it didn't matter. Dan's story was bound to be interesting and he'd enjoy it more with a good smoke.

The cigarette had long been reduced to ashes before Dan was through recounting his spectacular exit from Big Green. Tom accepted a Balkan Sobranie from Dan and lit it with his brother's gold Dunhill.

"So what are you doing now?"

"I scraped up the money to buy a small cable station but we can talk about that later. First, let's eat."

Dan snapped open his briefcase. Inside was a bottle of Porto Guedes '63, Tom's favorite port, and two glasses. Tom had never been able to afford port this fine and he hadn't tasted it since the last family dinner at Dan's house.

Dan's briefcase seemed to contain an unlimited supply of surprises. Tom's mouth watered as his brother brought out two Bosc pears, a package of thin crispy crackers, and a whole wheel of sharp cheddar. Next came a crock of Beluga caviar and a bottle of Dom Perignon that Dan explained was "for later." There was also a box of good cigars and a package of chocolate truffles.

Dan placed everything on the table and rummaged through his briefcase again. He looked up with a frown. "Damn! I forgot the cheese knife."

Tom jumped up. A knife was one thing he had. By the time he got back to the couch, Dan had opened the port.

Tom took a sip and tasted the cheese. Both were delicious. He tried not to make an absolute pig of himself as he wolfed down the pear and tried several crackers. The caviar was every bit as excellent as he had known it would be and the chocolate truffles were heaven. After several minutes of silent chewing, Tom looked up to find Dan watching him with some amusement.

"Low on food money?"

"You could say that." Tom poured himself a bit more port and lit one of the cigars. Then he leaned back against the couch cushions and sighed contentedly. "Tell me about this new cable station of yours."

"My lawyer and I were going over the F.C.C. regulations and we found a couple of important loopholes. I figure I can expand to the limit with the right kind of help. Are you willing to listen to a proposition?"

"Sure, I'll listen, but that's all I can do. Look around. You can see I'm not exactly rolling in cash right now."

Dan laughed. "I don't need money. The bank's already approved my master plan and I've got plenty of operating capital. I need your talent."

"For what? I don't know beans about television. Film's always been my baby."

"And what do you think they show on television? Live action went out with Uncle Miltie. Before I came here I stopped by the Walker and watched the print of *Snow* they have on file. You're a damned good film-maker, Tom. And that's why I'm offering you a job."

"Doing what?" Tom was interested in spite of himself.

"Doing exactly what you're doing right now with one important difference. You'll have a generous budget with state-of-the-art equipment and you can hire a bunch of assistants to do the donkey work. That'll free you up for the creative end."

Tom stared hard at his brother. "The whole thing sounds like a dream. Are you sure you're not already swacked on that port?"

"If you accept, you'll be head of my film division. I'll need a lot of product, Tom, because I just finished affiliating thirty-two other independents and I expect to triple that in the next two years. I'm talking network television, Tom. We're going to give the big three a run for their money!"

Tom was too rattled to say anything. He took another sip and shook his head.

"Well?" Dan grinned at him. "Aren't you going to ask me the salary?"

"How much?" Tom's voice came out in a croak.

"Eighty thousand to start, plus a third of my stock. But don't rush into it, Tom. Take your time and think it over."

Before Tom could react, the door opened and Tom's landlord barged in. His eyes went immediately to the coffee table.

"All right, Courtney. If you can afford a spread like that, you can damn well pay your back rent!"

Tom took one look at his landlord's face and turned to Dan. "I've thought it over and I accept."

"Smart move!" Dan popped the cork on the champagne and filled three glasses. Tom picked up one and handed it to his landlord.

"Drink up, Oscar. My brother will write you a check and you can rent this rattrap to somebody else. I just sold out . . . for eighty thou a year!"

2

A Year and a Half Later
Los Angeles, California

JOANNA COURTNEY LEFT the kitchen at a run, blond hair flying out in a cloud behind her as she raced to the office to catch her private business line. It was nine-fifteen in the morning and the big thermometer by the pool was already climbing past the eighty-degree mark. It would be another scorcher in Southern California. She looked down at the path again, just in time to sidestep a snail making its slow way across the path to the garden. All the rest of her neighbors had solved the problem by using snail poison but Joanna had refused. And this year Joanna was sure every snail on Cliffwood Drive had migrated to the Courtney garden. It took a sharp eye and a nimble foot to walk the flagstone path without stepping on at least one.

As a concession to the heat, Joanna was wearing cutoff jeans and a red law school T-shirt. The phone had rung before she'd had time to arrange her long hair in the twist she usually wore in hot weather. With her long, well-shaped legs, tanned from Saturday tennis at the club, and the faded T-shirt, which had shrunk from too many washings, she looked more like a teenager than the thirty-nine-year-old wife of a successful cable television producer. Since Joanna had no clients or court appearances scheduled for today, she didn't have to dress the part of a sophisticated, career-minded lawyer.

As Joanna unlocked the door to her office, she heard the answering machine pick up the call. Her recorded voice, sounding exceedingly professional, was saying,

You have reached the law offices of Joanna Courtney. Please leave your name and number at the sound of the tone and I will return your call. There was a beep and Alice Dolinski's voice, Dan's assistant at Empire Cable, came out of the speaker.

"Joanna? Are you there, Joanna?"

Joanna switched on the air-conditioner with one hand and reached for the phone with the other.

"Alice? I'm here."

"Thank God! I really hate to talk to machines. My lifeguide thinks it dates back to the third grade, when my teacher made us all sing a song for her tape recorder and I . . ."

"Did you hear from Dan this morning?" Joanna interrupted before Alice could go into a long discussion of her childhood memories. There was no one more efficient and hardworking than Alice and Joanna was very glad Dan had hired her as his administrative assistant after she'd been fired from Big Green over the Ned Richards incident, but Alice's current fascination with her lifeguide was ridiculous.

Alice had flung herself gung-ho into a fringy holistic therapy group led by a middle-aged, frizzy-haired woman who billed herself as a "guide to the inner life." She'd even attempted to look like her lifeguide, shearing off her lovely auburn hair and wearing it in a perm so tight, she had to comb it with a plastic pick that resembled a miniature pitchfork. She'd gone from a perfectly reasonable weight of a hundred and twenty pounds, well distributed on her five-foot, six-inch frame, to a little over a hundred pounds, the result of her lifeguide's health-food diet that was especially formulated to reduce stress and open the mind to higher consciousness. Neither Dan nor Joanna had been overly concerned at first. In the three years that Alice had been with Empire Cable, they'd watched her go through several phases, from a totally awesome

Valley Girl to a punk rocker, complete with technicolor wig and silver high-top tennis shoes. Alice's previous phases had lasted no more than a month but she'd been a lifeguide disciple for almost a year and there was no sign of the usual disenchantment.

"Dan? Oh yes, Joanna. That's the reason I called you. I just finished talking to him in Kansas City and he said to tell you he's catching the noon flight tomorrow. He's got two new affiliates wrapped up already and he thinks he can sign the third tonight so you can start the paperwork."

"It's already started, Alice. Anything else?"

"Not from Dan. He was really in a rush. But Tom signed Amalgamated Motors for a whole series of thirty-second spots. He says they want real commercials with a decent budget, not the our-operators-are-standing-by-to-take-your-order / not-available-in-any-stores type thing we've been doing."

"That's wonderful, Alice. Is Tom there now?"

"Yes, but he's out on the lot, taking a group of sponsors through our facilities. You were right about our new offices, Joanna. The sponsors are really impressed, especially when they catch a glimpse of a famous star. That stubborn husband of yours would never have moved if you hadn't pushed him."

"You're probably right about that."

Joanna smiled, bringing warmth to her classic Scandinavian face. Her parents were second-generation Americans from Swedish stock who had settled in Minnesota and she had the high cheekbones, light blond hair, and blue eyes of her ancestors. She had learned, from an early age on, that she could look imposing and regal if the occasion demanded. She had used her best imposing look when she'd negotiated Dan's rental contract with Tri-City studios and they'd bent over backward to please her. Empire Cable's sign had been placed in a prominent place at the main studio gate and Dan had been given several choice parking spots, close to his office suite. Both Dan and Alice had been impressed. Newcomers usually got the leftovers but their suite was large and spacious.

It had taken Joanna months to talk Dan into the move. He had argued that since he rented work space at various studios all over town, an office in a small trailer was all he needed. Joanna had agreed that the trailer was perfectly adequate; it just wasn't appropriate. In show biz, appearances were everything and Empire Cable had grown from the one small independent station Dan had originally purchased into a cable network of over a hundred affiliates. It would be much more impressive to have everything in one place, especially if that place was a studio with a prestigious address. Affiliates and sponsors wanted to see glamour.

Joanna had won her argument, the move had been accomplished, and now even Dan admitted that their new offices helped to generate more business.

"How about lunch, Joanna?" Alice sounded eager. "After all, the boss is away."

"I'm tied up today, Alice." Joanna smiled. She was having a precelebration lunch with Stan Lorman, Dan's anchorman on the "Nite News." The end of his complicated legal case was in sight. "How about Monday?"

"Monday's fine. We can eat right here at Tri-City's executive dining room. One of the secretaries told me they serve a great health food salad."

Joanna frowned slightly. She much preferred the commissary with its orange plastic tables. There everyone stood in line for their food, from grips and gaffers up to name actors in full costume. The executive dining room was reserved for boring MBAs in three-piece suits, but she could understand Alice's fascination with the building itself. It had been used as a location for several feature movies.

"Sure. Wherever you like, Alice."

"Great. I'll make reservations. Empire's approval for the executive dining room finally came through but I had to call every day for the past two weeks to get it. There's a real caste system here. The movie people are royalty, network television's landed gentry, and cable's somewhere down with the serfs."

"Are you sure you're not exaggerating?"

"Absolutely not. I had lunch with Evelyn from Joe Henry's office last week. They're working on a detective series for HBO. She told me she sent in an order for Kleenex and it was refused. Movie people get all the Kleenex they want, network television gets one box per office, and cable people have to buy their own."

"But why?"

"I don't know. That's just the way it is. The movie division doesn't mix with television and television doesn't mix with cable but I'm not complaining. I'm just glad to be in an office that has a bathroom. That reminds me . . . I'd better put in a call to central supply and see if cable people can get toilet paper."

Joanna was smiling as she hung up the phone and got out the master file for affiliate contracts. She was glad to help with some of Dan's legal work, but when he'd offered to put her on the staff at Empire, she'd turned him down. One of the reasons she'd gone back to law school was to have her own career. Working exclusively for her husband would be defeating that purpose. Instead, the moment she'd passed the bar exam, she'd signed on as a junior lawyer with Bartleman and Ekert in Beverly Hills. And the fees she'd generated in her two years with them had gone toward helping Dan build Empire into a thriving cable network.

She had finally gone into business for herself, six months ago, converting the Brentwood guest house into a spacious office. Floor-to-ceiling bookcases, filled with law books, lined two adjoining walls. A round conference table at one end of the room was surrounded by six leather swivel chairs, and a new, cherry-red Swedish fireplace had been installed in the corner to provide additional warmth for the rainy season. The floor was covered with a beautiful beige hand-woven carpet, Dan's office-warming present.

Joanna pulled Stan Lorman's file and leafed through it. Everything was in order. Then she leaned back in her chair and remembered the day she'd unlocked the door to her brand-new office and waited to greet her first private client.

Joanna's hands shook just a bit as she'd restacked the neat pile of papers on her antique rolltop desk and waited for Stan to arrive. At promptly ten, a knock sounded on the door and Joanna opened it to find herself face-to-face with Dan's "Nite News" anchorman.

Stan was even more handsome in the flesh than on screen delivering the evening news. He had dark brown hair, deep brown eyes, and the sort of open, guileless face that inspired trust, exactly the right sort of image for a newscaster. Most viewers felt that if Stan Lorman said it, it had to be true. He had one of the highest integrity ratings in the business.

"Mrs. Courtney? Thanks for seeing me on such short notice. I called Bartleman and Ekert and they referred me to you."

"Sit down, Stan." Joanna made a mental note to send Allen Bartleman some of his favorite brandy as a thank-you for the referral. "Since you work for my husband, I have to make sure there's no conflict of interest. Does your legal matter relate in any way to Empire Cable?"

Stan shook his head. "No, it's strictly personal. And I'd appreciate it if no one at Empire ever finds out about it."

Joanna nodded. "Whatever you tell me is completely

confidential, Stan. Dialogue between a client and a lawyer is privileged. Would you like a cup of coffee before we start?"

"I could use it."

Stan watched as Joanna poured him a cup of coffee, placed an ashtray on the coffee table, and took out one of her preprinted forms. "The first thing we have to do is fill out this information sheet." Joanna smiled at Stan to put him at ease. "Your full name, please?"

Stan hesitated. "Uh . . . I'm not sure how to answer that. Maybe I'd better explain before you write anything down."

Joanna put down her pen and gave Stan her full attention. She had expected her first private case to be a routine matter; she'd never heard of a client who couldn't answer the first question on the form.

Stan cleared his throat and started to recite the facts of his case in the same sort of clear, concise manner that he used to deliver the news. In less than five minutes, Joanna knew all the particulars.

Stan Lorman was born in Hungary under the name Stanislaus Lormagdian. When the Russian tanks rumbled into Budapest, young Stanislaus and his father were given false papers and smuggled into America by friends. Soon after, Stan's father found out that some refugees had been shipped back to Hungary because of their false papers. Rather than risk that fate for himself and his son, Stan's father decided not to notify the authorities of their arrival. Father and son were quickly assimilated into New York's thriving Hungarian community.

Jobs were plentiful for men who wanted to work and Stan's father had no difficulty supporting them. The problem arose when he attempted to enroll Stanislaus in an American school and found that a birth certificate was required. Other fathers might have kept their child out of school but Mr. Lormagdian believed in the value of a good education. A forged birth certification was readily available, for a price.

Stanislaus was enrolled as a first-grader in Sacred Heart Elementary School a month after he had first set foot on American soil. According to his birth certificate, his name was Stan Lorman and he had been born in New Jersey. Stan had lost his Hungarian accent by the time he finished elementary school and he'd excelled at his high school studies, earning an academic scholarship to U.C.L.A.

Stan and his father had moved to Los Angeles and at U.C.L.A. Stan had developed an interest in the university's thriving performing arts program. While working at the college television station, Stan had discovered that he had a real aptitude for announcing and soon he was doing most of the news broadcasts for the station.

After graduation, Stan took a position as a newscaster with an independent television station, the same station Dan had purchased a year ago. Dan had recognized his talent and Stan had climbed to his present position as the anchorman on Empire Cable's "Nite News."

Joanna reached out to fill Stan's coffee cup. From the way his voice tightened, she knew he was about to get to the crux of his legal problem.

Up until two days ago, Stan had almost forgotten that he wasn't born in this country. His last link with the old country had disappeared when his father had died last year. Stan was a registered member of the Democratic party, voting in every election. And his wallet contained, in addition to Visa, American Express, and Master Charge, a Social Security card and a California driver's license. The trouble started when Dan had assigned him to fly to Europe to interview several internationally famous authors for an upcoming series. The components that complicated Stan's problem were a restless three-year-old child and an over-worked clerk in the passport office.

The passport clerk had been ready to approve Stan's papers when the woman standing next to him had grown tired of holding her child and boosted him up to sit on the counter. The clerk, called back early from her lunch break because of the long lines, had brought her coffee with her. The child had reached out for the cup, the clerk had pulled it back, and the coffee had sloshed out, drenching Stan's phony birth certificate.

Naturally, the clerk apologized for the inconvenience but she couldn't send in the document in this condition. She would have to secure a new copy from the New Jersey Department of Vital Statistics.

Stan stalled for time, offering to send for the copy himself. But the clerk refused to penalize Stan for an incident that was entirely her fault. She would keep his application on file, and as soon as New Jersey responded, she'd complete his file and expedite the passport.

"And, of course, New Jersey has no record of your birth." Joanna sighed deeply as Stan nodded. "It's a serious problem, Stan. Technically, you're an illegal alien who's never reported his status. The penalty for that offense is deportation."

Stan's face turned white. His father had lived with that fear all his life.

"I'm sure it won't come to that, Stan." Joanna hurried to reassure her client. "Under any other circumstances, I'd pay a visit to Immigration and Naturalization and we'd work something out between us, but the situation is tricky right now."

"The I.N.S. crackdown? We had a story on that last Tuesday."

"Right. And don't forget the congressional bill."

Stan nodded. Congress was considering a bill to

penalize employers of undocumented aliens and the Latino lobby was screaming discrimination.

"Normally, your case would be a formality, Stan. I'd secure a temporary visa to protect your status and, after a few months, we'd make application for citizenship. Right now, I'm not sure that's a wise move."

Stan's eyebrows rose and Joanna went on. "To submit our application, we'd have to first admit that you're an illegal alien. Don't forget that the I.N.S. is anxious to find enough token illegal Anglos to pacify the Latino lobby. Someone in the department could decide that your case was perfect for that purpose. We might have to stall until the time is right to submit our application and that means working around your clumsy passport clerk. Let me think a minute." Joanna went over the possibilities in her mind as Stan waited anxiously.

"That birth certificate with the coffee on it . . . did the clerk save it?"

"No. She crumpled it up and threw it in the wastebasket."

"Good! And it stated you were born at home?"

Stan nodded.

"Even better. When the clerk calls you and says there's no record of your birth, tell her you'll try to contact the doctor who signed the certificate if she can give you the name."

"But she didn't write it down."

"Exactly! That means you'll experience all sorts of difficulties trying to locate people who were witnesses at your birth. It's a stall, Stan. As long as that clerk thinks you're working on the problem, she'll put a hold on your file. Meanwhile I'll try to make contact with someone at I.N.S. to discuss the problem without giving them any names."

"I guess I'd better level with Dan. He's expecting me to fly to Europe next month."

Joanna winced at the reminder that her husband was involved. Prudence dictated that she refuse Stan's case but she couldn't bring herself to turn down her first client.

"If you tell Dan that you're an illegal alien, he's required by law to ask for your green papers. Since you can't produce them, he has to file a report stating that one of his employees is an undocumented alien. We can't let that happen or the I.N.S. will be on our back before we're ready."

"What should I do?"

Joanna hesitated. She didn't want to advise her client to lie to her husband. This situation was definitely getting sticky but it wasn't exactly a conflict of interest.

"Tell Dan you're having trouble getting your passport, problems with missing documents, that sort of thing. Suggest that you do some segments with American authors first. And I'll do my best to push through your citizenship just as fast as I can."

During the next six months, Stan Lorman's case had dragged on. Joanna'd taken other cases, but most were quickly concluded. She'd drawn up a half-dozen wills, looked over several contracts, sued a Beverly Hills cleaners for ruining a client's expensive leather jacket, negotiated a cash settlement in a conflict between a tenant and his landlord, and changed the name Agatha to Anne. Dealing with the U.S. government, however, always took time.

If Joanna hadn't been so busy with her legal practice, she would have been lonely. Dan spent more time signing up affiliates than he did at home. It seemed he was always off on another business trip. When Stan managed to catch him between trips and give him the story about missing documents, Dan had quickly decided to change the series to exclusively American authors. It seemed that the matter of Stan's passport was completely forgotten except by Stan, Joanna, and the passport clerk.

Stan had stalled the clerk while Joanna contacted an acquaintance who worked at the I.N.S. She'd learned that the situation was still tight and a citizenship request was impossible at this time but she'd managed to secure a temporary visa for one Stanislaus Lormagdian. Luckily, no one at I.N.S. had guessed that Stan Lorman was the recipient of the visa and the accounting department at Empire Cable had no idea they'd had a Stanislaus Lormagdian on the books.

Now the wait was almost over. Joanna's contact at the I.N.S. had called her last week and urged Stanislaus Lormagdian to apply for U.S. citizenship. The heat was nearly off and the procedure would slip through the I.N.S. wheels slowly but smoothly. And when Joanna had called Stan to give him the good news, he'd insisted on taking her out to an expensive lunch. The end was in sight and he wanted to celebrate with the lawyer who had made it all possible.

Joanna glanced at her watch and got to her feet. She'd been doing what her mother called "woolgathering" again and it was time to get dressed for her lunch with Stan. It was a real treat for Joanna to be invited to an expensive restaurant. Dan had been out of town on business trips much too often to suit her and when he came home the last thing he wanted to do was go out to a restaurant. Joanna's social life had been practically nonexistent and Stan's invitation had lifted her spirits considerably.

Joanna dressed with care in the Chanel suit Dan had given her for her birthday. It was made of heavy raw silk in its natural golden-beige color with a tight skirt that hugged her hips and then widened to a flare at the knees. The jacket was simply cut and fell to just below waist level, with long raglan sleeves. Under the jacket was a high-necked, cream-colored blouse that tied in a fashionable bow at the neck. Joanna had pinned her grandmother's antique gold broach to the jacket and she wore soft, kid-leather shoes with a medium heel that matched her all-purpose shoulder bag.

Stan had chosen one of Joanna's favorite places, En Brochette, in Beverly Hills. The moment Joanna arrived she was shown to Stan's table in the gazebo garden, where they started with champagne, a lovely bottle of Tattinger. The cool, flower-scented air of the patio was pleasant and Joanna sipped her champagne, thoroughly enjoying the combination of the sunshine, the wine, and the strolling classical guitar minstrel who had stopped by their table. They had just finished toasting the progress Joanna had made when a photographer approached their table.

"James Collins, from the *Times*. How about a picture, Mr. Lorman? It'll make tomorrow's edition."

Stan turned to Joanna and she nodded. She knew how important publicity was in the show business world and Dan was always pleased when Empire Cable was mentioned in the paper. The photographer grinned as he stepped back to focus. Three quick flashes, a polite thank-you, and he was gone.

"I hope my eyes were open." Joanna laughed as she remembered her parents' photo album. "My father used to say I had the quickest blink in Minnesota. He took hundreds of pictures of me with my eyes closed."

"I don't believe it. There must be one exception." Stan smiled as he refilled Joanna's champagne glass.

"Well . . ." Joanna thought for a moment. "There's my wedding picture. That turned out just fine. Maybe that's why Dan and I are happy together. I have proof that I entered into marriage with my eyes open."

3

THE PHONE WAS ringing when Joanna got home from her lunch with Stan and she ran to answer it. It was Dr. Whitney with good news. She was pregnant at last.

Joanna rushed up to her room in a state of euphoria. Dan had left his number at the hotel in Kansas City but she didn't want to tell him news like this over the phone. She'd wait until she could tell him in person.

It was difficult for Joanna to sleep that night, alone in their bed. The only thing that made it bearable was knowing that Dan would be home tomorrow. She'd make his favorite dinner and they'd open a bottle of champagne. Then she'd tell him. Joanna smiled as she pictured Dan's face when he heard the wonderful news.

The next morning she put in an early court appearance, only to find that her case had been delayed. Ordinarily, she would have been upset but today the delay was a blessing. She checked her calendar, rescheduled an appointment, and rushed to Jorgensen's gourmet market for a tenderloin. Dan loved her beef Wellington and she had just enough time to make the brioche dough.

By noon, the house was filled with fresh flowers and white asparagus was marinating in chilled vinaigrette. Joanna sat down at the kitchen table to take a break and picked up the newspaper she hadn't had time to read. Perhaps they'd published the picture taken at En Brochette.

The entertainment section was in the middle of the paper and Joanna turned to it eagerly. The first thing she saw was her own face, staring up at her from the page. *"Joanna Courtney, wife of Empire Cable's Dan Courtney, enjoys an intimate lunch with anchorman Stan Lorman."*

Her eyes were open! Joanna laughed as she folded the paper, picture out, and placed it on Dan's side of the table. The picture covered almost a quarter of the page and the *Times* had over one million readers. Perhaps Dan should fire his publicist and hire her!

Taking the shuttle from the airport, Dan arrived at his office about noon. The receptionist's desk was deserted and so was Alice's small adjoining office. In his own office he found a foil-wrapped sandwich on his desk with a note letting him know his receptionist was at lunch and all calls had been transferred to sound stage three where Alice was helping with some script revisions.

The previous occupant of this suite of offices at Tri-City Studios, the producer of a series revolving around an African safari, had left his complete office furnishings behind when the series had been canceled. There was no money in Empire's budget for redecoration, so Dan had decided to leave everything just as it was. Alice had been speechless at her first glimpse of their new offices. The hat rack by the door was topped with antlers from some African deerlike creature and its base was a gnarled baobab tree. The entire floor was covered with a wall-to-wall leopard-print carpet. There was a zebra-striped couch in the corner, a four-drawer file cabinet covered in what looked like tiger skin, and the walls sported two fiercely grimacing African masks, a blow gun, and assorted spears. The *pièce de résistance* was a stuffed elephant's head with a desk built under it.

The giant pachyderm stretched across a twelve-foot expanse with tusks that extended another eight. Since they were stuck with the beast, Alice had named him

"Jumbo" and decided to use him as a message center. Jumbo's left tusk was designated for personal messages and the right one for business. Alice used sticky Post-It blanks and arranged them by priority: the closer to the point of Jumbo's tusk, the more important the message. Dan could see at a glance exactly which calls he should return first and all he had to do was reach up to grab them.

The phone rang before Dan had eaten half his sandwich. It was always like this when word got out that he was back, and Dan sat in his swivel chair feeling as if the telephone were a permanent appendage to his left ear.

Gary Bekins, Dan's affiliate in Austin, Texas, wanted more sports. His subscribers were clamoring for all-star wrestling. Two of the affiliates in Illinois thought the sports coverage was excellent but the third was disappointed that the Chicago Bowling Championship Tournament hadn't been televised. Kevin Miller reported that the subscribers in Scranton were enthusiastic about Dan's new sit-com but they didn't care for "The Down Home Cookin' Show." Minneapolis wanted more detective shows, Sacramento fewer and Sioux Falls thought the number of detective shows was perfect as long as Dan changed the time slot to seven P.M. and showed first-run movies at eight. In the survey of his affiliates, only one program consistently outdrew the rest. Everyone loved the "Nite News" with anchorman Stan Lorman.

Dan finished his calls and stood up to stretch. He had requested two windows but neglected to specify the view. Tri-City had given him two windows. One overlooked the side of a trailer parked no more than a foot from the wall, the headquarters of Rocking Horse Videos. Dan's other window faced a cinder-block editing complex, where an hour-long pilot for "Horror Incorporated" was in post-production. Since the air conditioning in Producers' One was worse than useless, Dan's windows were open. Today he was treated to rock music from the left and a series of chilling screams, played over and over, from the right. It was difficult to work in these surroundings but Empire Cable couldn't afford to build its own facility and Dan readily admitted it was a lot more convenient than the trailer.

There was a knock on the door and Alice came in. "Hi, boss. Did you have a good trip?"

Dan opened his mouth to reply but Alice went on without waiting for an answer.

"Lorraine Kale just called. She says there's going to be a price hike so we'd better get in our order before the weekend. And the telephone man's here to work on the console, so don't expect to make any calls for at least an hour. You've got two back-to-back meetings scheduled, one with Ken Maxwell at two and the other with Keith Doric at the bank at two-thirty. At three Tom wants you down in screening room ten to see a cut of that western he's doing. After that you're clear until four-thirty, when Roger Pearson is coming in to pitch ideas for that new detective show. Oh, and this week's products are here. I called a meeting and everyone's waiting."

"Thanks, Alice . . . I think."

Dan got up and went to the conference room where his key personnel were already assembled. The conference room had originally been a storeroom for office supplies, a ten-by-fourteen windowless space. Since Dan needed a conference room more than a storeroom, he'd torn out the shelves and given Alice the job of decorating it. The next time he'd walked into the room, it was a pale purple. Lavender, not purple, Alice had corrected him. She'd heard that mental institutions all over Europe were painted lavender because it was touted to be the most restful of colors. Did that mean

Alice thought Empire employees were psychotic? Of course not! But Dan knew how tempers flared at their weekly staff meetings. The lavender would keep people calm and receptive to suggestions.

Dan knew how useless it was to argue with Alice but he'd seriously considered having the room repainted with a nice ivory or a nondescript tan. To his surprise, after the first few staff meetings, he'd grown to like the color. Alice had scavanged through the Tri-City prop room and appropriated a long white plastic table with twelve matching chairs. She'd also draped one wall with sheer white drapes and pasted up a giant poster of a city skyline behind them to give the illusion of a window. The finishing touch was a white vase with plastic violets in the center of the table and lavender plastic cups for coffee.

Today's staff conference started the usual way. After Dan had greeted everyone and listened to progress reports on their various projects, Alice placed a large box on the table in front of him. It was Empire's policy to personally test all the products they advertised on the air.

"Great!" Dan smiled as he drew the first product from the box. "This one's for you, Sherrie." Dan handed a spray bottle down to Sherrie Vernon, Tom's assistant editor.

"More spray-on eyeglass cleaner?" Sherrie, a pretty girl in her late twenties wearing thick glasses, stared down at the bottle in her hand. "This is the third one I've tried. I'm going to wear out my lenses if I'm not careful."

"That's all right, Sherrie. I'm working on getting you a pair of extended-wear contact lenses."

"Contact lenses?" Sherrie winced. "I don't know, Dan. I've got this built-in phobia about sticking things in my eyes."

"Don't worry about it, Sherrie." Dan smiled at her.

"It'll be a while; they're still in the experimental stage. In the meantime, just clean your glasses with Sparkle and tell me how you like it." He paused. "Alice? Here's yours."

"I just hope it's not more dog food," Alice spoke up. "My sister's dog hides under the bed when she brings out another new can."

"No dog food, Alice. This week you'll try Whisk Off." Dan passed a package down the table to her and Alice looked at it dubiously.

"*'Cleans oil spills from concrete driveways'?* I live in an apartment, Dan."

"How about your brother's place?"

"Okay, boss." Alice sighed in resignation. "I'll drive out tomorrow and we'll try it out this weekend."

"Here's yours, Mike." Dan pulled out a green and gold box and passed it down to his line producer. "It's an after-shave that's supposed to turn women into animals."

"I'll try it."

There was a ripple of laughter as Mike dabbed it on and Alice made a grab for him.

"Tom? You get another toothpaste. It's called Rainbow."

Tom took the cap off the tub and squirted a little into an ashtray. "I'm not sure I can brush my teeth with something that's purple and red."

"Just try it, Tom. And take it in with you when you get your teeth cleaned tomorrow. I want to know what Doc Harris thinks of it."

Tom nodded soberly. He'd forgotten all about his dental appointment and he wished Dan hadn't mentioned it.

"Okay. Here's yours, Barry. Dinner for two at Caesar's. Alice said your first anniversary is this Friday."

Barry Snyder, Dan's head cameraman, looked surprised. "I didn't know we were doing Caesar's commercials."

"We're not." Dan smiled at him. "But I figure you'll give us a plug while you're there."

"Thanks, Dan. Trudy'll love it."

"Okay, that's it. Except for the women, of course. Alice? You and Sherrie can split these up."

Everyone except Sherrie and Alice hurried off to whatever they had been doing before the staff meeting was called. Dan tossed Alice the box of makeup and went off to his own office. A second later he realized that he'd forgotten to ask her if Keith Doric expected him to bring a copy of the operating budget. He had his hand on the conference-room door when he heard the two girls talking inside.

"Just what we need. More flavored lip gloss. This one tastes like a banana. You know what my therapy guide says about women who—"

"Not now, Alice." Sherrie interrupted. "Just take out half and leave the rest for me. I sure wish we'd hire another woman—"

"Oh, no! Here's another eye-shadow sampler. I've got eye shadow coming out of my ears."

Sherrie laughed. "That's a weird place to wear it. Why don't they advertise booze on television? Tom's been an absolute bear today and I could use a little sample of that about now."

Dan grinned, turned around, and went back to his office, leaving the two women arguing over who got what. He'd just poured himself a cup of coffee and was settling down to read the script for a new pilot when Alice came through the door with a package from his clipping service.

"It looks like good news this week." Alice leaned over Dan's shoulder as he opened the package. "We've never gotten a package this heavy before."

Alice was right and Dan grinned as he read the summary sheet. Empire Cable had been mentioned in thirty-seven newspapers around the country this week. Dan glanced through the clippings quickly, pulling out the most important ones. The *Las Vegas Sun-Times* had devoted two inches to his coverage of the blackjack tournament at the Sahara, the *Denver Post* had published a quarter page in their Sunday supplement featuring a prominent Colorado businessman who had invested in Empire Cable, and the *New York Times* had given him four lines in the business section chronicling Empire Cable's acquisition of two New York–based independents.

There was a manila envelope on top of the pile and Dan reached for it eagerly. The clipping service always treated photos with extra care, supporting the homily that a picture was worth a thousand words. He drew it out of the envelope and found himself staring at his wife's smiling face. Sitting at a table next to Joanna, returning her happy smile, was Stan Lorman.

"That one's a winner, Dan!" Alice spoke up. "We've never gotten a photo that large in the *Times* before."

"Yes. Good publicity." Dan placed the photograph on the corner of his desk and stared at it. Joanna and Stan were obviously at lunch. There was a bottle of champagne next to the table in a silver bucket and that meant they were celebrating. Dan felt a surge of unreasonable jealousy as he looked down at his wife's happy face. What was Joanna doing with Stan Lorman while he was out of town?

"See if you can get Joanna on the phone, Alice. I need to talk to her."

"Oh, she's not in, Dan. The message is right there on your desk. She'll be in court until five and she asked if you could meet her at home for dinner at seven."

Dan managed to keep a perfectly blank face until

Alice had left. Then his eyebrows met in an angry frown as he reached for the phone to cancel his evening meetings. Joanna had some explaining to do!

All through his busy afternoon, Dan's anger built. It escalated by increments each time he glanced down at the newspaper photograph. By the time he left the office and hopped on the crowded 405 freeway, he was shaking with rage. There was no need to look at the photograph again. It was etched firmly in his memory.

Usually a careful, courteous driver, Dan found himself honking at other cars and changing lanes without signaling. Finally, when he came dangerously close to sideswiping a red Pinto on the Mulholland Pass, he realized that he had to calm down or he'd never make it home to confront Joanna. He turned the car stereo to an easy-listening station and took deep, calming breaths as he took the off-ramp at Sunset Boulevard, but his hands were still trembling when he pulled into his driveway and shut off the engine. After reminding himself to behave sensibly and logically, he walked up the brick sidewalk and let himself in the front door.

Joanna rushed out to meet him, dressed to the teeth in a new blue lounge outfit that clung to her body. Dan's breath caught in his throat at the lovely vision she made. Was it possible that he was overreacting and her lunch with Stan was perfectly innocent?

Dan held himself in tight control as Joanna threw her arms around his neck and kissed him. Naturally, he wanted to kiss her back but first he had to find out about that photograph.

"Hi, honey! I'm so glad you're home! Why don't you jump in the Jacuzzi and relax for a while. Dinner'll be ready in forty-five minutes."

"I have to talk to you, Joanna."

"And I have to talk to you too. Just let me get dinner on the table first. Do you want a drink?"

"I'll get it myself."

Joanna shrugged as Dan headed for the bar in the family room. It must have been a rough day. He hadn't even kissed her back, but Dan was often tired and crabby when he came home from the office. It was a miserable commute from Studio City in the San Fernando Valley to the house in Brentwood.

"Did you have a good trip, honey?" Joanna stuck her head out the kitchen doorway but Dan wasn't in the family room. She hoped he'd taken her suggestion and gone out to the Jacuzzi in the backyard. A few minutes in the swirling hot water always restored Dan's vitality. He'd be in a better mood for her wonderful news at dinner.

Forty-five minutes later, exactly as she'd promised, dinner was on the table. Joanna stared at her husband uneasily as he picked at his asparagus. Something was definitely wrong.

Joanna brought out the beef Wellington and set it on the table. Dan looked up but he didn't even comment on the fact that she'd served his favorite dinner.

"There's no sense going through the charade of eating." Dan shoved his plate aside and stared at her. "I want to know the meaning of this photograph, Joanna."

Joanna glanced at the newspaper Dan handed her and turned to him with puzzled eyes. "But I thought you'd be pleased! The reporter mentioned Empire Cable."

"Why were you having lunch with Stan Lorman?"

Suddenly Joanna understood. "Oh, darling! You've been so busy that I never thought to tell you. Stan's a client of mine. And he took me to lunch, that's all."

"That doesn't look like a business lunch to me. Isn't that a bottle of champagne?"

Joanna fought down an angry retort. Dan was acting like a child but she refused to fight over something as silly as a lunch with Stan Lorman. Dan had lunch with potential backers often, some of them female, and she was sure they had wine at the table. "We were celebrating the progress we're making on his case. Come on, darling, this is silly. If I had anything to hide, I certainly wouldn't have given permission for the photographer to take a picture!"

"It was only a business lunch?"

Joanna sighed. "Yes."

"How many of these business lunches have you had with Stan?"

"Only one."

"He's really a client of yours?"

"Yes. I've been working on his case for almost six months now."

"Why haven't you mentioned it?"

Joanna sighed. Her perfect dinner was sitting on the table, untouched, and this evening was turning into a disaster. She had all she could do to hold her temper as she explained. "You've had so much on your mind lately that I hated to bother you with the details of my work. And, honey, you've got to admit you haven't seemed all that interested."

Dan winced. What Joanna said was true. He'd cut her off several times when she'd tried to tell him about her practice but he'd had a lot on his mind. He'd offered to put her on the legal staff at Empire Cable so they'd have a common interest but she'd turned him down flat. That still hurt a little. Any other lawyer only a couple of years out of law school would have jumped at the opportunity. If he hadn't shown the appropriate interest in her career, it was only because she'd refused to get involved in his.

"Okay, I admit I haven't been all that interested, but you should have told me about Stan Lorman right away. He's my employee and I have a right to know about any legal problems he has."

"This case doesn't involve the station, honey. It's purely a personal matter."

"Well?" Dan leaned forward and stared at Joanna. "Go ahead. Tell me about it."

Joanna sighed. "I'd like to, darling, but I can't. You know the client-lawyer relationship is privileged."

"For Christ sake, Joanna, you sound like F. Lee Bailey! What can be so damned confidential that you have to keep it from your husband? I'm not going to tell Stan."

Joanna was about to give in when she remembered the trouble Dan would have if the congressional bill passed and he knew about Stan's illegal status. She had to smooth this over somehow, without giving Dan any particulars that might hurt him in the future.

"Really, Dan, it's nothing that should concern you. And telling you about Stan's case might actually harm you in the long run. I'll be glad to tell you the details *after* the case is settled but not before."

"Okay, okay." Dan's lips tightened. "I won't ask you to tell me any more about it but I insist you call Stan right now and tell him you're referring his case to another lawyer."

Joanna couldn't believe her ears. "I can't do that, Dan. Another lawyer would have to start procedures all over again and I've got everything almost tied up. I can't believe you're asking me to give up one of my clients because you're upset about that silly picture in the paper!"

For a full minute Joanna and Dan glared at each other. Finally Joanna couldn't stand the tension any longer. "Really, honey . . . let's forget it until after we've eaten. Then we can discuss the whole thing calmly and rationally. I made a special dinner tonight because I have some wonderful news for you."

Dan seemed to thaw just a bit and Joanna pressed her advantage. "Let's drop it for now, Dan. Please?"

Dan nodded grudgingly but Joanna could tell he wasn't satisfied. Even though this wasn't the particular moment she would have chosen, she decided to tell Dan about the baby. At least it would get his mind off Stan Lorman.

Joanna reached for the champagne and popped the cork. She filled two glasses and handed one to Dan.

"How about a toast, honey. To our new baby."

"What?" The expression on Dan's face was one of pure shock and Joanna laughed.

"That's right, darling. The doctor called me yesterday with the news. I'm six weeks pregnant! Isn't that wonderful?"

"Yes. Wonderful." Dan glanced down at the newspaper, still lying on the table, and then back up at Joanna's radiant face. "Why are you pregnant *now*?"

"I don't know." Joanna laughed again. "The doctor says he sees this sort of thing all the time. I relaxed and stopped worrying and it just happened. Remember that lady I told you about? Mrs. Fairchild? She adopted a baby and a year later she had one of her own."

"Hmmm." Dan took a sip of champagne. "You had all those fertility tests, right?"

Joanna nodded.

"And they turned out just fine?"

Joanna nodded again.

"So naturally you figured that there was something wrong with me. Correct?"

Joanna smiled happily. "That's right, honey, but obviously there wasn't!"

"It seems pretty strange that things should change overnight, especially since you got pregnant six weeks ago and I spent most of that time in New York!"

Joanna's smile faded quickly and her face turned white. Her voice quavered slightly as she forced out the words. "Exactly what are you implying, Dan?"

For a moment, Dan almost relented. Joanna was

gripping the arms of her chair so hard, her knuckles were white, and her eyes were brimming with tears. He knew how much she wanted a baby, but after all those years of trying, it was pretty certain that it just wasn't in the cards. Now they had all the ingredients for a classic tragedy. A beautiful woman, desperate for a child. A husband, too busy trying to run a successful business to pay the proper attention to her. And another man who had a reputation for being handsome and virile. As he stared at Joanna, he wrote the scenario in his mind.

It had been strictly a business relationship at first. Joanna was smart enough to recognize Stan's type. While he had been out of town, they'd met often to discuss the legal case. Maybe, one particular night, Stan had suggested that they continue their discussion over a drink. Joanna had a low tolerance for alcohol and Stan certainly wasn't the type to let an absent husband stand in his way. It might have only happened once and then bingo! Joanna was pregnant. Would she go in for an abortion, like most women would under those circumstances? Of course not. She wanted a baby more than anything. She'd do exactly what she was doing now, trying to convince him that, against the odds they both knew were impossible, the baby was his.

Dan felt his compassion beginning to override his anger. If Joanna would only admit the truth, they might have a chance. He'd slipped a couple of times on those lonely business trips but it hadn't meant he loved Joanna any less. And he longed for a baby too. Was he mature and understanding enough to forgive Joanna if she admitted the truth and promised never to see Stan again?

"Look . . . Joanna . . ." Dan reached across the table and took her hand. "I know I've ignored you lately and I haven't been a very good husband but I do love you. And I know how much you want a baby. I do too. But we have to be truthful about this, honey. It's

63

the only way. Just admit that you made a mistake and that you'll never see Stan again. And I promise I'll do my very best to accept the baby as mine."

Joanna was so still and so white that Dan wondered if she were going to faint. She blinked once and her mouth opened but no sound came out. Then she swallowed hard, pulled her hand from his as if she'd touched something repulsive, and stared at him with eyes that had turned suddenly icy.

"Dan! Surely you don't believe that I . . . that Stan . . .?"

"Come on, Joanna." Dan reached out for her hand again but she pulled it back against her chest. "You can play the injured wife, but both of us know it's just an act. Let's not insult each other's intelligence. I'm willing to forgive and forget as long as you promise me it won't happen again."

Joanna took a deep, shuddering breath. "I can't do that, Dan. I can't promise you that something won't happen again if it didn't happen in the first place. This baby is yours. And right now, I'm not so sure I like that!"

As Joanna's lower lip began to tremble, Dan realized that she was about to break into tears. He wanted to take her in his arms and comfort her but that wouldn't solve their problem. Somehow he had to force her to tell the truth or they'd never be able to go on together.

"This isn't doing us any good, Joanna." Dan stood up and headed for the door. "I'm going to Tom's. You can reach me there when you're ready to tell me the truth."

At the time Joanna had been too shocked to react. She sat there at the table, staring at the congealing dinner on Dan's plate for a full half hour before she could move. Marriage was based on trust and Dan had demonstrated very clearly that he had none.

Joanna stacked the plates in the dishwasher, trying to

keep busy. Then she poured the champagne down the kitchen sink. As she watched it bubble and fizz its way down the drain, she shuddered at the symbolism.

In the days that had followed Dan's hasty exit from the house in Brentwood, he'd waited in vain for Joanna to call and beg him to come back. The only communication between the two of them had been accomplished through Tom, who'd been stuck in the role of middleman against his wishes. Tom loved his sister-in-law. And he loved his brother too. When he'd had left his loft in Minneapolis and moved to California, he'd felt that he was part of a family again. Now that family was dissolving and there hadn't been much he could do to prevent it.

Tom had done his best to talk sense to his brother. He was sure that Joanna had been telling the truth when she swore that Stan Lorman was no more than a client. But Dan had refused to listen to reason. And Joanna had been every bit as stubborn as Dan. She told Tom, in no uncertain terms, that if Dan refused to believe that the baby was his, there was no point in going on with their marriage. And Dan agreed with her on that point, at least. Despite Tom's best efforts to bring about a reconciliation, Dan consulted a lawyer to file for a divorce.

The lawyer had researched the case and told Dan that a divorce would be difficult because of jointly owned stock and commingled assets. Dan would have to buy out Joanna's share of Empire Cable and he was in no position to do that. Dan hadn't liked the lawyer's suggestion that the divorce be tabled until after Dan's planned expansion, but there was little choice. He had moved into a one-bedroom apartment near his office and obtained a legal separation. Joanna would remain his wife until at least the end of the year, when he could raise the money to buy her shares.

4

The Present
New York City

DAN COURTNEY, PRESIDENT of Empire Cable Network, slouched in his seat watching three beautiful models parade down the staircase in floor-length linx, sable, and mink. He was attending a *haute couture* fashion show at the Westford Club. No expense had been spared in staging this exclusive fashion show. A full magnum of vintage Piper Heidsieck, well over a hundred dollars per bottle at retail prices, chilled in ice by each table of four.

The Westford had once been an exclusive gentleman's club. Its address, on Murray Hill in the East Thirties, had become less fashionable over the years and the converted mansion had recently been purchased by a consortium of American fashion designers who had turned it into a showroom for their creations. Dan took his attention from the models for a moment and looked around him with an appraising eye. The renovation was truly remarkable.

The old circular staircase had been fully restored and its intricately hand-carved newel posts glowed with the sheen of well-preserved mahogany. The wainscoting had been carefully stripped of old varnish and renewed with the utmost of care. The heavy leather chairs, virtual thrones of comfort, had been recovered with the finest leather. The antique gaslight fixtures on the walls had been converted to electricity and the old and obviously priceless Persian rug that covered the floor had been completely rejuvenated. Items worth preserving had been perfectly restored to maintain the ambience of a gentlemen's club. Dan half expected a silver-haired butler to pour him a glass of port from a dusty bottle and offer an array of fine cigars.

The men in the audience seemed comfortable and at ease. This was, for them, a welcome change from the spindly chairs and feminine furnishings at most fashion shows. The women were also delighted. Dan had heard several ladies remark that stepping inside the Westford, something their grandmothers would never have been allowed to do, was like traveling back in time to the turn of the century.

Dan sipped his champagne and re-focused his attention on the show. Personally, he didn't give a damn about fashion but over seventy percent of his female viewers did. And that was the reason he was here.

When Dan had gone into the non-network television business, there was no reliable way of knowing how many people watched his shows. The yardstick of the television industry, the Nielsen rating system, had only listed the big-three networks. Of course it was possible to add up the percentage points and arrive at a fourth category, non-network, but there had been no way of judging how many people chose Empire over the other channels like HBO or Disney. It was clear that the non-network category was growing since network ratings had been dropping steadily. The viewing audience was watching something, but exactly what was anyone's guess.

It had taken the Nielsens awhile to catch up but they now measured Empire's audience. The Nielsen company used three polling methods for arriving at their numbers.

The first method was electronic. Black boxes, installed in sample households, kept track of which programs the viewer watched. Since this was a direct method, it was the most reliable.

The second method relied on people's integrity.

Viewer logs were sent to a much larger sample of households and a cover letter asked people to write down what they watched. Since a person might write down what he was intending to watch, or what he thought he should watch, this method wasn't as reliable as the first.

The third method was accomplished by spot check. A Nielsen interviewer called homes at random and asked what the viewer was currently watching. This was a way of checking the validity of the other two methods.

The Nielsens had tremendous impact. They were so critical to the success or failure of a show that most television producers rushed to their offices the morning after their program was aired to nervously await the overnight ratings. Television's chief revenue came from selling blocks of time to advertisers and higher prices could be charged for the commercials that aired during a highly rated show. It all translated into dollars and cents. A peak rating meant big bucks from advertisers. A low rating meant a loss of profit. If an episode received a consistently low rating, the writing was on the wall. The series was canceled and something that could draw more viewers was put in its place. Television was a business, not a public service, and quality was almost always sacrificed for popularity.

Dan resented this system of priorities. He believed that people wanted quality but it took time to build up an audience. Network television was so profit conscious, quality programs didn't get a fair chance. At the same time it was painfully true that you just couldn't generate any revenue airing fourteen hours of Wagner's *Ring Cycle*. Dan's goal was to show the people what they wanted to see and mix in a little quality along the way. He believed there was a middle ground and he intended to find it.

The former owner of Dan's first station had stocked

up on old reruns of sitcoms. Dan had aired those at first but gradually he'd started to produce his own shows.

The small independents had cornered the market on "how-to" programs. There was a series on how to do almost everything, from remodeling an old house to gourmet cooking. Dan had produced and aired a weekly half-hour series called, "How to Fake."

"How to Fake" had been an immediate success. By watching the show every week, the viewer learned how to pretend in any situation. There was a segment on contemporary literature, a brief synopsis of twenty important works that everyone should have read and probably didn't. The following segments included how to order from a French menu without asking the waiter what every item was, how to choose an appropriate wine that wouldn't deplete your pocketbook, when and how much to tip, common foreign phrases and how to use them in conversation, and a final episode on acceptable etiquette in various social situations. The whole series was instructional but it was also humorous, and Dan's viewers had loved it. He'd received hundreds of suggestions for future shows and he was still producing new episodes.

His next series had been the "Star Builder" show, Joanna's brainstorm. Each episode introduced a specialist who was in the business of creating celebrities. There were makeup experts, hairdressers, fashion and fitness consultants, on-screen sessions with diction and acting coaches, even a segment with agents and publicists. The series revolved around Linda Mae Karnowski, a pretty but not glamorous girl, who was gradually transformed by the "Star Builder" professionals into real stellar material. It was every woman's fantasy and every woman in the audience identified with Linda Mae.

After the first year, when Dan's small station had

fought its way out of the red and showed a profit, he hadn't been content to lie back to rest on his laurels. He had borrowed every cent he could for operating capital and worked night and day to affiliate other independent stations across the country. Now, Dan was the owner of a thriving cable network and he had sold his last block of convertible debentures this morning. Although he was in hock up to his eyeballs, Dan was confident that Empire, the "Everything Network," would be a success. Tonight would be the acid test. Empire was scheduled to air its first four hours of original expanded programming opposite the big-three network's highest rated shows. Tomorrow's ratings would tell whether Dan was a success or a failure.

It was true that he was presently overextended—a polite banking term that meant there was too much money going out and too little coming in. But the future looked promising if he could only get through the next few months. In Dan's personal life, however, the future was nothing but bleak.

Dan clapped politely as the three models made their exit and another three took their place. His eyes were fixed on the stage, but his mind was far away, thinking about Joanna.

When had his marriage begun to falter? Dan remembered the day Joanna had passed the bar and the celebration he'd arranged for her at her favorite restaurant. They had been happy then. And the day he'd bought the first station in what had now become the Empire chain. They had been happy then, too. Was it when he had started to travel across the country, attempting to line up affiliates? And when Joanna got so immersed in her law practice that she no longer had the free time to go on those long trips with him?

The sound of applause brought Dan out of his memories of the past and he tried to concentrate on the fashion show, but reminders of Joanna were everywhere. Just last night he had rushed to intercept a woman on the street with long, blond hair, only to realize that it wasn't Joanna at all. Then the dull ache of loss had consumed him. He was furious at Joanna's betrayal but even his righteous anger couldn't ease the pain he felt when he thought of her.

There she was. The woman he had come to see. As the featured model, she was wearing the best of the line. Unlike the other outfits he'd seen, this dress was classically beautiful but she could have been wearing a gunnysack as far as Dan was concerned.

Dan hastily scribbled a note and handed it to a passing usher. It was time to put his personal problems on hold and concentrate on his work, and this was part of it.

Dan watched the stage impatiently, as he waited for an answer to his note. This segment featured something called "the ethnic Milanese look," something that looked absurd even on a model. It seemed that ordinary women with ordinary faces and figures didn't stand a chance this year. Next came a camel-hair coat that reminded Dan of a worn bathrobe and a fur and denim ensemble that was described by the announcer as "a work of art," definitely not the words that Dan would have chosen. The "fun formal ballgowns with Oriental emphasis" were just coming on when the usher came back. Miss Dubois would be delighted to join him for lunch.

The maître d' at the Marquis Room greeted Dan politely enough, but he was told that there would be an hour's wait before a table was free. A discreetly folded bill reduced the waiting time considerably. In less than five minutes Dan was ushered to a banquette covered in rich-looking dark green velvet that nestled into an alcove at the corner of the room. The waiter remarked that it was one of the most coveted locations and Dan could easily see why. The banquette afforded a perfect view of the rest of the room while maintaining a maximum of privacy by bordering the lovely, interior rose garden.

The Marquis Room was a relatively new restaurant in the Dynasty Hotel. The chef had earned rave reviews from New York's finest restaurant critics and the room was beautifully appointed with crystal chandeliers and snowy-white tablecloths covered by a top cloth of bright pink linen. The dark green fabric of banquettes and drapes set off by the pink carpet and tablecloths served to highlight the spectacular rose garden. The whole room was a peaceful and lovely sanctuary in the heart of the city. A white marble fountain in the center of the room added to the illusion of dining *all fresco,* and Dan was satisfied that he'd chosen a setting that would charm his guest.

Dan smiled as he studied the twenty-page leather-bound wine list and wondered whether he had earned this choice table on the strength of his name or just the size of his billfold. Perhaps it was best not to know. He had just enough time to order a bottle of Dom Perignon before the head waiter rushed up to tell him that Miss Dubois had arrived.

Dan rose as Maree appeared in the doorway. She was dressed in an original from the House of Françoise, the same outfit she'd modeled in the show. Dan could almost hear the announcer's description as he gazed at her.

The skirt was ankle length, made of a pearly-mauve suede as delicate as tissue paper. It caressed Maree in a way that made Dan suspect she'd been sewn into it. The top was a rich black taffeta with huge puffed sleeves that made her look fragile and feminine. It was nipped in at the waist to show her perfect figure and had a deep V-neck, softened by a delicate silk ruffle that matched the color of the skirt. A rope of pearls was clasped around Maree's long, elegant neck, supporting a stunning diamond pendant that nestled between the rise of her breasts. The jewelry was part of the outfit, especially designed to call attention to the low neckline. Maree looked sexy and demure at the same time. Her lovely dark hair was arranged in a charming disarray of curls that made it seem as if she'd just rushed from a romantic liaison.

As Maree swept past the tables on the arm of the maître d', all conversation stopped. Not until she was settled at Dan's banquette, did a low, excited murmur break out. Maree Dubois was a celebrity. Her picture had been on the cover of most American magazines and her name was synonymous with glamour and high fashion.

As he filled Maree's tulip-shaped champagne glass, the waiter's hand trembled a bit and Dan could understand why. He had to concentrate to keep his own hand steady as Maree raised her glass. Such beauty in close proximity was breathtaking.

"To you, Dan Courtney. And to the proposition I hear you will give me."

Dan smiled as he gently touched the rim of his glass to Maree's. He had no doubt that every man in the room would like to offer her a proposition, but he wasn't about to correct her choice of words. He had expected to lead up to his proposal over a leisurely lunch but it appeared that Maree was just as eager as he was to open negotiations.

Before Dan could begin their conversation, another solicitous waiter arrived with their caviar appetizer.

"Oh, wonderful!" Maree's eyes sparkled at the sight of the caviar tray. "Caviar is . . . how you say . . . a less-weight food?"

Dan was thoroughly puzzled for a moment. "Do you mean a *diet* food?"

"Yes, that is the word. I have long English for short time here, no?"

73

"No . . . I mean, yes!"

Dan smiled. Maree's problems with the English language would be charming on camera.

Maree's mouth watered as the waiter served the caviar. At only seventy-four calories an ounce, provided she judiciously bypassed the sour cream and the toast tips, caviar was a blessing for a model.

As Dan began to explain the details of the contract, Maree spooned a generous helping of caviar into her mouth and crushed the delicious eggs with the tip of her tongue. Eating caviar was a sensual experience and Maree fought to keep her mind on Dan's words. There was a beguiling openness in his face and Maree was sure she detected a streak of carefully hidden sexuality. The thought of seducing Dan Courtney made her shiver slightly in anticipation. One of the American models had told her he was separated from his wife and the dresser said he was a minor celebrity in the television world. Some people called him a "Ted Turner with class." She'd always been attracted to tall blonds with rugged good looks, and her last two lovers had looked much like Dan.

With a start, Maree realized that she was giving more interest to Dan Courtney, the man, than she was to his business proposal. There would be time for that, later. She deliberately put all thoughts of romance out of her mind and concentrated on what he was saying.

". . . so we tallied the results on the Empire computer and we found that sixty-three percent of our women viewers are interested in a weekly fashion show. And since your name had the highest recognition factor, I want you to host the show. I'm prepared to give you a contract for twenty-two episodes. That's a full year."

"A full year?" Maree frowned. "In France a year counts fifty-two weeks. It is different here, yes?"

"It's different in television." Dan smiled at her puzzled expression. "Twenty-two episodes with one rerun apiece. That's forty-four weeks. Then we allow for eight preemptions for various specials and that takes us through the year."

"Oh. I see." Maree nodded. "And which amount of time does it take to make one of these episodes?"

"That depends. We'll try to tape three shows on the same day. It's cheaper that way. But the preparation before we shoot could take anywhere from two weeks to a month."

Maree nodded again. "And you ask me to produce these shows? To be a television producer?"

"Well . . . I guess you could say that. For all practical purposes, you'll be the producer."

"Then I should have what you call a producer's credit on the television, no?"

Dan sighed. Signing Maree wouldn't be quite as easy as he had anticipated. She obviously knew more about television than she was admitting.

"All right. I'll give you producer's credit."

Maree smiled happily. "And now that I am producer, the contract must be made to fit."

"Made to fit?"

"Yes. It should not say a year. Instead we must put it for twenty-two episodes. The monies will be right as they are written."

Dan threw back his head and laughed. Someone had coached Maree carefully. He had been prepared to give her a year's contract at eighty thousand dollars. Now she was negotiating the same salary for work that might take her only twenty-two weeks. And to further sweeten the deal, she'd have a producer's credit that could lead to a slot on another show.

"I am funny, no?" Maree pouted charmingly.

"You are smart, yes. All right, Maree. I'll rewrite your contract. But you'll have to sign an exclusive for Empire Cable. If the ratings are good when we air the fashion series, we'll talk about creating another show."

"This is fair, Dan Courtney. But talk of business before lunch is not good. We will discuss details later, yes?"

Dan nodded and Maree gave him an approving smile. Then she leaned back and sipped her expensive champagne. She was glad that Dan had agreed to her terms but she'd been prepared to accept his contract as it was initially written. Maree was wise enough to realize that at twenty-eight, she was already one of the "grandmas" in the modeling business. Currently the "high priestess of the fashion world," Maree could look forward to canceled bookings and lowered rates, tapering off to an occasional spot in a cheap mail-order catalog. Smart older models got out before that happened, traditionally opening an agency or marrying one of their rich accounts. Maree had rejected both of those possibilities.

Modeling was a tough job with very little glamour involved. Maree was yelled at by temperamental photographers, required to hold ridiculous poses that would have taxed a gymnast, and subjected to a minute inspection of nearly every inch of her body by anyone associated with the shoot. She had to adopt the mentality of a Barbie doll as she was prodded and poked by people who often forgot her name and called her "honey" or "sweetie." The hours were grueling and the pay ridiculously low unless a model was lucky enough to make it to the top.

Maree had made it, but the rigors of her profession had taken their toll. There were mornings when she literally had to force herself out of bed to make a five A.M. call. She was weary of donning bikinis in twenty-degree weather and sweltering under hot studio lights dressed in heavy ski clothes. The final straw was the dieting. Maree had eaten enough green salads without dressing to last her a lifetime and, for the past year, she had experienced hauntingly erotic dreams about chocolate.

"Dan?" Maree looked up at him impishly. "Do you suppose we could jump the entrée?"

"Do you mean *skip* the entree?"

"Yes." Maree gave him a brilliant smile. "I would very much like to skip the entrée. I find I am killing . . . no, *dying*, for dessert."

The sky was beginning to darken outside the window as Maree picked up the gold Cross pen to sign her contract. They were seated on the leather sofas in the living room of Dan's hotel suite, where they'd been for the past four hours. Dan had discovered that Maree was a shrewd businesswoman. The original contract that Dan had brought with him was covered with negations and addenda. Still, Dan was pleased with the contract and so was Maree. They would work well together.

Dan's hotel suite was modest compared to the mammoth, six-room suites on the floor above, but it was a far cry from the single rooms he used to rent when he'd first started traveling for Empire. It had taken two years of traveling on a shoestring before he'd finally decided to indulge himself and stay at hotels that didn't bolt the pictures to the walls. Now he always rented a suite and most of his business was conducted there. This suite at the Dynasty was perfect for wooing affiliates and financial backers alike.

The living room was large enough to hold two ivory-colored leather sofas and three matching barrel-backed chairs. A chrome and glass table with six chairs overlooked the terrace and several original oil paintings hung on the walls without benefit of bolts. A large color television was part of an oak entertainment center against one wall, along with a stereo setup complete with radio and tape player. In the drawer beneath the tape deck was a selection of tapes to suit any taste. The color scheme was blue and ivory and the room had been done by a decorator who was determined not to offend anyone's taste. As a result, it had ended up being totally nondescript.

The bedroom was another matter. There the decorator had obviously been given free rein. The massive king-size bed was covered with a bright rose satin bedspread and the walls were papered in a huge floral pattern, predominently shades of pink with a smattering of green. The drapes matched the walls with their riotous flowers and the design was repeated again on the sheets and the pillowcases. Last night, when he'd gone to bed, Dan had dreamed he was sleeping in the middle of a giant flower.

The bathroom was gold and pink with a gold tile floor, gold faucets, and bright pink towels to match the bowl and the tub. The shower enclosure was mirrored on both sides and Dan had been subjected to the reflection of his naked body countless times as he stepped into the shower, It would have been perfect for someone with narcissistic tendencies but Dan had been greatly relieved when the mirrored surface had clouded up with steam.

"I am finished, Dan Courtney." Maree looked up from the papers and massaged her cramped hand. "I have monogrammed the line-throughs and also by the words you have put very small."

"You've initialed the deletions and the insertions?"

"Yes. That is what I said. And I put my name on the line where it is typed at the end. Are we now legal?"

"We're legal and it's time to celebrate. This time we'll drink California champagne," Dan took the bottle from its bucket of ice and held it up so Maree could see the label. "You're going to have to get used to it, now that you'll be living in California."

Maree read the label and laughed.

"I do not think so, Dan Courtney. This is Chandon Napa Valley Brut, made by Dom Perignon. The grapes, they may be grown in California, but the *chef de caves* is a Frenchman."

Dan gently dislodged the cork and poured two glasses. He held his up to toast Maree. "To the beauty you bring to Empire Cable."

"And to my new handsome boss which makes me very happy."

Maree took a sip of her champagne and turned the full force of her stunning smile on Dan. Then she stood up and slipped out of her taffeta blouse, revealing a thin lace teddy that left little to the imagination. Dan's breath caught in his throat as she wiggled out of her skirt and stood before him in nothing but a wisp of fine black lace.

Dan cleared his throat. He knew he should stop Maree before things went any further. "I'm flattered, Maree, but I'm a married man."

"I know. The best lovers are."

Maree turned her back to him and slipped the thin satin straps off her shoulders, then lowered the lacy garment slowly to her waist.

Dan felt very uncomfortable as he feasted his eyes on Maree's silky bare back. He'd never dreamed that bare shoulders could be so erotic.

"Actually . . ." Dan fought to keep his voice under control. ". . . now that we're working together I should tell you . . ."

Dan stopped in midsentence and swallowed with difficulty as Maree turned to face him again. He had all he could do not to gasp out loud at the lovely sight. "Maree . . . you don't have to do this!"

"But I want to, Dan Courtney."

Dan tried to concentrate on Maree's face but his eyes were drawn to her full, lovely breasts. They gleamed in the golden afternoon light, and he knew if he reached out to touch them, they would feel like warm silk.

Maree hooked her thumbs in the lacy fabric and pulled the teddy down slowly, revealing inch after inch of creamy skin. The lace stretched taut over the rounded globes of her buttocks and then slipped down to fall in a crumpled ball at her feet. Then she bent over deliberately, legs straight and slightly spread, to pick it up and place it neatly on a chair.

This time Dan did gasp out loud. For the first time since they had separated, Dan forgot all about Joanna. A slight sound of protest died in his throat as Maree walked toward him slowly, stopping just short of brushing her breasts against his face.

"I . . ." Dan cleared his throat again. "I know I'm probably being a ridiculous fool, Maree, but I . . . I really don't think I should sleep with you."

Maree smiled and cupped his face in her hands. "That is good. I, also, do not want to sleep. I am not at all tired."

"Dan Courtney! What is that annoying sound?"

Maree's voice roused him and Dan realized that the rhythmic beeping had been going on for some time. For a moment he was totally disoriented but then he recognized the sound of his alarm watch, tossed carelessly on the table by the bed.

"Oh, Christ!" Dan rolled off Maree's body abruptly and jumped out of bed. He grabbed his robe and left her to watch in astonishment as he dashed out into the living room and switched on the television set.

Maree sat up and tried to figure out what had happened. Other lovers had been full of tender words and compliments after an interlude in bed. They had plied her with flowers. And food, and wine, and kisses. They had even offered to draw her bath, and more often than not, they had climbed in the tub with her to prolong their mutual pleasure. If the men in this country were as strange as Dan Courtney, perhaps she'd made a drastic mistake in coming to America.

The sound of the television drifted in from the living room and Maree's bewilderment turned to anger. Her other lovers had ignored ringing telephones and urgent messages for her. One had even refused to leave her bed when a fire broke out in the apartment next door. Never, in her wildest imaginings, had she expected to be left for a television program!

Maree stood up and grabbed the first thing handy, a rose-colored bath sheet monogrammed with the initials of the hotel, and wrapped it tightly around her body. Then she strode purposefully into the living room.

"Dan? I must talk with you." Maree's voice was clipped but Dan didn't seem to notice.

"Quiet, Maree! Sit down and watch this."

"But Dan . . . it is an advertisement."

"That's right!" Dan paid no attention to Maree's indignant flounce as she sat down on the couch; his eyes were glued to the screen. Maree was so angry she was speechless. She took a cigarette from the silver box on the table and puffed furiously, staring with narrowed eyes at the offending television set.

A smiling baby's face filled the screen and an announcer came on with a voice-over. *"They say the baby has your mother's eyes?"* A set of brown eyes wearing glasses twirled in from the left and settled over the baby's eyes.

"And your father's nose?" A square, mannish nose cartwheeled in from the right and took its place on the baby's face.

"And your Aunt Ida's forehead?" An elderly woman's forehead, complete with wrinkles, whisked in from the top.

"And Uncle Jerry's chin?" A man's chin with a goatee rolled up from the bottom of the screen.

"Prove your baby's face belongs to your baby, alone. Eagleson and Sachs, Baby Photographers for the past twenty years, will be happy to give you the true picture."

The image on the screen switched back to the face of the baby—who gave a delighted gurgle.

Maree couldn't help laughing out loud. It was impossible to resist a baby's chuckle. Dan grabbed her hand and gave it a quick squeeze. "Just wait, Maree. The next one's my favorite."

The scene opened on a peaceful, pastoral scene with green rolling fields. It reminded Maree of the French countryside near Mont Saint-Michel, on the Normandy coast. A classical flute piece was playing in the background.

Sheep entered the picture one by one, until there was a small flock frisking and gamboling. They looked so cute as they gave little half hitches and jumped straight-legged into the air that Maree found herself smiling.

The music grew a bit more sinister as an oboe took up the refrain. Then it gained momentum and the camera pulled back to a wide angle, revealing a circle of wolves who were watching intently. The sheep, completely oblivious to the danger, continued their frolicking as the voice-over came on.

"The National Council of Sheep Breeders urges you to eat more lamb. Forty thousand wolves can't be wrong."

"Oh, Dan! This is terrible!" Maree's laughter belied her words. She was still laughing as the screen flashed a logo and the announcer's voice continued.

"This hour-long block of commercials is brought to you by Empire Cable, the Everything Network. There will be no further interruptions for programming."

Suddenly Maree understood Dan's hasty exit from the bedroom. He had told her that Empire was airing its first four hours of original expanded programming. She reached for his hand and brought it to her lips in a kiss that was meant as an apology. Then she settled back to watch.

The next commercial opened with a city sidewalk scene and the Andrews Sisters singing "How Much Is That Doggy in the Window?" in the background. A basset hound ambled into the frame, sniffing his way past the shops. He paused outside a huge laundromat and appeared to ponder the scene through the front, plate-glass window with great interest.

"There are special shops to wash your clothes." The basset hound turned sad eyes toward the camera for a moment and then ambled on until he came to a busy, automated car wash.

"And special places to wash your car."

Again the sad eyes faced the camera and Maree had to smile. There was nothing in the world as sad as a basset hound.

"But how about me, man's best friend? It's demeaning when you drag me out to the front lawn and give me a bath with the garden hose!"

The basset hound turned a corner and stopped in front of an open door. A sign on the window read RALPH'S DOG GROOMING and the camera zoomed in on the telephone number. A smiling young man dressed in white appeared in the doorway. He beckoned to the basset hound, who trotted obediently inside, tail wagging joyously.

"Ralph's! Fourteen Hundred Ventura Boulevard. The only grooming service your dog can ask for by name."

Maree laughed and Dan slipped his arm around her shoulders.

"Hairdressing a dog is very difficult." Maree snuggled a little closer. "I had to look very long in Paris to find the best hairdresser for Robespierre, my poodle."

"Robespierre?"

Maree nodded. "You have heard of the Reign of Terror, no? I give the name Robespierre before I take him to obedience training. Now that he is a good boy, I call him by Robby. Is it good to trust this Ralph to cut his hairs when I send for him?"

"Absolutely. I want people to know that if they see a product on Empire, it's reliable. We tested Ralph's with five dogs before I agreed to film their commercial."

"You have five dogs?"

"No, I had to borrow them for the day. My staff took them out to a field to roll in the dirt and then we made appointments for all five of them. They came back from Ralph's with their clean tails wagging."

"Then how did you test the baby photographer? You loaned a baby?"

"Borrowed. Yes we did, in a way. We used one of the film editor's grandsons, a secretary's niece, and one baby from central casting."

"And the lamb?"

"Oh, we served it in the cafeteria. We had lamb burgers, lamb chops, lamb stew, shish kabob, and Gyros. Everyone except my brother agreed it was delicious. Tom won't eat anything that doesn't moo or oink."

As Maree watched the screen eagerly, waiting for the next segment, Dan reached for the phone to call Tom. He wanted to congratulate his brother on a job well done. Any block of commercials that could pacify a passionate Frenchwoman was bound to be a success.

5

TOM COURTNEY SAT in his den with the door closed for privacy. He was home, at his beach house in Malibu, and the den was the only room that felt totally his, even though he'd purchased the house two years ago. The previous owners had decorated. And when Tom took possession of the two bedroom home, he hadn't had time to redo the rooms to his taste. The wall-to-wall white carpeting in the living room showed every sandy footprint and Tom knew he'd have to replace it some-day with a color that blended with the beach outside. For the present, he'd hired a cleaning service to come in twice a week. They cleaned the glass walls that overlooked the water and treated the redwood decking that ran all around the house on the ocean side so it wouldn't turn white with the salty air. The bedrooms could stay as they were until he had time to figure out what to do with them. The blue and silver wallpaper in the master bedroom was horrid but the room was large enough to accommodate a huge heated waterbed, the kind he had always wanted. After the cold winters in Minnesota, Tom had a horror of climbing into a cold bed. This one was a constant ninety-two degrees and meant he never woke up shivering.

The second bedroom, done in a circus motif for the previous owner's daughter, wasn't being used as a bedroom anyway. It was Tom's studio at home. And every time Tom went in to work on a project, he was amused by the clowns on the wallpaper and drapes.

Television was a lot like a three-ring circus. The decor was really quite appropriate.

The den, however, was exactly the way Tom would have done it with wood paneled walls and built-in bookshelves. There was a place for his film library and the shelves were large enough to accommodate oversized books. The room had a masculine feel with a polished wood floor and Joanna had given him a huge bearskin rug with the head attached to go in front of the stone fireplace. It was a restful retreat and Tom found himself spending most of his time in the den. Tonight, in particular, it was a virtual haven.

Tom clicked the remote control to turn up the volume another notch on his twenty-four-inch, high-resolution, color television monitor. The party in his living room was growing loud and he could tell that his guests had worked their way through the champagne and were well into the mixed drinks.

Two weeks ago Vanessa Atchison, one of Tom's girlfriends, had asked if she could give a small party for the premiere of his television commercials. Tom had been flattered and, since Vanessa hadn't landed the job she'd expected in a television soap, he had graciously offered to pick up the tab.

Before he knew what was happening, the intimate party had grown into a massive undertaking. Vanessa had worked for hours on the guest list. They simply had to invite representatives from the major networks and all the important people from the studios. Tom had tried to warn her about the division between movies, network television, and cable. People in those fields just didn't mix socially. Vanessa told him to leave that to her. She'd only invite the people she knew personally. They'd be delighted to come. And Tom wouldn't mind if she filled in with some of the kids from her acting classes, would he? Tom's party would be a great place for them to make contacts.

The guest list had swelled like a sponge in water and finally Vanessa had admitted that she had a slight problem. Her apartment simply wasn't large enough to hold such an important affair but Tom's Malibu beach house would be perfect. Could she possibly hold it there?

Tom had agreed and Vanessa had been effusively grateful. She'd promised not to bother him with the details unless she simply couldn't help it.

Vanessa had called Tom at least once a day to discuss the party. First there was the matter of the menu. Should she hire Lars Hansen for a smorgasbord or go with someone like the Beverly Hills Catering Service? Or maybe, since Tom was wild about corned beef, he'd prefer platters from a Jewish delicatessen? Tom had told her he didn't care one way or the other but Vanessa had pressed for an answer. It was his party, after all. Tom had opted for the smorgasbord.

The knotty problem of liquor had come up next. They could have a punch bowl but that was terribly midwestern. The liquor store had suggested two kinds of wine, a chenin blanc and a sauvignon but it reminded Vanessa of those dreadful testimonial dinners. There was always the option of a full bar but that meant hiring a bartending service. Perhaps Tom would rather to do the thing with champagne? Definitely, Tom had wanted champagne. He'd read about show biz parties and they all started with champagne. Vanessa could hire a bartending service to serve mixed drinks after the champagne ran out.

The next call had concerned the floral arrangements. They really had to have flowers. Vanessa had been in love with the idea of redwood tubs with birds of paradise but Harvey Bloomfield had done that at his last party. One of the florists she'd consulted had recommended scattered arrangements of orchids and driftwood. Unless, of course, Tom had a favorite flower he'd rather use? Tom had been good and not mentioned dandelions. Orchids and driftwood were fine. Now, if she'd excuse him, he really had to get back to work.

The next morning, Vanessa had called back. She was sorry to bother Tom at work every day, but she wanted to make sure this was a night Tom would remember for the rest of his life. This time the subject was music. Should they have a live band out on the patio? Or do something classy like hire strolling violinists?

Tom had been due in editing and two people were waiting in his outer office. Enough was enough. If the guests were coming to watch his commercials, they could damn well listen to the sound track of the broadcast.

Vanessa had conceded that Tom had a valid point. Of course they'd set up a huge projector television in the living room. But what about *after* Tom's commercials? Would he prefer the violinists? Or would he rather go with jazz or pop? Weary of the whole business, Tom had given her full authority to make all the decisions and the result was tonight's black-tie affair. And Vanessa had arranged a wonderful party. There was only one problem. Tom knew only a smattering of his guests, and the ones he recognized he didn't like very much. It seemed that most of them were too busy cultivating each other to care about the premiere. They had no real interest in Tom's work and Tom had none in theirs. He had retired to the den the moment his commercial block was announced, and no one had even missed him.

The phone rang and Tom picked it up. It was Dan, calling from New York with congratulations. Would Tom meet him for lunch tomorrow at Bruno's Chartreuse? Dan would be alone but Tom was welcome to bring a date if he wished.

Tom hung up the phone with a smile on his face and

watched the last of his commercials. He didn't really feel like going back out to the party to accept the phony praise. He poured a snifter of his favorite port and settled back in his recliner chair, wishing that the party were over.

"Tommy, honey?" Vanessa pushed open the door to the den. She was dressed in a Bill Blass original of poppy-red silk and she looked stunning. "Aren't you coming out? Your program's over."

"I have to make a couple of calls first. Go back and enjoy yourself, Vanessa. I'll be out later."

Vanessa gave a charming little pout but Tom didn't seem to notice, so she backed out of the room and closed the door noisily behind her.

The moment she was gone, Tom picked up the phone and punched out his sister-in-law's number. He wanted to invite her for lunch at Bruno's Chartreuse tomorrow. It didn't take a mind reader to see that Joanna and Dan were still in love and Tom figured if he threw them together often enough, they'd eventually resolve their differences. Tom readily admitted that his motives for trying to reconcile them weren't entirely altruistic. He missed the family dinners at Dan's house in Brentwood. None of his girlfriends could make a chocolate soufflé like Joanna's.

"Hi, kid. How's the weather in Minnesota?"

Joanna Courtney laughed as she leaned back on the couch and propped her feet up on the low coffee table. Her ankles were swollen again tonight and her doctor had told her to keep her legs elevated as much as possible.

"Ninety-two degrees and muggy, Tom."

Joanna didn't have to ask who it was. Her brother-in-law made a point of asking about the Minnesota weather every time he called. He knew she called her mother every week at the family farm.

"Are the mosquitoes bad?"

"Watch it, Tom. You're talking about the Minnesota state bird."

Tom laughed. He loved to give Joanna a hard time about her home state, especially now that they were all Californians.

"Be honest, kid. Aren't you lonesome for the four seasons?"

"What four seasons? Minnesota has only two . . . Winter and Road Repair!"

Joanna tucked back a strand of long, blond hair and cradled the telephone between her ear and her shoulder. She knew what was coming next.

"Joanna?"

"Hmmm?"

"Why do they use artificial turf on a Minnesota football field?"

"I don't know, Tom."

"It keeps the cheerleaders from grazing at half-time."

Joanna groaned. "Oh, Tom . . . That's awful!"

Tom's voice dropped down to a serious register. "Did you watch Empire's premiere, Joanna?"

"Of course I did. Your commercials were fantastic! Do you think you'll get an Emmy?"

"Not a chance. They don't give Emmys for commercials, kid. They give something called a Clio. Which commercial was your favorite?"

"That's hard . . ." Joanna thought for a moment. "I think the one with the baby's face. Do people really act that silly around babies, Tom?"

"That's what I'm told."

"Do you think my baby'll have its Uncle Tom's nose?"

"I hope not. I need my nose. It comes in handy for sticking in other people's business. And speaking of that, have you heard from Dan?"

"Not a word." Joanna sighed. "You know more about what he's doing these days than I do."

"You sound a little depressed, kid." Tom's voice was warm and sympathetic.

"I'm just feeling sorry for myself, Tom. The doctor says I have to start watching my weight or I'll look like the Goodrich blimp."

"You can't get me on that one. Goodrich doesn't own a blimp. Tell you what, kid . . . I'll treat you to a nice dietetic lunch tomorrow at Bruno's Chartreuse. By then we should know the ratings and we'll either celebrate or commiserate. One o'clock?"

"It's a date."

When she hung up the phone, Joanna was smiling. She was sure Bruno's menu didn't contain a single low-calorie item but she'd give herself one last splurge before she went on that diet. Seeing Tom always cheered her up and right now he was her only link with Dan.

Joanna pulled out the yellow pages and flipped through the *C*'s. She found a likely listing and dialed the number of Sweet Memories on Wilshire Boulevard. Their ad said they made confections to order and she was well acquainted with Tom's sweet tooth.

After a few minutes of describing the two Emmys of solid Swiss chocolate, Joanna gave the clerk her credit card number and hung up, smiling. The clerk had assured her they would be delivered to the Empire Cable offices tomorrow morning. Perhaps she'd been foolish to order a second Emmy for Dan, but old habits died hard and Joanna knew that her husband was a bona-fide chocoholic. The Courtney brothers had grown up on nickel Hershey bars and gone on from there. Dan had been in the Toffler bar stage when she had met him, and on their honeymoon in Europe, they had gone on what amounted to a holy quest for the very best in chocolate. They had agreed on a three-way tie:

the hot chocolate in the restaurant at the Aalborg Zoo in Denmark, the Parisian éclairs with chocolate filling encased by chocolate pastry and covered by chocolate frosting, and the so-rich-I'll-die-if-I-take-another-bite-but-it's-worth-it sacher torte in Vienna.

Even though it was only eight in the evening, Joanna was exhausted. As she climbed the staircase to the master bedroom on the second floor, she had to half pull herself up by the railing.

The bedroom felt huge and empty without Dan's things scattered around. The patchwork quilt Joanna's grandmother had made was spread over the four-poster bed. Joanna had found a woman to add a plain border around the outside so it could be used as a bedspread. The bed, made of bird's-eye maple, with its matching twelve-drawer dresser and vanity, had been shipped from Minnesota at considerable expense. Both Dan and Joanna had agreed that cost was no object. Grandfather Sorensen had made the furniture himself, and every piece was a family heirloom.

Joanna had spent weeks looking for just the right wallpaper. It was textured cream-colored satin and the drapes were slightly darker with sheers to match. Grandma Sorensen's spinning wheel sat in a place of honor by the window and the hardwood floor was covered with the huge braided rug that she had made. The only jarring note was the television and Joanna had converted her grandmother's washstand to conceal it. A blue enamel pitcher and bowl sat on top, and the moment the doors below were closed, the room seemed to recede to the early nineteen-hundreds.

Now Joanna opened the washstand doors and switched on the television. Empire's new series, a western, was just going on. Everyone had warned Dan that producing a western was crazy. They said the days of *"Gunsmoke"* and *"Bonanza"* were long gone. Dan had gone ahead with the project anyway and tonight it was airing for the first time. The hero was an American Indian, living on a reservation in Montana. The bad guys were the local sheriff and a man from the Bureau of Indian Affairs. Even though Joanna had never been a fan of the traditional western, she found herself watching with pleasure as she changed into her nightgown.

When Joanna and Dan had first moved to the big house in Brentwood, Dan had installed a television set in every room. Joanna had thought it was pure craziness, but Dan had reminded her that television was his bread and butter. There was a console in the living room, a huge projection television in the family room, a portable on the enclosed patio, and a monitor in the dining room. A small nine-inch set was in the kitchen on top of the refrigerator. Joanna had remarked that he'd forgotten one place. Perhaps they should install a set in the bathroom? Dan had missed the irony and gone out to buy two more, one for each bathroom.

Since Dan had left, Joanna had found herself watching more and more of the programming on Empire. She knew that it would be wiser to forget about Dan and get on with her life but she still switched on the television every night, watching for the shows he'd created.

When she had finished her nightly ritual, Joanna got into bed and propped pillows behind her so she could watch the rest of the western. Next came Dan's detective show starring a husband-and-wife catering team who served up solutions to murders along with their potato salad.

The hour flew by much too quickly and then it was ten o'clock, time for Empire Cable's award-winning "Nite News." Before Stan Lorman's face could appear on the screen, Joanna switched the channel. Although Stan was an innocent party to the breakup of her marriage, the sight of him always brought back painful memories.

Stan had become a citizen at last. His papers had gone through last week. Joanna knew she could have called Dan with an explanation of Stan's case but it wouldn't have accomplished much. There was nothing she could say to convince him that he was the father of her baby.

Channel eleven was showing a rerun of "I Love Lucy." It was one of the shows where Lucy was pregnant with little Ricky. Joanna snuggled down under the covers and closed her eyes, half listening to the soundtrack. There was a funny bit when Lucy got stuck in an overstuffed chair and Ricky had to pry her out. As she dropped off to sleep, Joanna was filled with envy for the red-headed comedienne. Pregnancy certainly had its comic side if you didn't have to go through it alone.

6

JOANNA OPENED HER eyes as the bright morning sun flooded the bedroom. It was past nine in the morning and she had work to do before her luncheon with Tom.

Fifteen minutes later, Joanna headed for the kitchen. About to pour herself a cup of coffee, she remembered that she was limited to three cups a day. She settled for a glass of orange juice and carried it out to her office. She was making a motion for change of venue. The judge she'd drawn was notoriously prejudiced in cases involving blacks and teenagers and Joanna's client was a seventeen-year-old black girl. Joanna had to present a good argument for changing venue without mentioning that the judge was the true reason for her objection.

As she shut the office door, she caught sight of herself in the mirror over the desk. Her long, blond hair was caught back in a silver barrette at the back of her neck, one of the products Dan had brought home for her to test. It was intended to hold long hair neatly, without pulling or crimping, and Joanna had given it an excellent rating.

Joanna's hairstyle was a simple one and it accentuated her high cheekbones and Scandinavian profile. Just the other day, one of her clients had remarked that she looked a lot like Liv Ullmann in *Forty Carats*. Naturally Joanna was flattered at being compared to the beautiful Swedish actress but she wished that her client had picked one of Miss Ullmann's earlier films. Joanna wasn't delighted at the reminder that she was pushing forty. Her doctor had assured her that having a first baby at thirty-nine was no problem for a woman in good health but Joanna was still a bit worried, especially since she had to deal with every aspect of her pregnancy alone. Her mother couldn't come out to stay with her because of her father's illness. Ed Sorensen was still recovering from his heart surgery last month, and although he was doing just fine, he needed constant care.

Since she'd had no appointments scheduled for today, Joanna had dressed in a pair of worn maternity jeans and an old MGM sweatshirt that Dan had left behind. She could see that she wouldn't be able to wear the sweatshirt much longer. It was stretched so tightly over her midsection that Leo the lion's face was misshapen. Alice's lifeguide would have a field day explaining her choice of clothing, but wearing Dan's sweatshirt made Joanna feel that he was taking some part in her pregnancy.

Joanna paged through the file for her teenaged client. Then she pulled several heavy volumes from her bookshelf and began to track down precedents. An hour passed quickly as it always did when Joanna was involved in a case.

The phone rang and Joanna shook her head to clear it. Her body felt stiff and she stood up, did a quick stretch, which made the baby kick with a vengeance, and reached for the phone. She hoped it wasn't Tom, cancelling their lunch date.

"Joanna? I'm glad I caught you. It's Allen Bartleman."

Joanna sat back down and reached for her pen. Allen usually called to refer clients. The case of brandy she'd sent him after the Stan Lorman referral had definitely been worth its weight in gold. "Hi, Allen. How's business in Beverly Hills?"

"Busy. Everybody's suing. I've got another case for

you, if you want it. Say yes now, before I have to tell you the particulars."

Joanna began to laugh. Allen was a frustrated practical joker and the last case he'd referred to her had been downright ridiculous. It involved a pure-bred female Afghan, named Patricia, who had been impregnated by the mongrel who lived next door. In short, it had been a doggy paternity suit and Joanna blushed every time she thought about presenting it in court. The judge had been unable to control his laughter and the spectators hooted as she presented the evidence, a video tape the client had made of "Patricia's rape."

"One question, Allen." Joanna sighed. "Does this case involve animals?"

"Some say yes, some say no. It's a relatively simple divorce proceeding."

"I'll bet!" Joanna laughed out loud. "All right, I'll take it. Now tell me what I've gotten myself into."

"Mrs. Sally Bowman is suing her husband, Georgina Bowman, for divorce. Your client is the husband."

"Well, that sounds simple enough." Joanna began jotting down the names. "Wait a second, Allen. Did you say my client's name was Georgina?"

"Right!" Allen gave a great booming laugh. "The husband had a sex change last year. He's agreed to the dissolution but he's demanding half of his wife's wardrobe."

"I should have known."

Joanna was thoughtful as she hung up the phone. Divorce cases tended to be filled with emotional tension and there were no winners. Even her professors in law school had been divided on their views of divorce, one maintaining that the law takes an interest in the preservation of the family. Public policy dictates that the lawyer, as an officer of the court, is charged with the duty of affecting a reconciliation, if at all possible.

Another professor's position was diametrically opposed. He said that a lawyer's sole duty was to protect the interests of his client. Justice arose out of the conflict of adversaries and was not well served by bleeding hearts or altruistic intentions.

A third professor maintained that it was all very well to help the parties reconcile but the smart lawyer got his fee up front.

Joanna still wasn't sure how she felt about the subject. Divorce cases were difficult and she had avoided taking them for personal reasons. She had plenty of work without them. Pictures of her former clients lined one wall. There were the Monrreal brothers in their gardening truck, who had successfully sued the finance company for repossessing their vehicle on a bookkeeping error. Corrine Chambers in the new mink coat she had been given by the furriers after they had improperly stored her old one. So many clients. Only one picture was buried in the back of her file cabinet. It was the newspaper photograph of Joanna and Stan Lorman that had led to so many tears.

Joanna switched on her answering machine and headed toward the house. The sprinkler system was acting up again. There was a standing puddle of water under the rosebushes and the dahlias looked like they were drowning. Yesterday, the sprinkler heads had switched on five times despite the gardener's attempt to reset the system. Dan seemed to be the only one who understood the complicated twenty-four-hour clock with its interlocking gears, and Joanna refused to call him like some helpless female and ask him to come over and fix it.

The sight of her waterlogged garden made tears come to Joanna's eyes. Dan had always taken care of minor repairs around the house. Now that he was gone, she'd just have to learn to do things for herself. First thing tomorrow morning she'd comb the garage shelves for the instruction booklet that had come with the sprinklers. And if she couldn't find it, she'd rip out the whole damn garden and plant water lilies.

He knew she was inside the house in Brentwood but every time he managed to move forward a few inches, someone pushed him back. He could hear music floating out of an open window and the sound of a party inside. Clinking glasses, the deep rumbling voices of the men, and the higher-pitched musical laughter of the women all blended together in the night air. Silhouettes moved past the drapes and he knew the guests were dancing.

"Excuse me. Let me through please." He tried to make his way past a man in a white linen suit but the man shoved him back with a harsh, "End of the line, buddy!" His words contrasted sharply with his genial southern accent.

The crisp night air was growing cold and he realized that snow was swirling around his ankles. Dropping to his knees, he began to crawl through the hedge that blocked off the front door, hoping to bypass the crowd. He was halfway through when he met a waiter, also on his knees, holding a silver platter piled high with baby shrimp above his head. "Would you care for an hors d'oeuvre, sir?"

Rather than hurt the waiter's feelings, he took one. It made crawling difficult but he managed to use his elbows to crawl up the steps, where he was accosted by a butler.

"Do you have an invitation, sir?"

"I don't need one. I'm her husband."

The butler laughed. "I beg your pardon, Sir. You were her husband."

Before he could frame a reply, two burly bouncers grabbed him under the arms and bum-rushed him out of the door. The people standing in line began to applaud.

"No status! No status! You have no status!" One by one the hostile strangers took up the chant.

"Excuse me, sir. Is anything wrong?"

Dan awoke to find a pretty stewardess staring down at him in concern. He was on flight 218, nonstop from Kennedy to LAX.

"No, nothing's wrong. I guess I must have been dreaming." Dan sat up a little straighter and blinked a couple of times to clear his head. "When do we land?"

"We're on the approach now, sir. ETA is twenty-two minutes. You slept through our brunch."

"Did I miss anything?"

The stewardess leaned a little closer and lowered her voice. "Not really. The orange juice was warm and the eggs Florentine were cold. The coffee wasn't bad though. I've still got some left if you want a cup."

"I could use it, thanks."

In a moment she was back, carrying a plastic cup with the airline's insignia on the side. The coffee was hot and strong and Dan barely had time to finish it before they landed. He took the shuttle to the parking lot, reclaimed his car, and drove to the office. A vague uneasiness, no doubt a result of his dream, stayed with him as Alice ended her running account of what had happened in his absense.

". . . so I told Jerry to send it over right away."

"Send what over?"

"The promo tape I've just spent five minutes telling you about." Alice looked up from her notes and frowned. Dan was staring out the window and she knew he hadn't heard a word that she'd said.

"Oh . . . that tape."

"Is there something wrong, boss? You look preoccupied. My lifeguide says that if you've got a problem you should—"

"I don't have a problem, Alice. Everything's fine. It's just jet lag. Locate Tom for me, will you? And tell him to meet me here, at twelve-thirty."

"Sure, boss." Alice gathered up her notes and

headed for the door. "Are you sure there's nothing wrong?"

"Nothing's wrong! I had a nightmare on the plane and woke up disoriented, that's all."

Dan breathed a sigh of relief as Alice left his office without asking about his dream. She loved to talk about psychic symbolism but Dan wasn't in the mood for that now. His dream had been pretty obvious. It meant that he missed his life with Joanna. And he felt guilty about making love to Maree. After the divorce, he wouldn't feel guilty anymore and he wouldn't have these damn nightmares. Then he could enjoy other women again without comparing every last one of them to Joanna.

"Boss?" Alice came back in, carrying a large, gift-wrapped box. "This just came by messenger. Can I watch you open it?"

Dan nodded. Alice loved surprises. She leaned over him while he unwrapped the package and gasped as he drew out the chocolate statue.

"What is it, boss?"

"It's an Emmy. A solid, milk chocolate Emmy."

"Here's the card." Alice picked up the card that had fallen out of the package. "It says, *You'll probably win another one of these but it won't taste this good.* And it's signed, *Joanna.* Isn't that sweet, boss?"

Dan nodded. He'd call Joanna to thank her. Or maybe he should thank her in person. Things were strained right now, but there was no reason why they couldn't remain friends.

"I could get Joanna on the phone for you but you'll probably want to thank her in person. Just because you're getting a divorce doesn't mean you can't stay friends."

Dan sighed. As usual, Alice had read his mind. There were times when she reminded him of Radar on "M*A*S*H."

"Right, Alice. Get Ingrid Reese on the phone for

me, will you? I need to sign Woody Herman for our big-band special."

"I already did. They'll be here at ten tomorrow morning to discuss terms."

"Then type up the shooting schedule for the western and distribute it."

"It's done."

"How about getting my new parking sticker? I forgot to remind you before I left."

"It's right there, on your desk."

"Fresh coffee?"

"Already perking."

Dan racked his brain to think of something Alice hadn't anticipated. It was uncanny the way she managed to stay one jump ahead of him.

"Then stop playing Radar and take a coffee break with me."

"Thanks, boss." Alice smiled. "And while we're drinking our coffee, you can tell me all about that dream you had on the plane."

"Here we are, ma'am." The young taxi driver, probably an unemployed actor, got out of the cab to open the passenger door. "Do you want me to see you in?"

"Oh, no thank you."

Joanna smiled and gave him a generous tip. She'd found that most people were very courteous to pregnant women, especially to women who were as pregnant as she was. She waved the taxi on and checked her appearance in the plate-glass window of Bruno's Chartreuse before going in. She was wearing her favorite maternity outfit, an ice-blue linen dress with a wide yoke at the shoulders decorated with little sprigs of hand-embroidered flowers. From the yoke down, the material was draped artfully to hide her enlarged figure. She had worn dark blue leather shoes with a heel that was just a bit higher than was sensible and she carried a dark blue leather clutch purse. Her hair was done in its usual style, swept up and back with the silver barrette Dan had given her. There were only so many tricks a designer could use to conceal a pregnancy, but all in all, she was satisfied with her appearance.

The moment she opened the door, Bruno spotted her. Of course, she was pretty hard to miss.

"Mrs. Courtney! It's good to see you again."

Dressed in immaculate chef's whites with a pink scarf tied around his neck for color, Bruno rushed through the crowded little bistro to greet her. He was smiling broadly and Joanna smiled back. She hadn't been in Bruno's Chartreuse since Dan had left and it felt almost like coming home.

"The gentlemen are already seated in your favorite booth."

Joanna's smile faded a bit as she followed Bruno. Tom hadn't said anyone was joining them. Perhaps she had misunderstood Bruno's heavy Swiss accent.

The booth in the corner was raised on a pedestal and Joanna had always loved it. White lace curtains hung above the wooden enclosure and it seated up to five people in an intimate setting despite the proximity of the other tables. Bruno reserved the booth for special customers and it took on the importance of a gourmet Academy Award.

"Here's my date." Tom saw Joanna coming and waved. Then he turned and spoke to his companion who had his back to Joanna. "Shove over a bit and let her in your side. I think there's more room."

Joanna stepped up on the pedestal and gasped as she faced Tom's dining companion.

There was a moment of tense silence and then Dan moved to the center seat, Joanna took a deep breath and slid in on the end. She shot Tom a look of pure exasperation but he was smiling at her obvious discomfort. Joanna cleared her throat and decided to make the best of the situation.

"Hello, Dan. It looks as though Tom is up to his usual tricks. Think we can get through lunch without stabbing each other with the bread knives?"

Dan looked just as uncomfortable as she felt but he laughed. "I'll be good if you will. Actually, I'm glad to see you, Joanna. I wanted to thank you for that chocolate Emmy."

"Did you bite the ears off first?"

Dan laughed again. They'd started a tradition the first year of their marriage by exchanging solid chocolate Easter bunnies. Dan had always bitten the ears off first, while Joanna had started with the feet.

"If you want the truth, I bit off the whole head."

"That means your pretty head is safe today," Tom broke in.

"Did you get the overnights yet?" Joanna picked up her water and sipped it.

Dan shook his head. "Not yet, but I told Alice to call if they came in before we got back."

Joanna began to smile as she pulled a paper out of her purse. "I've got them. One of my clients works at Neilsen. When I told him how important it was, he sent out a messenger the moment they were tallied."

"Joanna, you're a wonder." Dan grabbed the paper and glanced at the ratings. Then he gave a delighted whoop. "Two point seven! Bruno? Bring us a bottle of Chandon Brut. We've got something to celebrate!"

Dan's high spirits were infectious and Joanna began to relax. They polished off the bottle of champagne and started the meal with Bruno's rich beef stock chock full of succulent onions topped with broiled cheese and a dash of grenadine. Joanna knew she'd never tasted anything so delicious and she was sure her enjoyment had nothing to do with her impending diet. Next Dan ordered *petit roste* for all three of them. The crisp little patties of potatoes with sour cream and two kinds of caviar were heavenly and Joanna ate every bit. She had just about decided to pass on the entrée when Bruno stopped by to tell her he had fresh chicken livers in wine sauce and she suddenly discovered her appetite again.

They had just finished their entrées when there was a stir in the restaurant. Joanna pulled back the curtain to see a party of three being seated quite close to them.

"Red alert!" Joanna nudged Dan. "Look who just walked in."

Dan leaned over and peered through the curtain. Then he dropped it back into place and turned to Tom, who was watching the whole cloak-and-dagger scene with obvious amusement.

"John, Frank, and Ralph." Dan spoke in an undertone.

"As in Big Green, Bigger Green, and Biggest Green?"

Dan nodded and Tom started to grin. "Why don't you invite them to join us for a drink?"

"I can just pull back the curtain and ask," Joanna spoke up. "We're practically sitting on top of them."

Dan hesitated. He'd worked for Ralph Barton for five years and he still had the urge to rise when his old boss walked into a room. Old habits were hard to break, but he was in business for himself now and there was no reason not to invite Ralph and his executives to join them.

Joanna was watching him intently and Dan had the feeling that she knew exactly what was running through his head. Finally he nodded. "Go ahead."

Joanna pulled back the curtain and leaned out.

"Excuse me . . . Mr. Barton?"

Ralph Barton looked up with a startled expression. Joanna could tell he didn't recognize her even though she'd attended countless GRN functions with Dan.

"I'm Joanna, Dan Courtney's wife. We're celebrating the overnights for Empire Cable and Dan wants to know if you'd like to join us for a glass of champagne."

Dan gestured to their waiter, who was watching the exchange from his place behind the bar. The champagne bucket was quickly replenished, and a moment later Ralph, John, and Frank arrived at their table.

"Dan! Long time no see!" Ralph extended a hand. "I'm afraid I don't keep up with the cable ratings. What were the numbers?"

Before Dan could reply, Joanna handed Ralph a copy of the sheet with Empire's ratings marked in red. Ralph glanced at it and nodded.

"Two point seven, hmm? Of course that doesn't sound like much to a network man. I just canceled a show with a fifteen point six. Are you working for Empire now, Dan?"

"He owns it." Joanna smiled sweetly and slid over so Ralph could get into the booth. There were introductions all around and the waiter opened the champagne. As soon as everyone was served, Dan raised his glass in a toast.

"Congratulations on Sweeps Week, Mr. Barton. I noticed that GRN came out on top again."

"Of course we did, but it was a battle." Ralph Barton smiled, displaying his perfectly capped teeth. "It would have been a lot easier with one of your specials, Dan. Too bad we lost you."

"Right, Ralph." John and Frank spoke, practically in unison. They had obviously had a lot of practice agreeing with their boss.

Joanna almost choked on her champagne. They hadn't lost Dan at GRN, they'd fired him!

"I heard a little rumor last week." Joanna turned to Ralph with a guileless smile. "Someone said that westerns might come back to television."

"Ridiculous!" Ralph Barton laughed. "Some poor

fool comes in to pitch a western every season and we always tell him that the last cowboy died when Lorne Green started doing Alpo commercials."

"What about a western from the Indian point of view?"

"It'd never make it." Ralph reached for a cigarette and John and Frank immediately produced lighters. "GRN watches the market trends and westerns are definitely out."

Joanna shot a look at Tom. Dan's western had done beautifully. Tom locked glances with her for a second and spoke up.

"What do you think of the European television system, Mr. Barton? They run their commercials in a block so their regular programming is uninterrupted. Could that work for network?"

"Never! There's no way a network could sell advertising with a setup like that. People'll just tune in when the regular shows come on."

"I did that last night . . . Ralph." Dan almost choked over Ralph Barton's first name. "And we got pretty good ratings . . . for cable."

"Well . . ." Ralph looked slightly uncomfortable but he quickly recovered. "I'm not saying it won't work once. The novelty and all that. But take some advice from a man who's been in the business for years. Stick to the regular cable programming and you'll be just fine."

"It's really nice of you to give Dan advice, Mr. Barton," Joanna spoke up, "especially since he's a competitor."

Ralph reached out and patted her hand in a very patronizing way. "Oh, my dear, that's funny. Big Green's not worried about some little cable station cutting into our ratings. Everyone switches to network at prime time."

Another few minutes of conversation and the champagne was gone. When Ralph's party left to return to their own table, Tom was grinning.

"I think he's worried."

Dan looked thoughtful. "Take a peek, Joanna. Are they sticking around to order lunch?"

Joanna raised the curtain slightly. Ralph Barton's table was empty. She caught a glimpse of his silver hair through the outside window as he got into a studio limousine.

"I think he lost his appetite. They just drove off."

"Good!" Dan nodded. "Now I can enjoy dessert. Do you suppose Bruno has any of those enormous strawberries dipped in chocolate?"

Ralph Barton paced the floor of his conference room in the GRN Tower. It was an impressive room, half the size of a football field. The carpet was a rich deep brown that showed every speck of lint, but Ralph Barton didn't concern himself with that. He had several employees who were kept on the books simply to keep the conference room in immaculate condition. Dan's whole office suite could have fit into this space with room to spare.

Ashtrays with the Big Green logo sat at each place on the highly polished ebony table, but they were merely for show. Last year Ralph had fired a top executive for smoking a brand of cigarettes he didn't like, and his other executives had taken the hint. Ralph was the only one who smoked during meetings.

Photocopies of the overnight ratings had been placed on each chair and GRN's twelve top executives would be arriving shortly. Ralph had called this emergency meeting the moment he'd returned from Bruno's Chartreuse.

Ralph walked over to look out at the spectacular view. The GRN Tower, a gold-tinted edifice, rose thirty-five stories and his penthouse offices were on the top floor. Ralph had demanded clear glass walls; he'd had visions of standing at the apex of his empire watching his employees work.

The architect had explained that birds were confused by transparent walls and flew into them, so Ralph had quickly agreed to gold-tinted two-way mirrors instead, even though the cost was much higher. The architect spread tales about Mr. Barton's humanitarianism and Ralph had laughed when he'd heard them. If the truth were known, he just didn't want to be bothered with hiring a team of window washers to keep the feathers and guts off his view.

The intercom at his end of the table buzzed and his executive secretary's voice came through the electronic box, tinny and high-pitched. "Everyone's here, Mr. Barton."

"Send them in."

The door opened and twelve high-ranking GRN executives nodded to their boss and took their places at the conference table like obedient schoolboys. There was a bit of throat clearing and then the room was silent again, all eyes fixed on Barton.

"You've all been told why I called this meeting." Ralph Barton let his eyes roam over the seated executives. There were several nods. "I trust you're prepared?"

This time every head at the table nodded. There was a shuffle as several men reached for their briefcases and snapped them open.

"Fine." Ralph permitted a ghost of a smile to appear on his face. "Let's hear from programming first. Robert?"

As Robert Stein, a thin, balding man in his early fifties, began to give his report, Ralph let his eyes wander around the room. It pleased him that his top executives looked nervous. It was his responsibility to keep them alert and on their toes. Every man at this table knew there was no such thing as tenure in show business.

Each department head was alloted five minutes for his report. Exactly sixty minutes had passed when George Curtis, a young Ivy League MBA who was vice-president of the advertising department, concluded. "That's all, Mr. Barton. Empire Cable's two point seven share is statistically insignificant but it does represent what could be a small but critical loss of revenue to GRN."

Travis Alcourt's hand shot up. It was time for open discussion. "I can't agree with you on that, George. Our computers show an entirely different picture."

Ralph nodded to Travis and he stood up to take the floor. He was a deeply tanned man in his thirties who looked more like a tennis pro than the vice-president in charge of comptrolling. Ralph had hired him when old Sam Malinow, an accountant from the old school, had retired. The noisy old comptometer that had occupied a prominent place on Sam's desk had since been relegated to the prop department along with his supply of old-fashioned green eyeshades. The voluminous ledgers were replaced by a shiny new mainframe computer and the main terminal on Travis's desk was hooked directly to the computers at the New York Stock Exchange. It had cost a fortune but now every department was computerized. Ralph admitted that the new system was efficient but it still took brains to interpret the numbers.

Travis pulled out a stack of computer printouts and pointed to a series of figures, circled in red. "The proof's right here, Mr. Barton. Our figures show that the rating drain Empire represents will *not,* under any conditions, impact GRN earnings. The danger lies elsewhere. The Nielsen's could affect stock options."

Ralph nodded. The value of stock options was a matter of market pressure. If the market overreacted to the ratings, GRN's stock could plummet even though there was no real threat to the company.

"I say your data is skewed!" George jumped to his feet. "You haven't taken into account the latest trends in advertising."

"Hold it a minute, boys."

The moment Ralph held up his hand, George sat down. There was silence in the room as Ralph drew out another cigarette and accepted a light from John Weisner, VP in charge of expansion and development, who was seated on his left. Three other monogrammed lighters were returned to their respective pockets.

"You boys may be experts but you're giving me bullshit. This isn't a question of charts and numbers, it's a study in human nature. Dan Courtney's two-point-seven share may be insignificant right now, but it shows the other independents and affiliates that network is vulnerable. We've got the start of a war here, boys, whether you realize it or not!" Ralph smiled and every one of his chief executives started to sweat, despite the efficient air-conditioning system. When the boss smiled like that, it meant heads were going to roll.

"While you boys were jacking off with your computers, I made a few telephone calls. Did your fancy printout tell you that Dan Courtney is overextended, Travis?"

Travis Alcourt turned pale beneath his perfect tan as he shook his head.

"How about you, George? Did your overpaid advertising consultants tell you that Courtney ran that fucking commercial block of his for free, just to hook his sponsors for the next time around?"

This time George Curtis blanched and shook his head.

"You boys are green, that's the problem!" Ralph smiled again as he noticed that no man at the table could meet his eyes. "While you were out eating your yogurt and pine nuts, I figured out a way to end this war without any bloodshed. It takes money to establish a network, right boys?"

"Right, Mr. Barton." Every man at the table spoke in unison and Ralph smiled again. They sounded like a fucking Greek chorus.

"And we know Empire's finances are shaky, right?"

"Right, Mr. Barton."

"So we'll buy Courtney out at top dollar. It'll save us money in the long run, right?"

"Right, Mr. Barton."

Ralph smiled. He was ready for his punch line.

"So we'll offer him an executive post right here at GRN. Say, vice-president in charge of advertising . . . or maybe comptrolling . . . We'll offer him any VP post he wants, right?"

"Right, Mr. Barton."

This time the Greek chorus was noticeably ragged. "I'll approach Courtney personally, of course. We should have the results in a couple of days and you'll be informed. That's it. Meeting's over."

Ralph was still smiling as his executives picked up their briefcases and left the room. He knew they were heading back to their offices to call emergency staff meetings. All twelve men would attempt to prove they were indispensable and there would be peak production in every department. There was nothing like a good scare to keep the wheels turning smoothly.

The moment the last man had left, Ralph went into his private office and shut the door. He took three swigs of Maalox, directly out of the bottle, and pressed his hand to his stomach. His ulcer had been killing him ever since he'd returned from lunch and taken the call that was waiting from the king.

The king was a nickname for Everett Kingston, the majority stockholder and chairman of the board at GRN. When the king spoke, everyone not only listened, they jumped. The king had told Ralph to put Courtney out of business and he wanted results immediately. He enjoyed scaring his boys but Ralph knew they couldn't work miracles. He would have to get rid of Courtney by other means.

It was almost four in the afternoon when Tom and Joanna pulled up in front of the StarBrite Cleaners on Sunset. They'd talked for an hour after Dan had left and now Tom was taking her home.

"Are you sure you have time for this?" Joanna looked worried.

Tom nodded. "Of course I do. I don't have anything scheduled for the rest of the day. Go ahead, Joanna. I'll be right here, waiting."

Joanna got out of the car and hurried inside. She presented the claim ticket for the suit she wanted to wear in court tomorrow and shifted from foot to foot as the counter girl found it on the revolving rack. She had just come out of the store, the suit draped over her arm, when she heard someone call her name.

"Joanna, darling!" Pinky Calvert came rushing over. As usual, the overweight, carrot-haired woman was dressed from head to toe in her favorite color, pink. Pinky's first name had been Margaret but she had legally changed it when she became the Hollywood gossip columnist on Empire's "Nite News." There was no denying that Pinky was good at her job. Dan's affiliates loved the frizzy-haired matron and her thinly veiled references to famous stars. The first time Alice had seen Pinky Calvert, she had quoted her lifeguide. Red-headed women who made a habit of dressing in pink were subconsciously rebelling against society's conventions.

Since there was no escaping her, Joanna put on her best smile. "Hello, Pinky. I haven't seen you in a while."

"You've dropped out of sight, darling, but I certainly don't blame you. I want you to know that I'm just sick about the whole thing with you and Dan. It must be just terrible losing your husband!"

Pinky's phrasing made Joanna smile.

"I haven't *lost* him, Pinky. You make him sound like a missing wallet."

Pinky gave Joanna a sympathetic smile. "You're so brave to joke about it, darling. I'd never be able to do it . . . and in your condition too! Tell me, honestly, Joanna. Aren't you a tiny bit worried, having a first baby at your age? They say the risk increases with every year over forty."

Joanna bit back a sharp retort about being *under* forty but she couldn't hold back the sarcasm that crept into her voice. "My doctor says I'm doing fine, Pinky; especially for a woman of my advanced years."

"I didn't mean *that*, darling. I just thought you might be worried, that's all. Mongoloid children, birth defects, that sort of thing. Do you know if there are any genetic problems on the father's side?"

"No, Dan comes from strong stock, Pinky. And he *is* the father."

"Oh, dear! I'm really putting my foot in it, aren't I?" Pinky looked distressed as she reached out to pat Joanna's hand. "I want you to know that I *never* believed those awful rumors about you and Stan Lorman. Whenever anyone asks me, I tell them that I know you personally, and you simply wouldn't *do* such a thing!"

"Thank you, Pinky."

"Have you considered moving, darling? I mean after the baby's born, of course. There's bound to be gossip, you know how people are. Perhaps you could go back to the Midwest and open a nice little law office. I'm sure it would be better for the baby."

"Actually, I haven't even thought of—"

"Hi, Pinky!" Tom got out of the car and took the cleaners bag from Joanna. "We'd better get going. I'm parked in the red."

Pinky watched as Tom dropped an affectionate arm around Joanna's shoulders. Then she cleared her throat. "Well . . . I'd better be off. I have to find some material for tomorrow's show. Nice seeing you, Tom. And think about what I said, will you, Joanna dear? They say a small town is the perfect place to raise a child."

Tom waited until they were out of earshot.

"What was all *that* about?"

"Just Pinky's usual advice to the masses. She thinks I ought to move because people will gossip about the baby."

"You mean *she'll* gossip about the baby." Tom shook his head. "Someone ought to put a muzzle on that woman. Come on, kid . . . back to the car. I wasn't kidding about that red zone."

Joanna was quiet on the way home. Even though she didn't like to admit it, Pinky had upset her. When Tom dropped her off, she hung the suit in her closet and stretched out on the bed to take one of the afternoon naps Dr. Whitney had recommended. As she fell asleep, Joanna was still thinking about what Pinky had said and wondering if she was right.

7

SHERRIE VERNON, TOM'S assistant editor, zipped along Pacific Coast Highway in her new red convertible. Actually, it wasn't new, and it hadn't been red when she'd bought it yesterday, but a lot had happened in the past three days. On Friday she had gone in to be examined for the new contacts Dan was testing for Empire Cable. The optometrist had said she was a perfect candidate for extended-wear contacts and Sherrie had seen herself without glasses for the first time in her life when the optometrist had put in a pair of test lenses. Her green eyes had been hidden behind glasses for so long, she'd forgotten that people said they were her best feature. And without glasses . . . why she felt like a different person!

Sherrie had been so delighted she'd begged to take her lenses home with her that day but the optometrist had explained that she had to wait for him to prepare her correct prescription. If she could be patient until Monday, he'd have them ready for her after work.

Monday seemed weeks away and Sherrie had tried to keep busy over the weekend. On Saturday afternoon she had gone shopping with her roommate, Marge. Sherrie, who usually bought sensible things, splurged on a new string bikini and a satin negligée. The contact lenses were changing her whole outlook on life and she hadn't even started wearing them yet.

Sunday afternoon Sherrie and Marge went down to a used car lot where Sherrie traded in her reliable gray Mazda for a small, sporty-looking convertible. The car dealer agreed to paint it red and have it ready for a Monday night pickup.

As Sherrie passed a truck, the driver beeped his horn. At first Sherrie thought he was objecting to her driving but then she saw he was flirting with her. She waved and stepped on the gas, feeling very sexy. She was on her way to Tom's Malibu beach house and she was determined that tonight would be more than the work session Tom had planned.

Even though it seemed fruitless, Sherrie had tried every trick in the book to get Tom to notice her. She'd deliberately let her breasts brush up against his arm when they were in the editing room but he'd just muttered, "Sorry," and moved away. She'd tried wearing her long black hair in a variety of styles but he hadn't once mentioned whether he liked her in braids or a chignon. Marge knew a lot of out-of-work actors who had jumped at the chance to get on the Tri-City lot, but even though a different "boyfriend" picked Sherrie up every day for two weeks, Tom hadn't even raised an eyebrow.

When Marge had told her to be more aggressive, Sherrie had geared up her courage and invited Tom to a party, but he'd told her he was busy that night. He'd also been too busy for a picnic, a lecture, and the opening of a new gallery. Sherrie had just about given up when she'd heard, via Alice, the office matchmaker, that Tom and Vanessa had broken up. And today, at the conclusion of a grueling session in the editing room, Tom had actually asked her to drive out to Malibu to see the work he'd done on the new sit-com. Sherrie had raced home in a dither and Marge had told her to gear up for an all-out attempt.

Sherrie turned off the highway and took the access road to the beach. She had no trouble finding Tom's house. She'd driven past many times before, wishing she had the nerve to go up and knock on his door.

Tom's car was parked in the garage and Sherrie pulled up behind it. Then she checked her hair and makeup in the rearview mirror and got out of the car. She was wearing a white jersey dress she'd borrowed from Marge and high-heeled sandals, a very different image than the usual jeans and Empire Cable T-shirt.

Sherrie was almost at the door when she remembered her tote bag and rushed back to the car to get it. Marge had insisted she carry along a never-fail secret weapon, a video tape Marge swore was very romantic. Five minutes of this movie was guaranteed to produce results.

"Sherrie. You look so . . . different." Tom stared at her as he opened the door.

"It must be my new contact lenses." Sherrie put on her sexiest smile. "Do you like the new me?"

"Very nice." Tom grinned as Sherrie whirled around like a model for his inspection. "Of course I liked the old you too. Come in. I mixed up a pitcher of daiquiris. I thought we'd have a drink before we start to work."

Sherrie frowned at the mention of work. Tom had been properly appreciative of her outfit but now he was treating her just like he did at the studio.

"Do you mind if I put on a video tape, Tom? It's one of my favorites."

"Go ahead," Tom answered from the kitchen. "What's the name of it?"

Sherrie floundered. She had no idea. "It'll be a surprise, Tom. Let's see if you can recognize it."

Tom came in carrying the drinks and sat down next to Sherrie on the couch. She grabbed the remote control and hit the play button. If this tape didn't work, she'd kill Marge.

Tom gasped as the title filled the large-screen television, then he laughed out loud. Sherrie was so embarrassed she almost crawled through the floor. It was *The Art of Erotic Massage!*

Sherrie grabbed the remote control to switch it off but Tom was quicker. He put it on pause and grinned at her.

"*This* is your favorite tape?"

Sherrie gulped, and even in the dim light Tom saw that she was blushing. He was ready to click off the tape and save her any further embarrassment when Sherrie decided to brazen it out.

"Yes, sometimes films like this are . . . uh . . . very enlightening."

Tom figured it would be interesting to see just how far Sherrie would carry this whole thing. "Okay, Sherrie. Since you brought it, we'll watch it."

Tom clicked on the tape again and Sherrie thought she'd die. She'd never seen anything like it before but the plot was very apparent when a nude couple appeared on the screen. Somehow she suffered through twenty-five minutes of instruction, complete with visual examples. She would have run back out to her car but Tom was holding her arm.

"Well, that was certainly enlightening." Tom rewound the tape, grinning all the while. "I never would have guessed you liked that sort of thing, Sherrie. You must have hidden depths."

That did it. Sherrie had suffered enough for one night. She turned to glare at Tom.

"I *don't* like that sort of thing! That's my roommate's tape and I've never seen it before. I just wanted you to . . . to notice that I was a member of the opposite sex, that's all. And now that I've made a complete ass of myself, I'm going home to arrange my roommate's funeral."

Sherrie tried to make as dignified an exit as she could but Tom held on to her arm. Naturally, he'd known that the tape had to be some sort of a mistake, but what Sherrie had said was all too true. And for the life of him, he couldn't understand why. How could he have spent eight hours a day without noticing her shining black hair or her lovely sea-green eyes. And her skin looked like burnished copper tonight, as soft and smooth as velvet.

"Hey . . ." Tom reached down to wipe off a tear that was shimmering on Sherrie's long eyelashes. "I'm sorry, Sherrie. I was just teasing you. You don't have to go home yet, do you?"

Sherrie took a deep breath and shook her head. "No, not if we have to work."

"Work can wait until tomorrow. I think we ought to have a few drinks. I don't think I've ever talked to you about anything except editing."

Five minutes later, Sherrie was laughing at something Tom said. Her embarrassment had evaporated and she felt comfortable again. And when Tom bent down and kissed her, she felt even better.

Dan turned onto the freeway in the bumper-to-bumper evening traffic and swore softly under his breath. The lunch with Joanna had been fun, almost like old times with the three of them together, but he'd been forced to leave at two-thirty to meet with his banker. Dan's happy mood had dissipated abruptly after the first few minutes in Keith Doric's Century City office.

Keith was a chief loan officer at First World Bank and he looked the part. He'd been wearing a gray three-piece suit that was obviously expensive with a white dress shirt and a conservative gray-and-blue-striped tie. At thirty-three, Keith had a smooth, unlined face that was a drawback in the world of finance. Most people wanted their bankers to look older and wiser, so when Keith had risen to the position of First World's chief loan officer, he'd instructed his personal barber to frost his naturally dark hair with gray.

Dan had gone into Keith's office in a confident frame

of mind. He'd assumed that selling the last of Empire's convertible debentures in New York would straighten out their financial problems. As usual, Keith had been more cautious.

"Your loan application goes before the board next week but I don't think they're going to approve it." Keith had shifted uncomfortably behind his glass and chrome desk. "Cable television is a high-risk venture and First World Bank is a conservative institution."

"How about the ratings?" Dan had handed the small, gray-haired man the Neilsens that Joanna had provided. "Doesn't that show that Empire has growth potential?"

Keith nodded. "To me, it does. But you can't assign a figure to the future. There'd be no problem if you were in a regular business, say hardware. If you owned a chain of hardware stores, you'd have real property and inventory to list. First World always looks at tangible assets and you don't have any. You rent your facilities and you have no inventory to speak of."

"How about the shows? I've got nineteen episodes of my western in the can. That ought to count for something."

"Not really." Keith had sighed. "You have to think about this whole thing with a banker's mentality. You can't assign a fixed monetary value to the shows you've made. Again, it's speculative. The board needs to make sure you're in a position to make your loan payment every month."

"But I have a perfect payment record." Dan had sat up a little straighter in his chair. "Look at the last loan First World gave me. It was a five-year loan and I paid it off in six months. Doesn't that prove that Empire Cable is a good risk?"

Keith had winced. "No, Dan. Your repayment record might actually hurt you. You paid off the principal so rapidly that the bank lost money on the transaction.

And you failed to establish a long-term credit rating. I know it's not fair, but I don't expect the board to approve your loan until Empire shows a profit on the balance sheet."

"But then I won't need the loan! It's a fucking catch twenty-two!"

Keith had nodded. "I know, Dan. And I can't think of any advice to give you right now. Just remember a few basics for the future and you won't get into this situation again. Always borrow more than you need and use the extra to make a down payment on a tangible asset that the bank can use for collateral to secure your next loan. You can keep up a running line of credit that way."

Dan had stared at the palm trees gently waving outside Keith's window for a moment and then he'd nodded. "I need a tangible asset to use for collateral for the bank to approve my loan, right?"

"That's right."

"Is a car considered a tangible asset?"

Keith had shrugged. "Only if it's a staff car, used for Empire Cable business."

"How about a limo with an Empire Cable emblem on the door?"

"Yes. That would be considered a staff car. But Empire doesn't own a limo."

"It will by tonight. I'll give you the figure for the full market value tomorrow. You can list it as an asset on the balance sheet before you present my application to the board."

Keith had raised his eyebrows. "That might just work. But, Dan . . . you can't afford an Empire limo!"

"I know, but you taught me something, Keith. I'll put the down payment on my credit card. And as soon as the bank approves my loan, I'll be able to make the payments on it."

Dan had left Keith's office and gone straight to

Beverly Hills Limousine where he'd purchased their best black stretch model. Now he was seated behind the wheel of Empire's new staff car, listening to the big engine purr. Driving the limo was quite an experience. When other drivers saw him, they dropped back courteously so he could change lanes whenever he wanted, probably trying to catch a glimpse of the passenger behind the tinted glass windows. Dan made up his mind not to disappoint them in the future. He'd tell Alice to pick up one of those cardboard cutouts of Laurence Olivier to prop up in back. On second thought, no one would recognize Lord Larry, who looked different in every part he played. Sylvester Stallone was safe or John Travolta. They didn't have to be great actors, just recognizable stars.

It took a full hour to get over Mulholland Pass, and Dan breathed a sigh of relief as he took the freeway exit at Barum Road and zipped past the apartment buildings that nestled up against the side of the mountains. Another five minutes of driving and he arrived at the security gate at Tri-City studios.

Dan put on a fresh pot of coffee and settled down behind his desk. Alice had arranged his calls with efficiency and Dan reached up to take them off Jumbo's giant tusks.

The three on the left were personal messages. His suit was ready at the dry cleaners and Pinky Calvert, his Hollywood news commentator, had called in. Everyone was talking about his success in the ratings. The third message was from Alice. It read, *My father tried the new deodorant you gave me. Pit Stop. He says it's a terrible name and it makes him smell like a French whore but it works.*

Dan chuckled and stuck the message back on Jumbo's tusk. Nothing was there that couldn't wait until tomorrow. The four business messages on the left, however, were urgent. Both Ben Santini of NNT and

123

George Askos of USAT had called. They'd left their private numbers.

Fifteen minutes later, Dan hung up the phone grinning, his good humor completely restored. Ben, the president of the number-two network, had offered Dan a half-million dollars a year to join his company. George's offer from the number-three network had been even higher. Naturally Dan had turned them both down, but it showed that they were sweating.

The next message made Dan laugh out loud. Ralph Barton had called and requested an appointment. And Alice had given him one . . . at nine tomorrow morning. Everyone in the industry knew that Ralph Barton hated morning meetings but Alice noted that he'd agreed to this one immediately.

The last message was just as important in a different sense. Dick Zastrow, the owner of four independent stations in the Midwest, was here in Los Angeles. Dick had told Alice that he was impressed with the overnights and wanted to discuss an affiliation with Empire Cable Network. He was staying at the Century Plaza and Alice had written down his room number, circled in red ink. She'd also added a little note for Dan that said, *I think you can sign him tonight, if you work on him— Take him to Rex's party. Invitation's on your desk. Tom got one too.*

Dan was smiling as he dialed Tom's number. They'd treat Dick Zastrow to a night on the town, show him Hollywood dining at its finest, and end up at Rex's party. By the time the night was over, the little businessman from Kansas City would be more than ready to sign on the bottom line.

"Don't answer it, please!" Sherrie held Tom as tightly as she could. They were locked together on the deep-pile white rug in front of the fireplace in Tom's living room.

"It might be important." Tom reached for the phone but he couldn't quite reach it. He was in an extremely enjoyable but awkward position.

"It's probably a salesman anyway." Sherrie's voice was breathless. "Just ignore it, Tom. It'll stop."

Sherrie reached up and wrapped her arms around Tom's neck, silencing him with a passionate kiss. They had enough of ringing phones at the office, and now that she'd finally gotten Tom to make love to her, she wasn't about to stop for a phone call.

"Honey . . . I really think I should answer that. . . ."

Sherrie raised her legs and locked them around Tom's back. It was all the persuasion he needed. She had just enough time to grab the cord and pull the phone plug out of the wall before she was lost in a whirlwind of delicious sensation.

It seemed as if hours had passed before Sherrie finally opened her eyes and gathered the necessary energy to sit up. She could hear Tom blending drinks in the kitchen and she felt as lazy and content as a well-fed cat.

"Here you go, Sherrie." Tom came back into the room carrying a fresh daiquiri and stopped cold as he noticed the unplugged phone.

"I'm sorry, Tom . . ." Sherrie looked terribly guilty. "I know I shouldn't have, but the ringing was distracting you . . . right when it was really important."

Tom grinned at her. He supposed she had a point and he certainly wasn't complaining about the way they'd spent the preceding hour. He set their glasses down on the mantel and reached out to plug the phone back in again.

Both Sherrie and Tom groaned in unison as the phone began ringing. Sherrie reached to pull the cord back out again but Tom was quicker.

"No, you don't. I'll get rid of whoever it is as soon as I can."

"Okay."

Sherrie gave in good-naturedly. Tom had already picked up the receiver. She made a teasing little grab as she walked past him and was relieved to see that at least one part of his anatomy was more interested in her than in the phone conversation.

"No, you're not interrupting a thing." Tom chuckled and captured Sherrie's hand. "The phone got accidentally unplugged and I didn't realize it."

Sherrie raised her eyebrows and Tom made a helpless little gesture. She knew what that meant.

"Dick Zastrow's ready to sign? That's great, Dan! Thirty minutes? I'll see you then."

Tom turned to explain the conversation to Sherrie but she was already putting the video cassette back in her tote bag.

"I'm really sorry about this, Sherrie, but—"

"I know." Sherrie interrupted, "The voice of the master, right?"

"Right."

Sherrie sighed and began to put on her clothes. "I knew something like this would happen if you took that call."

"Maybe we should have left it unplugged."

"Or off the hook." Sherrie took her time about dressing. Tom was watching her with obvious relish and that made her feel good. Then she picked up her tote bag and headed for the door.

"Hold it, Sherrie. Where are you going?"

"Back home. You're going somewhere with Dan, aren't you?"

Tom nodded. "We're taking a new affiliate out to dinner and then we'll drop by Rex Watson's party. I want you to come with me."

"Is that an invitation or an order?"

Tom gave her a long level look and then he grinned.

"It's an invitation. The orders come after the party when you come back here to spend the night."

"What can I say? You're the boss." Sherrie smiled ecstatically. A fancy dinner, plus one of the biggest parties of the year as Tom's date. She wouldn't miss it for the world. Of course she'd have to go to work in Marge's white dress tomorrow and everyone would guess she'd spent the night with Tom, but she didn't care.

Tom bent down to kiss her and this time Sherrie kept her eyes open. She'd have to remember to give that optometrist a rave report but not to spell out the particulars. All she knew was that learning the art of erotic massage would be a snap without her old glasses getting in the way.

8

Dick Zastrow peered out the window of Empire's new limo in awe as they approached Rex Watson's mansion. Rex had purchased the old G. B. Forbes mansion, which sat on the top of the highest rise in the Hollywood Hills overlooking the city, surrounded by other homes of the rich and famous.

"That house used to belong to Bogie and Bacall." Dan pointed at a deceptively modest-looking house on King's Road. "It looks small from the outside but it goes down three levels inside. There's a fifteen-foot-deep sunken tub in the bathroom."

"Wow! Bogie and Bacall!"

Tom, who was driving, navigated the curved road and pulled over to the side so another car could pass them. As they passed an observation point, Dick gave his predictable response. "Wow! Look at that view!"

"There's an even better one from Rex's patio. On a clear day you can see the entire city."

Dan smiled in anticipation as they took the last curve. Rex had completely modernized the inside of the house but kept the original castle-type architecture. There were secret passages and strange round tower rooms with huge medieval locks and keys. Dan and Joanna had been invited to Rex's housewarming and Dan remembered that there were seventeen bedrooms, each with its own spectacular fireplace. The mansion came into view, and for a moment Dick was speechless.

"Uh . . . Dan . . . " Dick swallowed hard. "If you'd told me it was this fancy, I would have rented a tuxedo."

"It's not necessary, Dick," Dan reassured the Midwest businessman. "You'll see people dressed in all sorts of weird outfits here tonight, sweatsuits included."

"Wow!"

Dick Zastrow's one-word vocabulary was back. Dan grinned as the limo pulled up the circular driveway and stopped for the valet parkers. It was refreshing to show the sights of Los Angeles to someone from the Midwest. They had taken Dick to dinner at Chassen's and the overweight little man had almost passed out cold when he'd caught sight of Joan Collins. Dan had made the introductions and Dick had been practically incoherent when he'd asked for her autograph.

Dick's eyes almost popped out of his head as they entered the front door. Dan introduced him to several minor starlets and Dick's normally ruddy complexion turned even redder as one of them kissed him on the cheek. They made their way to the ballroom and Dick just gasped. Rex had set up a complete gambling casino with crap tables, roulette wheels, baccarat alcoves, poker tables, and blackjack pits. There was even a gilded cashier's cage in the corner of the room. A butler met them at the door and handed them each two crisp hundred-dollar bills.

"Mr. Watson welcomes you to his casino. Have a profitable evening."

Dick looked down at the bills in his hand and blinked as Dan led him over to the cashier's cage.

"Wow! Is it real money?"

"I'm sure it is. Cash it in for chips, Dick, and try your luck. How about blackjack first?"

Dick's eyes began to gleam as he noticed the poker tables. "You go ahead, Dan. I think I'd better stick to poker. We play every Friday night at the Elks Club."

Dan found a place at a poker table for Dick and sat in on a couple of hands. He was ready to turn over his chips if Dick lost. But after the third hand, when Dick raked in a seven-hundred-dollar pot on a gutsy bluff, Dan wandered away and left him to his own devices. Friday nights at the Elks Club had been good practice.

Tom was standing next to the blackjack table, his arm around Sherrie's waist, watching several of Rex's guests lose.

"Where's our friend? Getting fleeced at the poker table?"

"I think you've got it backward."

Dan gestured toward the poker tables and Tom's eyes widened when he saw the pile of chips Dick had accumulated.

"Guess he's set for the night. He looks happy enough."

"So do you, Tom."

Tom looked down at Sherrie and grinned. "And why shouldn't I be? I've got the prettiest woman at the party on my arm."

Dan nodded. He was glad his brother was finally showing some sense when it came to women. Sherrie was one hell of a good film editor and she looked smashing tonight in that slinky white dress. He'd never really noticed how pretty she was.

"Oh, Dan?" Tom reached out to stop him as Dan moved away. "Did you run into Cici yet? She heard you were doing that Civil War thing and she's definitely interested. She says she wants to broaden her repertoire."

Dan grimaced and Tom laughed. He'd heard all about Coral Connors in the last special Dan had done for Big Green. Both men found it hard to believe that the bubbleheaded dancer had become a major star.

"You'd better go look for her, Dan. She'll pop the ratings right up over the top."

"I know it's the smart thing to do, Tom, but I'm not even sure she'll sign with me after our little run-in on the last show."

"Bite the bullet. You may have to eat a little crow but it'll be worth it. I saw the last balance sheet and we need a big draw."

"Okay, okay. You two keep an eye on Dick. I just hope Cici can handle a southern accent."

"Be serious, Dan," Sherrie spoke up. "The only accent Cici Connors can handle is the kind you sprinkle on meat."

Dan laughed as he walked away but he soon sobered. Tom was right about the balance sheet. There was a stockholders meeting on Friday. The ratings from the new expanded programming looked good, but they wouldn't translate into dividends until Empire Cable pulled out of the red. One way to boost the stockholders' confidence was to show them he had good product that would attract advertisers. The "Nite News" was an excellent draw and the new western looked promising, but his backers were clamoring for a big series that would bring in more affiliates. Everyone in the industry knew that Cici was a lousy actress, but *People* magazine had put her on the cover two weeks ago and the issue had sold out overnight. If he could produce a signed contract at the meeting, his board members might be more generous with operating capital.

Dan checked but Cici wasn't in the buffet line or sitting at any of the indoor tables. He passed through the library where several studio execs were holding court on comfortable couches and walked out on the patio. The night was crystal clear. Dan picked out the twinkling line of lights on Sunset Boulevard where it intersected with Mandeville Canyon Road and wondered what Joanna was doing tonight. He had the impulse to call her and invite her to join him, but it was almost eleven and she was probably sleeping.

Steve Trainer, a handsome young actor who'd made his name in the afternoon soaps, was looking out over the city. Dan pushed his way through the people and joined him. "Steve, just the man I wanted to see."

"About the southern-period series?"

Dan laughed. There were no secrets in this town. He'd mentioned yesterday that he was thinking of approaching Steve Trainer for the part of the Union soldier and somehow the word had gotten out.

"Should I mail you a copy of the script?"

Steve grinned. "I've already read it, Dan. My wife goes to the same hairdresser as the writer's wife."

"And I suppose it was written with you in mind?"

"Definitely. Rachel wants me to do something classy for a change. She's sick of being asked whether I really knocked up Lorraine, the gorgeous deaf paraplegic, on 'To Each His Own.' Just call my agent and we'll work out a deal."

"Hold it a second, Steve. I'm not so sure you'll want the part when I tell you who I'm trying to sign as your costar."

"I heard already. Cici Connors, the workingman's wet dream."

Dan grinned as Steve made a gesture that was on the borderline of obscene. "Think you can work with her?"

"No problem, Dan. Cici has a unique style of delivery that I find personally intriguing and the emotional interplay in the script is a real challenge. As a dedicated actor I promise to maintain my highest professional standards."

"Cut the bullshit, Steve. You want the part for the three five-minute segments where you'll be on camera alone."

Steve flashed his famous grin and shrugged his shoulders. "Well . . . that's definitely a factor. Just between you and me, I think Cici's a no-talent cunt but I'd sign on with Eva Braun if the part was big enough."

"An honest actor, that's a real rarity in this town." Dan patted Steve on the back. "Now all I have to do is sign Cici. Have you seen her?"

"Sure. She was wearing a see-through top with no bra. I didn't actually see her face but I'd recognize those boobs anywhere. She was arm in arm with Dee Dee French and I heard them say they were going upstairs to the master suite to climb in the Jacuzzi and powder their noses."

"As in snort?"

"Yeah. You'd better try to keep her off the blow while we're taping, Dan. Rachel's tennis coach knows Cici's contact. She's doing at least a gram a day."

Dan frowned. "Do you think it affects her performance?"

"Maybe." Steve looked thoughtful. "I take back what I said about keeping her off the stuff. Anything that affects Cici's performance is bound to be for the better."

There was a crowd at the foot of the marble circular stairway and Dan stopped to say hello to several people before heading upstairs. If he remembered the floor plan correctly, the master suite with its projection room, den, pool-size Jacuzzi, indoor garden, and five-hundred-square-foot bedroom took up most of the second floor.

Dan opened the bedroom door by mistake and backed out quickly. There were four nude couples romping on the mammoth circular bed. Then he remembered that the Jacuzzi was in the garden room and he found it after opening three more doors by mistake. The instant Dan entered the garden, he heard Cici's girlish laughter. He stepped past potted palms and down the flagstone path where he found Cici languishing in the huge tub, her long auburn hair pinned on top of her head.

"Danny!" Cici raised herself partially out of the water and reached for her champagne glass. "You came just at the right time. I'm out of champagne."

Dan tried not to look at Cici's famous attributes as he

moved the silver bucket closer to the edge of the tub and filled her glass.

"Me too." Dee Dee French held out her glass. "We were just arguing about who had to get up and pour."

Dan decided to get right down to it. "Are you straight enough to talk business, Cici?"

Cici gave a little giggle. "I've never been straighter in my life, Danny boy. And I know about that series you're casting. Did you sign Steve Trainer?"

"He gave me a definite yes tonight."

Cici gave a little sigh and leaned back until her head was against the cushioned side of the tub. She didn't seem to notice that the whole upper half of her body was exposed.

"Steve Trainer . . ." She pursed her lips and looked serious. "I'm just not sure, Danny. He's a lousy actor but I guess I could make him look good."

"Cici, darling . . . you could make *anyone* look good."

Cici frowned slightly and Dan knew she was trying to figure out exactly what he had meant.

"Tell Cici I paid her a compliment, Dee Dee."

"It's true, Cici. Dan said it in kind of a funny way but I know he thinks you're a wonderful actress. Isn't that right, Dan?"

"That's exactly right, Dee Dee."

Dee Dee gave him a little wink and Dan quickly revised his opinion of her. Dee Dee knew exactly what he was doing. If Cici signed, Dan made up his mind to give Dee Dee at least a walk-on.

His unexpected ally jumped in again. "I think you should do it, Cici. Think of the great costumes: wide sweeping skirts with yards of material and those tight little nipped waists that show off your figure."

Dan could see that Cici was sidetracked and now was the time to cinch the deal. "I don't think the costumes really matter to a dedicated actress like Cici. It's the opportunity for career advancement that's important. The part of Annabelle is a lot like Scarlett O'Hara, and look what that part did for Vivien Leigh."

"He's right!" Dee Dee stepped in, right on cue. "Just think about it, Cici."

"Vivien Leigh?" Cici began to smile. "Oh, yeah. I remember her, the one that gets killed in the shower. I bet she's still getting residuals from *Psycho.*"

Dee Dee winced but neither she nor Dan was about to tell Cici that she had mixed up her Leighs.

"Well . . . what do you think, Cici? Are you going to follow in Miss Leigh's footsteps?"

"It's really tempting, Danny." Cici leaned back against the lip of the tub and pouted a bit. "I might do it if I could bring myself to forgive you for being so nasty to me on that Big Green special."

Dan bit his tongue. He had to play her little game if he wanted to sign her. "Come on, Cici. That's water over the dam. Ralph Barton screwed us all on that show."

"He screwed you too?" Cici looked astonished. "That's funny, Danny. I didn't know old Ralph swung both ways."

Dee Dee reached out and took her friend's arm. "Don't make the man suffer, darling. Tell him you'll do it. I'd sign in a flash if someone offered me a part like that."

"Well . . ." Cici wiggled a little and stretched. "I guess I might sign, Danny . . . but only if you do me a big favor in return."

Dan drew a great sigh of relief. It hadn't been as tough as he'd expected.

"Sure, Cici. Anything your little heart desires."

"Take off your clothes and hop in here." Cici giggled. "Dee Dee and I are dying for someone to massage our backs."

9

JOANNA WOKE UP at two in the morning. Another nightmare. Tears were running down her cheeks as she made her way to the family room and sat down heavily on the love seat. Here she was, pregnant and very alone. And even though she had shrugged off Pinky Calvert's comments at the time, they'd had an effect. She was having her first baby much later than most women. What would she do if there *was* some sort of complication?

The baby seemed active enough and Dr. Whitney told her that everything was just fine, but could she believe him? She had taken a tranquilizer before she'd known she was pregnant. What if the little blue pill had hideously marked her baby for life?

Joanna thought of the pictures of deformed babies and shuddered. Pinky had brought up genetics and that was another problem. Dr. Whitney had asked the standard questions and she'd answered them as best she could but she couldn't very well ask Dan about his family background when he didn't believe he was the father of her baby. Naturally, she'd asked Tom some questions but there might be things he didn't know. There could be something terribly serious, like congenital heart failure, lurking in the Courtney genes. Or Down's syndrome. Joanna had avoided thinking about that. She wasn't sure she could cope with a Down's syndrome baby. Or cystic fibrosis. Everyone said a cure was imminent but it might come too late for her baby.

Joanna swallowed hard. Barring genetic problems,

there were the usual complications of childbirth. Dr. Whitney had told her not to worry but she couldn't help it. Right now the umbilical cord could be wrapped around the baby's neck. Even if that didn't happen, the placenta could become separated from the uterus. Joanna wasn't entirely sure what that would do but it was bound to be horrible. And at this very moment she could be developing toxemia, causing premature birth.

Premies. The very word made Joanna shiver. She knew that babies who weighed less than a thousand grams at birth were prone to all sorts of problems. Sometimes their lungs were so undeveloped that they had to rely on a respirator for the rest of their lives. Undeveloped digestive systems were another danger. Often premies had to undergo radical surgery, and her baby could die on the operating table from any one of a thousand ailments.

Joanna sighed. It was absurd to worry about premature birth with only two weeks to go. Women had babies like clockwork and most of them were perfectly healthy. Carters wouldn't manufacture those cute little sleepers in ten graduated sizes if most of their customers died a week or two after birth.

Deliberately, Joanna forced herself to calm down and picture herself and the baby, perhaps a lovely little golden-haired daughter, playing in the backyard. She could make cookies—chocolate chip would be good or maybe peanut butter—and invite the neighborhood children in for refreshments . . . *if* the other parents would let their children play with a child whose father wouldn't even recognize her.

Suddenly Joanna was furious. How could Dan leave her with a child to raise, all by herself? And here she was, missing him like some sort of silly teenager, saving every piece of junk he'd left behind when she ought to be throwing it all in the garbage!

The moment she thought of it, Joanna was on her

feet. She dragged out the box of Dan's things, grabbed the biggest trash barrel she could find and settled down on the couch for a stint of long-due housekeeping. The first thing Joanna pulled out of the box was one of Dan's old Speedo swimsuits. She wadded the swim trunks up into a ball and threw them at the barrel. "Take that you lousy rat!"

Joanna picked up Dan's Dodgers' baseball cap. "And that!"

Dan's old electric shaver hit the edge of the waste-basket and bounced in. "And that!"

Joanna pegged Dan's broken tennis racket toward the basket, strings flapping. He had used it to play in the celebrity tennis match last year but he hadn't even gotten to the semifinals.

One by one Dan's discards hit the trash barrel. Joanna was growing tired as she picked up the last item, a gag gift she'd given Dan for his birthday. It was an executive decision maker, a box with a bouncing red light and three labeled categories. You asked a question, pressed the button, and the light landed on YES, NO, or MAYBE. Dan had taken it to the office and it had been on his desk until he'd moved to Tri-City studios. Then he'd obviously forgotten to pack it.

As she held the box in her hand, Joanna realized that she was more angry with herself than she was with Dan. She'd never had any trouble making decisions before. For the first time in her life, she was being ambivalent. She missed Dan and she wanted him back. That much was perfectly clear. But she also wished, just as strongly, that she'd never have to lay eyes on him again. How could she want two so totally opposite things? If Dan knocked on her door right now, admitted he'd been wrong, acknowledged that the baby was his, and begged to come back, would she let him? She honestly didn't know and her indecision made her furious.

Even though she knew it was silly and juvenile,

Joanna turned on the little box and asked her question. If all her conditions were met, should she take Dan back?

The bells rang, the red light bounced, and finally came to rest on the MAYBE category. Joanna shrugged and tried it again. The bells rang, the red light bounced, and again it landed on MAYBE.

"Three times and out." Joanna asked her question, pressed the button, and got a MAYBE for the third time.

"You're a big help!" Joanna threw the decision maker in the wastebasket and headed back to bed. She had a court appearance tomorrow and she simply had to get some rest. As she fell asleep she wondered if the decision maker was stuck or whether it was just as ambivalent about Dan as she was.

_____ **10**

IT WAS EIGHT-FIFTEEN in the morning when Dan pulled into his parking space on the Tri-City lot, easing his station wagon in, next to the limo. After they'd left Rex's party, he'd told Tom to drop him off and keep the limo for the rest of the evening. Sherrie had climbed in the back and claimed she'd play the part of a movie star while Tom drove them back to Malibu. Dan had a pretty good idea what Sherrie and Tom might have done in the spacious back seat but he wasn't about to ask questions.

"Dan! Dan, darling! I need to talk to you!"

Dan stopped in his tracks. It was Pinky Calvert and there was no chance to duck her. She was just coming around the corner of the editing complex and she was a show-stopper in a bright pink beaded jumpsuit. The color was so bright that Dan actually winced as she approached.

"Hi, Pinky. How's the show coming?"

Pinky placed one diamond-studded hand on Dan's sleeve. "I just finished taping, darling. An insider's view of Rex Watson's party but don't get upset. I didn't breathe a word about the deal that was made in the Jacuzzi."

"Uh . . . good!" Dan nodded but his mind was spinning. Had Pinky seen them? She seemed to have spies out everywhere.

"Cici told me. And I think it was a stroke of pure genius on your part to give the supporting role to Dee

140

Dee French. She's a charming little actress, don't you think? And such a stabilizing influence on Cici!"

"Yes. Yes, she is."

Pinky leaned a little closer. "I'm probably the only one who knows, but Dee Dee has a doctorate in psychology. She was Phi Beta Kappa at Stanford. I'm sure that's the reason she handles Cici so well."

Dan was so astounded he couldn't think of an appropriate reply but that didn't stop Pinky. She could gossip for hours to a blank wall.

"Actually, speaking on a purely personal level, I do hope you take an interest in Dee Dee now that Joanna's moving away. You're the type of man who needs an educated woman, and it can't be very much fun, living alone."

Dan spoke before he thought. "Joanna's moving away? But why?"

"Because of the gossip, darling. Surely you can't blame her. After all, there's the child to consider. Unless, of course, you've decided to reconcile?"

Dan was about to reply when he realized that Pinky was pumping him for information. "Excuse me, Pinky. I'm late to an appointment. Keep up the good work. Our viewers love you."

Dan hurried off as fast as he could. He didn't breathe easy until he'd closed the door of the producers' building behind him. Then he stopped and thought about what Pinky had said. Of course there was gossip about Joanna's baby and their divorce. And it was perfectly reasonable for Joanna to take action to protect her baby from people's malicious speculation.

His step was heavy as he walked toward his office. He didn't like the idea of Joanna moving out of his life. What if she went back to the farm in Minnesota? Then he'd never get to see her. Of course, after the divorce went through, she was free to go anywhere she wanted. And he'd waived all rights to the baby.

The baby. Dan tried to concentrate on that. Stan Lorman's baby, not his. Naturally, he'd waived all rights. But was that a mistake? If he'd demanded visitation privileges, at least he'd have an excuse for seeing Joanna on a regular basis.

"Good morning, boss." Alice took one look at Dan's long face and shook her head. "No, I guess it's not. My lifeguide says that morning depression is—"

"Not now, Alice," Dan interrupted. "I have to get ready for my meeting with Ralph. Has Tom come in yet?"

"He's over in editing and he said he'd be here at a quarter to nine."

"Alice? Has Joanna mentioned anything about moving?"

"Not to me, but it sounds like a good idea considering all the . . ."

"Gossip that's going around. I know. Is there any coffee, Alice?"

"Fresh perked. Sit down, take three aspirins, and I'll bring you a cup. Oh, Dick Zastrow is coming in at noon to sign the papers for affiliation. He's bringing some rhubarb plants for Joanna and I told him you'd make sure she got them. Miss Dubois comes in at twelve-thirty, but then you're free for the rest of the afternoon."

Dan nodded. Perhaps he could run those plants over to Joanna and ask her if she planned to move. Then he'd know for sure.

Alice was studying him intently. "I've got an idea, boss. Why don't you run those plants over to Joanna this afternoon, and ask her if she's planning to move? Then you'd know for sure."

"Dammit, Alice . . . just get me my coffee!"

Alice nodded and backed out of the room. Dan was in an awful mood. Maybe it was time to give Joanna a call.

"Ralph Barton is here to see you, Mr. Courtney."

Dan and Tom glanced at each other as Alice's voice came over the intercom. It was five minutes before nine. Ralph must be nervous.

"On your feet, Tom." Dan grinned at his brother. "Ralph hates to walk into a room with tall men. That's why all his assistants are short."

Ralph walked in, dressed impeccably in an expensive, summer-weight suit, and even though it was already in the low nineties outside, he managed to look as cool as if he'd just stepped from a refrigerated car. He probably had. One of the perks of Ralph's position was a personal limo with a full-time chauffeur. Dan and Tom exchanged glances. The word around town was that Ralph Barton never perspired and he was living up to his image today.

"Ralph! Good to see you." Dan gestured toward a chair and all three men sat down. "Coffee?"

"No, thanks. The ulcer's kicking up again."

"I'm sorry to hear that. You don't mind if my brother Tom sits in, do you? He minds the store while I'm off fishing for affiliates." Dan knew that Ralph probably felt outnumbered, but he took the intrusion well as he turned to Tom with a smile.

"That's fine with me. As a matter of fact, that's very good. So you're Dan's assistant, then?"

"Well . . ."

Dan stepped in smoothly. "Not at all. Tom's an equal partner in Empire Cable. He's in charge of production while I take care of the financial end."

Ralph winced. He'd probably have to offer Dan's brother a position at GRN too. It would run into money but he didn't want Empire Cable to stay in the Courtney family.

"Well, Ralph . . . I know you didn't come here just to chat." Dan leaned back in his chair. "What's on your mind?"

"A little business offer, Dan. The boys and I discussed it yesterday and we came to the conclusion that we need you back at GRN. I'm offering you the position of VP in charge of programming for Big Green."

Dan nodded. They'd already decided to string Ralph along just to see how high the stakes could get. Naturally they'd turn him down in the end.

"That's one hell of an offer, Ralph. What's the salary?"

"Seven hundred thousand a year plus the car and the expense account."

"That's a lot of money." Dan leaned back in his armchair. "What do you think, Tom? Head of programming for the largest network is nothing to sneeze at."

"I don't know, Dan." Tom went into the part they'd rehearsed for Ralph's benefit. "Do you think you can run Empire and work for Big Green at the same time?"

"Sure, as long as I've got you to help me. That would be all right, wouldn't it, Ralph?"

Ralph shook his head. "No, Dan. Conflict of interest and all that. And setting up Tom, here, to run it wouldn't meet our criteria. Actually, I'd like to hire both of you. We have an opening in our film department that would be right up Tom's alley. It pays three-fifty a year—plus expenses, of course."

Dan looked over and quickly averted his eyes, since Tom was having trouble keeping a straight face. "Let me get this straight, Ralph. Tom and I would have to sell Empire to accept your offer?"

"Right."

"That's a big step, Ralph." Dan frowned and turned to Tom. "What do you think?"

Tom shook his head. "I don't know, Dan. We're just getting rolling and I doubt if we could find a buyer who'd be willing to pay what it's worth."

"That's no problem." Ralph smiled and played his ace in the hole. "I happen to know of a group that's interested and they'd pay top dollar."

"Fascinating." Dan began to smile. "Does this group have any connection with GRN, Ralph?"

"Only peripherally. Let's just say it's a consortium of businessmen who know a good thing when they see it. I have it on good faith that they'd be willing to pay over two million."

"Two million!" Tom whistled. "That's pretty incredible for a fledgling organization like Empire. Our assets aren't worth a tenth of that on paper."

"They're interested in the potential, Tom. Empire Cable promises to become a major in the cable market."

"Wait a second, Tom." Dan stepped in. "I think Ralph's just done us a hell of a favor by telling us about that consortium. If Empire's got that much potential, we'd be fools to sell."

"That's true." Tom nodded. "Thanks, Ralph."

Dan stood up and walked around the desk to shake Ralph's hand. "You've been a real help, Ralph. I admit we were really tempted by your offer, but I can see that we'd better stick with Empire. Would you like a tour of our facilities before you go?"

"Uh . . . no, thanks. I've got to get back to a meeting."

Ralph rose to his feet and headed for the door. He'd hoped he could get Courtney the easy way but the whole thing had backfired and he wasn't sure how. It was time to call a meeting of the big boys.

Joanna did her best to look less uncomfortable than she felt. The courtroom was packed with a restless high school civics class and the air conditioning wasn't working. Even Judge Bassinger, who was usually the height of judicial fashion in an expensive, hand-tailored robe, looked rumpled and sweaty. The six high narrow windows, evenly spaced along one wall, had been opened to catch the slightest hint of a breeze, but the atmosphere inside the room remained stifling.

The jurors were practically falling asleep as the prosecutor droned on. He was a thin man in his fifties with a face that looked even older. A heavy drinker, he'd obviously tipped a few at the midmorning recess. His voice was pitched so low that it was difficult to hear over the street noises and his arguments made no sense. Unfortunately, the jurors seemed too bored or too exhausted from the heat to sort out the fallacies in his reasoning.

Joanna glanced over at her client and suddenly realized the one thing that might win their case. He looked alert, unruffled, and totally innocent.

The charge against him was unlawful conversion and the testimony had been extremely tedious and convoluted. It was unlikely that anyone on the jury fully understood the question. That meant the case would probably be decided on personalities and her client truly looked the part of an innocent victim.

At last the prosecutor finished and it was Joanna's turn to address the jury. She deliberately left her papers on the table and approached them empty-handed.

"Ladies and gentlemen of the jury," she began. "It's very hot, so I promise you my remarks will be brief."

There were several answering smiles and Joanna waited a beat before she went on. Now she had their attention.

"Since the case against my client is impossibly complicated and the testimony has been far too confusing to reach any clear-cut conclusion, it all boils down to one simple question. Do you believe my client?"

She gestured toward her client, who was watching the jury alertly. She had carefully coached him to make eye contact with each and every juror.

"Or do you believe the prosecutor?"

This time she pointed sharply at the older lawyer who had sprawled in his chair and was in the act of mopping his very red face with a crumpled handkerchief.

"As you make your decision, I urge you to carefully consider the prosecuting attorney. He wants you to buy his entire line of reasoning on simple faith. Then ask yourself this question. Would you buy a used car from this man?"

Dan sat down in an upholstered seat in the editing room and took a deep breath of the cool air inside. He'd rushed over the minute Tom had called to ask for a brainstorming session on the newest western episode. Tom and Sherrie had spent all morning working on the fight scene but they still weren't satisfied with the results.

The editing room was a plush miniature theater. It looked like the private screening room of an old-time Hollywood mogul with the exception of the electronic gear. A dozen video screens glowed with a variety of stopped-frame images or pulsed with vivid color test patterns. The control console, which Tom was manning, resembled something taken from the set of a space wars movie. It had more dials, switches, and blinking lights than were dreamed of in NASA budget proposals.

"Do you think it's a script problem?" Dan asked.

Tom took a moment to consider. "No, that's not it."

"Directing?"

"No . . . and the acting's fine too. It's something else, Dan, and we can't put our finger on it."

"The X-factor."

"That's right." Tom frowned. That was their name

for the intangible ingredient that turned a bad scene into something that worked.

"Okay, let's take a look at it."

Tom dimmed the lights and pressed a button to play the scene.

The apache's silent footsteps on Tombstone's wooden sidewalks contrasted with the thumping and jingling of Bart's boots and spurs. The Apache reacted, drawing his hunting knife. Bart chambered a round in his lever-action Winchester at the instant the Apache hurled his knife but the knife buried itself in his thorax before he could shoot.

Tom froze the image on the screen. "See what I mean, Dan? It just doesn't work!"

"Maybe there's too much intercutting," Sherry spoke up. "It's visually confusing. We forget whose side we're on."

"We tried editing out some of that but it didn't help," Tom reminded her. "I'm afraid we'll have to reshoot the scene. We just don't have enough coverage from the Apache's point-of-view."

"It's not POV footage we need." Dan sounded thoughtful. "It's something far more subtle. Run the master again, Tom. I'll show you what I mean."

Dan watched intently as Tom ran the master shot. It was the first shot a director made, a wide angle run-through of the whole scene from the vantage point of a person sitting tenth-row center at a theatrical play.

"There!" Dan called out and Tom froze the tape. "Cut to Bart's close-up. Okay . . . now spot the insert right there and let's see what we've got."

Tom grinned. The cut that Dan had just proposed would have entailed hours of labor if he'd been working with film. Film editing was still done by hand. Innumerable strips of celluloid were laboriously cemented together and the editor had to wait for it to dry before he could see the effects of the cut. With video tape, all

Tom had to do was punch up the change on the computer keyboard and hit the interlock play lever. The cut was done almost instantaneously. In seconds, the screens displayed Dan's version of the scene.

"Oh, that's much better!" Sherry was always impressed by how these minor changes made the same footage seem like a different take.

"Almost . . ." Tom was thoughtful. "How about a little sweetening? Maybe a snare drum to build tension during the approach?"

"Let's try it."

While Sherrie pulled open a huge flat drawer containing hundreds of audio cassettes, Dan thought about the magic of post-production. The director could be mediocre and the actors merely adequate but a good post-production man like Tom could turn the final product into award-winning material.

Sherrie handed him an audio tape and Tom pushed it into the control panel. He played expertly with the levers and knobs for several moments, advancing and retarding the sound track in relation to the picture. When everything was lined up to his satisfaction, he set the interlock, and rewound.

"Here goes."

All three of them watched the scene again. This time, the almost-subliminal snare drum built the tension so that the knife throw came as a thrilling climax.

"Pure genius!" Dan stood up and stretched. "Come on back to the office with me and we'll eat the rest of my chocolate Emmy."

It was one o'clock, Dick Zastrow had signed his affiliate contract, and Dan was walking back to his office when he saw the Empire limo come in through the gate. Alice was driving and she'd managed to talk the costume department out of a chauffeur's cap. Even though he couldn't see her, Dan knew Maree was riding in the back, behind the tinted glass. The long black car turned left and disappeared around the corner, bypassing the parking lot. Alice was taking Maree on a driving tour of the studio, exactly as he'd instructed. That meant he had at least fifteen minutes to figure out what to say to her.

When Dan got back to his deserted office, he poured himself a fresh cup of coffee and leaned back in his chair. He couldn't allow the affair he'd begun with Maree in New York to continue. It wouldn't be fair to either of them. He was still a married man and Pinky Calvert would be sure to get wind of it. Joanna was already being hurt by the gossip about them and he wasn't about to add more fuel to the flames. Dan was truthful enough to admit that the potential gossip wasn't the only reason he wanted to end the affair. Their relationship could go nowhere, not with the specter of Joanna haunting his dreams. But what was the best way to tell Maree that it was over? When his intercom buzzed twenty minutes later to announce her arrival, Dan still hadn't come up with a tactful way.

"Dan!" Maree ran into the room and hugged him tightly. "I am happy to see you!"

"I'm glad to see you too." Dan returned her embrace and then stepped back quickly. "Did you have a nice flight?"

"It took much time to find my luggage but I am here at last. Tell me, where should I put my things?"

"Alice arranged a bungalow for you at the Beverly Hills Hotel until you can find your own place."

Maree looked puzzled. "Then I am not to stay with you?"

"Uh . . . no. I'll explain that later when I drive you to the hotel. Right now I want Alice to show you the set and introduce you to the rest of the staff."

Dan buzzed for Alice who appeared much too quickly. He had the sneaking suspicion she'd been listening outside the office door.

"Will you show Miss Dubois the set, Alice? I have to make a few phone calls and then I'll join you."

"Sure. Come on, Maree. I've been meaning to ask you a question on fashion, anyway. My therapy guide says you can tell exactly how old a European woman is by the way she drapes her scarf around her neck. I don't think that's ever caught on in America. Dan's wife, Joanna, never wears them, but maybe that's because she's still so young and attractive."

Dan shook his head as the two women went out the door. Alice was incorrigible. Maree was wearing a patterned scarf to match her traveling suit and Alice had zeroed in on it like a homing pigeon, wasting no time in letting Maree know exactly where her loyalties lay.

Dan picked up the phone again and punched out the extension for Tom's office. A moment later, his brother came on the line.

"Yeah, Dan. What's up?"

"A little problem, Tom. Her name's Maree Dubois and she's the French model I signed for the fashion series."

"That's a problem?"

"It could turn into one. I need someone to show her around town, to do the typical tourist things."

After a long pause, Tom sighed. "That would be pretty awkward for me right now. I just invited Sherrie to spend the week with me and . . . well . . . I don't think Sherrie would exactly fall in love with the idea."

"I guess not." Dan grinned at the near-panic in his brother's voice.

"How about Alice? She knows all the tourist spots."

"I don't think that would work, Tom."

"Oh. Well, there's always you."

"I was hoping to avoid that. I know it's ridiculous, but it makes me feel a little uncomfortable."

"Why?"

"Well . . . Maree's gorgeous and unattached. There'd be gossip and that might bother Joanna."

There was a long silence and then Tom chuckled. "It sounds like you're having second thoughts about being single. Why don't you just make up with Joanna and both of you can show Maree the sights. That's what you really want to do, isn't it?"

"Cut it out, Tom. I don't want to hear that tired lecture again."

"Okay. You're a big boy. You'll just have to work it out by yourself."

Dan hung up the phone and sighed. When the phone rang again, it was Tom, calling back.

"Sorry, Dan. I guess I shouldn't have been so outspoken. I've been thinking and I *do* have one suggestion."

"Yes?"

"I've seen pictures of Maree Dubois and you can't ask one of the married men to escort her around town. That'd be asking for trouble. Since there's only one other single guy on the staff, we'll have to use Stan."

"Lorman?" Dan's voice turned cold.

Tom spoke fast before Dan could hang up. "You don't have to ask him. I will. Forget your personal bias for a minute and consider the free publicity we'll get. Stan can do a couple of spots for the 'Nite News' while he's showing her around town, a sort of Parisian's view of Hollywood. He'll be introducing Maree to the Empire audience and it'll be a dynamite promo for her fashion show."

There was a moment's hesitation and then Dan sighed deeply. "Okay, but you arrange it. The less I see of that bastard, the better."

Dan was frowning as he hung up the phone. It was

only right to provide some sort of entertainment for Maree but he'd have to warn her before she went out with the son-of-a-bitch who'd ruined his marriage.

Maree opened her suitcase and began to hang her clothes in the closet.

"White wine?" Dan handed the glass to Maree, who was standing in front of the mirror holding up a sheer peach-colored négligee.

"Thank you, Dan Courtney. This color is lovely, no? I spend long monies for this in New York."

Dan cleared his throat. This was no time to correct Maree's English. "It's very pretty, Maree. Would you stop unpacking for a minute? There's something we have to talk about."

"Of course." Maree sat down on the edge of the bed obediently. "What is it, Dan?"

"I just want you to know that I had a marvelous time in New York but—"

"Oh, also I did." Maree gave him a radiant smile. "You have changed my thinking of American mens."

"Well . . . that's quite a compliment." Dan cleared his throat again. "Maree? That's what I wanted to talk to you about."

"Yes?"

"It's just that New York was New York. And this is Los Angeles. I . . . uh . . . I find my situation here has changed over the past few days."

"Mon Dieu!" Maree looked crestfallen. "My contract . . . she is canceled?"

"No, nothing like that."

"It is the monies, then." Maree gave a sigh of relief. "You do not have to give me so many monies, Dan. I am willing to take a slice."

Dan smiled. "No, Maree. You don't have to take a cut. It's our relationship that has to change."

A puzzled expression crossed Maree's lovely face and then, suddenly, she laughed.

"Oh, that! You American mens must stop hitting around the bush."

"It's *beating* around the bush, Maree."

"Okay. Beating around the bush. You just say, *I cannot make love to you anymore.* And I say, *Okay.* Then all is straight. Alice told me you love your wife. That is unusual but it is also very romantic."

"But you're not angry?"

"Why should I be? We have one perfect evenings to remember. It will be our secret, yes?"

Dan stared at her for a moment in total disbelief. He'd spent hours trying to come up with exactly the right way to break off their affair and Maree had put it all into one simple sentence. All his worries about gossip had been just an excuse to hide the truth. He still loved Joanna.

"Thank you, Maree." Dan stepped closer and hugged her. "You've been very understanding about this whole thing and I'm grateful."

Maree smiled. "And I also must say thank you for arranging a fig for this evening."

"A fig?"

"Yes, with your charming newsman. I am looking forward to it."

Dan paused for a moment and then he laughed. "You mean a *date*."

"That is right, a date. He is inviting me to a Hollywood nightclub."

Dan picked up his car keys and turned back as he opened the door. "Maree?"

"Yes, Dan Courtney."

"Watch out for Stan Lorman. He's on the make. That means—"

"You do not have to tell me," Maree interrupted. "Alice gave me much instruction on these words."

11

RALPH BARTON HELD up one finger for the waiter, who saw the gesture and wasted no time in getting to the booth.

"Bring three piña coladas, Sam. George Askos and Ben Santini will be joining me any minute."

"Right away, Mr. Barton."

As the waiter rushed off, the corners of Ralph's mouth turned up. He always got the very best of service and it wasn't because he was an over generous tipper. From the day he had taken over as president of GRN, he had commanded a private booth in the main dining room, reserved especially for him.

The telephone, in a little niche next to the booth, jingled softly and Ralph picked it up. It was the desk, telling him that George and Santini had arrived. Several moments later, the two men walked into the restaurant. Even in a place like the Polo Lounge, where celebrities were commonplace, heads turned. Ben Santini was the head of NNT, the second network in the ratings. USAT was third and Anatole Askos, the Greek tycoon, had recently purchased it for his playboy son, George.

Ralph watched the two men follow the maître 'd through the crowded room. George Askos was wearing a leather jacket with his ever-present Greek fisherman's cap. He told people it reminded him of his roots but Ralph figured the closest George had ever been to a fishing boat was his father's yacht cruising on the Mediterranean. George was in his early thirties but his round face and pudgy body made him appear much younger. The word was that George had failed miserably at every job his father had ever given him. A little over a year ago, when George had fallen for a gorgeous, money-hungry showgirl and married her after a drunken weekend in Vegas, the old man had bought her off, purchased USAT, and installed George as president in a last-ditch effort to teach him responsibility. Insiders knew that George had little real power. His father made all the decisions.

Ben Santini was a different story. A small, dark man in his forties with a sharp-featured face, Santini looked dangerous. He wore a white suit, dark shirt, and sunglasses, which only added to the illusion. The advice around town was not to cross him and Ralph had heard that Santini had some powerful connections in the family. Whatever the reason, there was never any trouble on the NNT lot.

As they neared the table, Ralph fixed his face in a welcoming smile. "Glad you could make it. Santini? George? Sit down. The drinks ought to be here any minute."

The moment they were seated, Sam the bartender arrived with the drinks. Ralph's was garnished with a wedge of pineapple and a sprinkling of coconut, no cherry. The other two drinks had all three garnishes.

"No cherry, Ralph?" Santini raised his eyebrows in question.

"I never eat them, Santini. Not since that scare over red dye number four."

Santini took a sip of his drink and smiled. "They make a good drink here but I'm betting yours is nothing but pure fruit juice."

Ralph laughed. "That's true, Santini. I'm off the

booze for good. My doctor says it aggravates my ulcer."

"That's too bad, Ralph." George's cap was slightly askew as he downed his drink and held up his finger for another. "I'm glad I'm a Greek. We drink ouzo like water and we don't get ulcers."

Santini stared hard at Ralph. "It's not the alcohol that's getting to your ulcer. I heard you struck out with Dan Courtney this morning."

"So, did you, Santini. That's the reason I asked you to meet me here. I think it's about time we pool our resources."

"Courtney's a nothing." George dismissed him with a sweep of his hand. "That two point seven of his was a fluke. USAT's not losing any sleep."

"You might not be worried but your old man is." Santini spoke up. "I heard he made you offer Courtney a VP in development at six-fifty."

George looked a little sheepish. "Okay, but it wasn't my idea. The old man worries too much. He thinks there's a chance that Empire could knock us out of third place."

"Exactly!" Ralph brought his fist down hard on the table. "It's a long shot but Courtney could make it, and that would hurt all three of us. We have to stop him before he builds up momentum."

"How?" We know he can't be bought. All three of us have tried." George drained his second drink and held up his finger for a third. His cap had slipped a little farther.

Santini leaned back and lit up one of his smelly little black cigars, looking thoughtful as he blew a smoke ring toward the ceiling. "I could eliminate the problem."

"I'm sure you could." Ralph smiled at him. "But I don't think we need to do anything . . . uh . . . drastic. I've found another way but the people I talked to are expensive. Jacobi and Associates. They specialize in this type of thing."

"I've never heard of them." George frowned. "How about you, Santini?"

Santini shook his head and Ralph hurried to explain. "You haven't heard of them because they're good. Jacobi keeps a very low profile. He runs a team that specializes in subverting the competition."

"Hold on, Ralph." Santini looked surprised. "That's exactly what I proposed!"

Ralph smiled. "It is, Santini, it is. It's just that Jacobi and Associates play dirty but they stop short of major felonies. Why shoot a man when you can drive him to suicide? You see my point?"

"You're talking subtlety." George began to grin. "Okay, Ralph. The Greeks understand subtlety. Remember the Trojan horse? It sounds good to me, Ralph, but I want to know how much it'll cost. USAT's at the bottom of the heap and I'm not sure how much more I can get out of the old man."

"Forget your old man, George. The fewer people that know about this, the better. Just take the cash out of your allowance."

George's normally ruddy face turned even redder. It seemed that everyone in the industry knew about the monthly allowance his father still gave him in lieu of a salary.

"What sort of guarantee do I get?"

Ralph laughed. "No guarantees, George, but I give you my word that Jacobi and Associates are worth every penny. Remember that Union Tungsten take-over?"

Both men nodded. It had been in all the papers.

"Jacobi arranged that and he did it practically overnight. And everything he did was perfectly legal. The federal government launched a full-scale investigation but they couldn't find a single irregularity."

"Okay." George nodded. "I'm in if Santini is."

Ralph turned to the Italian. "Looks like it's up to you."

Santini let another lazy smoke ring float up at the ceiling. "I'm in, but if this doesn't work, Ralph, I'm holding you personally responsible."

"Consider it done." Ralph picked up his glass and held it aloft. "Let's toast the demise of Empire Cable."

George sat at the table after Ralph and Santini had left, staring down at his drink. This whole situation made him very uneasy. He pushed the drink aside, ordered a cup of coffee from the waiter, and thought about the two men who had just left. Barton didn't need money from them to hire Jacobi. It had been a ploy to involve NNT and USAT in case things backfired. And George had been around long enough to know the way Santini operated. He wouldn't just sit on his hands and wait for Jacobi to play his semi-legal dirty tricks. He'd take direct action, the Italian way. Suddenly George realized why he'd been invited to this meeting. He was the patsy. If anything went wrong, Santini and Ralph would finger him. He had to buy himself an insurance policy right away.

After the waiter had refilled his coffee cup, George considered what his father would do in a situation like this. Anatole Askos was seventy-eight years old but he was in robust good health and he controlled his many businesses with intelligence and cunning. Powerful men had powerful enemies but Anatole Askos was the exception. People said he had outlived them all but George knew that was only partially true. His father employed a network of experts who did nothing but compile dossiers on his business associates. Those files contained information that eluded even the C.I.A. If Anatole Askos had any doubts, he investigated . . . thoroughly.

George smiled. For the first time in his life, he had no doubt that he was making the right decision. He reached for the phone and dialed a number. Rumor had it that more than one million-dollar deal had been accomplished from the phones at the Polo Lounge. The call he was about to make might eventually net him even more than that.

Simon Jacobi, a tall, stoop-shouldered man with thinning brown hair and deep-set eyes, had often been compared to the man in *American Gothic,* the famous painting. He was perfectly nondescript and could easily fade into a crowd without notice. It was this very forgettable quality that brought him to the business in the first place. Simon specialized in corporate double-dealing, making a far better living at it than he had as an accountant.

While still in accounting school, Simon had learned the knack of obtaining confidential information without being remembered by the person who had obliged him. He had put himself through college by requesting student personnel files and substituting glowing recommendations for ones that might cause future problems. Simon had once estimated that in his college career he had doctored five hundred student files at fifty nontaxable dollars a pop.

Now, twenty years later, Simon sat in his chrome and glass office on Wilshire Boulevard and thought about his newest project. He was working late tonight. Quite by accident, Simon had discovered that key government computers were more willingly manipulated after midnight. He liked to think the flying heads and chips were tired after a long day's work and sleepily gave up information without bothering to demand every digit of the user's code.

Simon smiled as he went over the information he'd obtained from NUMAX, one of the newest electronic information networks. If his staff in the field came through, he could wrap up this project even sooner than he'd estimated. Ralph Barton had hired him this afternoon with a two-hundred-and-fifty-thousand-dollar retainer and his personal assurance that the remaining five hundred thousand would be delivered in the morning. It was a plum account and Simon was pleased. He always took a personal interest in his VIP clients and he knew that Ralph Barton could throw a lot of business his way.

The bell on Simon's computer rang and he shoved his desk chair back to watch as another report came in from the field. He had sent his expert team out right after Ralph Barton had left. Simon tore the paper off the machine and studied the material carefully. He now knew Dan Courtney's areas of financial and personal vulnerability and that gave him a perfect place to start in the morning.

It was well past midnight and Simon had been working since seven the previous morning. He knew it would be wise to go back to his apartment and get a good night's sleep but he was too excited about his new case to relax. Perhaps he'd drop by Leila's place on the way home to take the edge off his excitement.

Simon picked up the phone and punched out a Beverly Hills number. The phone was answered on the third ring by a pleasant female voice.

"Miss Pritchard's residence. Fay speaking."

"This is Mr. Adams. I'd like an appointment."

"Oh, yes, Mr. Adams. Just a moment and I'll see if accommodations are available."

There was a click and Simon drummed his fingers on the desk top in time to the innocuous recorded music. In less than a minute, Fay's voice came on the line again. "How soon could you be here, Mr. Adams?"

"Twenty minutes. I'm fairly close."

"Fine. Miss Pritchard will be expecting you."

Traffic was light as Simon turned right on Wilshire Boulevard toward Beverly Hills. In precisely eighteen minutes he pulled up in front of a handsome duplex, designed in the thirties. He got out of the car, activated the alarm system, and walked up the impeccably manicured walk. A small shutter opened in the door, someone looked out, and then the door was opened by a lovely blond girl dressed in maid's attire.

"It's good to see you again, Mr. Adams. Follow me, please." She led the way to a small sitting room and stepped aside so Simon could enter. A tall, gray-haired woman who still bore traces of striking beauty, commanded the room from a wheelchair.

"Ah, Mr. Adams, you're always so prompt. I'd like you to meet Luanne and Diane. As you can see they are twins and they just arrived from Seattle."

Simon gave an almost imperceptible frown and Leila Pritchard turned to the two girls who were sitting demurely on the couch.

"That will be all for now, ladies. You may be excused."

"It was lovely meeting you, Mr. Adams." Luanne and Diane spoke in unison, then rose and left, smiling sweetly at Simon on the way out. They were well trained.

Leila waited until the two girls had left before she turned to Simon. "So, it's Violet again, Mr. Adams?"

Simon nodded. Then he cleared his throat and hoped his nervousness didn't show as he forced out the words. "And . . . is Keith available?"

"Of course." Leila Pritchard smiled graciously as if it were the most natural request in the world to spend an hour in one of her tastefully decorated bedrooms with a thirteen-year-old girl and a black ex-con.

Ben Santini walked through the noisy passenger terminal with its bright purple carpet and yellow plastic chairs toward the oak-paneled door next to the small stand-up bar. Los Angeles International Airport had been remodeled for the Olympics three years ago, but the airport was still crowded. The waiting areas were filled with summer tourists, toting bulging packages with souvenirs from Disneyland and Hollywood.

Santini stepped to the side as a tanned college student, wearing a Fear T-shirt and cut off jeans, elbowed through the crowd carrying a surfboard. A few feet later he was almost knocked off his feet by a frantic young mother chasing her run-away toddler.

"They ought to furnish this place with cages," Santini muttered, eyeing a crowd of grubby young people, sprawled on the chairs with backpacks and sleeping bags. A red-faced tour director was trying to get their attention with a microphone but no one was listening. Something about another delay in their flight plans.

Santini reached the oak door at last and flashed his VIP card. A smiling airline employee closed the door behind him, effectively cutting off the crying babies and irritated travelers.

"Right this way, Mr. Santini. I have a table waiting for you." The smiling young woman led him to a table overlooking the tarmac and returned quickly with a plate of hors d'oeuvres.

"This is more like it." Santini leaned back in the overstuffed chair and sighed. "I don't understand why people fly tourist class."

"Money, Mr. Santini," the young woman answered. "First class is a lot more expensive."

"Not if you own the airline. Get a bottle of red wine and join me."

While he was waiting, Santini tried a sautéed mushroom in wine sauce and glanced around the room. The lighting was subdued, the decor very old money. Four men were sitting at a nearby table wearing expensive three-piece suits and carrying oversized leather briefcases. He decided they were high-powered lawyers, flying at their client's expense. At another table, an elegantly dressed woman sat holding her miniature poodle, feeding him bits of hors d'oeuvre with long red manicured nails.

"Your wine, Mr. Santini?"

The young woman set a bottle on the table and turned it so he could read the label. It was a 1978 BV Cabernet Sauvignon. She opened it effortlessly and poured a small amount in a crystal wineglass.

"Our bartender remembered that you enjoyed this on your last trip, Mr. Santini. I told them to load a case on the plane for you."

"Good." Santini smiled. "Now sit down . . . right next to me. I need to kill a little time before my flight."

The young woman blushed but she did as he asked. Though she'd been told what to expect, she gasped slightly as she felt his fingers brush her thigh.

"Talk to me, honey," Santini ordered.

"Yes, Mr. Santini. Are you flying for business? Or for . . . uh . . . pleasure?"

"Pleasure. Definitely for pleasure." Santini smiled guilelessly as he slid his fingers higher. "I try to get back to Chicago at least four times a year to visit my brother. Move a little closer, honey. That's right."

The young woman's face was very pink by the time her beeper went off, announcing the flight. "Uh . . . excuse me, Mr. Santini, but flight seventeen is boarding its preferred passengers now. If you'll . . . uh . . . just follow me?"

"Anytime, honey." Santini moved his hand and rubbed her bottom as she stood up. "What's your name?"

"Bunny Roberts, Mr. Santini. It's right here on my nametag."

Santini pinched her bottom again. "I wasn't looking at your nametag, honey. You like Italian food?"

"It's my favorite, Mr. Santini."

"Then get your ass in gear and change into something sexy. I'll tell them to hold the plane. You're coming to Chicago with me."

"Oh, Mr. Santini!" Bunny gave a little squeal of delight. "It'll only take me a minute to change."

Santini smiled at her obvious excitement. "Take your time, honey. They'll hold this fucking plane forever if I say so."

The delighted expression stayed on Bunny's face until the door to the employees' locker room closed behind her. Then she was all business as she rushed to the pay phone on the wall. She dropped a quarter in the slot, dialed quickly, and tapped her foot impatiently as she waited for her call to go through. She didn't dare leave Santini alone for too long. It would be a disaster if he left without her.

The phone was answered on the first ring. "Jim? This is Joyce. I'm on my way to Chicago with our man. Flight seventeen. Have someone waiting to tail us and pick the best. He's a bastard, no question, but he's got sharp eyes."

In less than five minutes she was boarding the plane, wearing a low-cut minidress and high-heeled boots. Her smile was firmly in place and she gave a sexy little wiggle as she settled down in the first-class seat beside him. It would be a rough night but she was well paid. And the information she got in Chicago could wrap this thing up tight.

12

THE AMBIENCE WAS unmistakably Italian, opera playing softly in the background, red-checkered tablecloths with wine bottles in the center holding candles and the pungent mouth-watering scent of garlic permeating the very walls. People came to this small restaurant in Chicago to assuage their homesickness for the old country and Ben Santini knew that if this place closed its doors tomorrow, twenty years from now the building would still smell of fine Italian cooking.

Santini and Bunny sat in a back booth, separated from the main dining room by a red curtain. This private spot was reserved for business, and Ben was with the owner, his brother Guido.

"Maria made your favorite, *gnocchi alla Romana*." Guido set down a steaming platter and went off for a bottle of wine. By the time he came back, his brother was deep into the plate of dumplings and Parmesan.

"Here's a nice Ruffino. Seventy-nine. It was a good year. You like the *gnocchi*, Ben?"

"Mmmm!" Santini looked up and grinned at his brother. "You sure Maria doesn't have an unmarried sister?"

"I'm sure. I'll go tell her you like the food. She says you're getting too thin out there in California."

"*Zabaione* for dessert?" Santini smacked his lips as he anticipated the wine egg custard that was Maria's specialty, and Guido laughed.

"She already knows. I heard her ask Tony for the best bottle of Marsala in the house."

166

There was silence while Guido sipped his wine and watched his brother and the girl eat. Enjoyment of food was almost as sacred as high Mass to the Santini family. When the plate was empty, his brother broke off a crust of Italian bread to mop up the last of Maria's *Romana* sauce and pushed his plate back with a sigh. Now the discussion could begin.

"Take a hike, honey." Santini nudged Bunny with his elbow. "My brother and I have some business."

"Anything you say, Mr. Santini. Is it all right if I go back and visit with your sister-in-law in the kitchen?"

"Sure." Santini reached out to squeeze her breast. "I'll send Guido for you when we're through."

"Nice piece, huh?" Santini chuckled. He was so busy watching her rounded bottom under the short mini-dress that he didn't even notice that she'd left her purse behind. It was a tiny shoulder purse of white leather to match her boots. And inside, concealed in a cleverly designed pocket, was a miniature, high-quality, voice-activated tape recorder.

"You need any more cash for the business, Guido? It's been a good year for me."

"We're doing fine, Ben. You saw the lounge area when you walked in?"

"There must have been thirty people waiting for tables."

"We're thinking about changing our policy. No street traffic, reservations required."

"Good idea." Santini nodded. "This is turning into a high-class operation."

Guido smiled at his older brother but there was a question in his eyes. "So what can I do for you, Ben? You didn't fly out here just to ask if I needed any more money."

"That's right." Santini's voice lowered and Guido leaned closer to hear him. "I've got a little problem, Guido, and I'd like to take care of it . . . our way. I'll need some help from Mario. You still see him, don't you?"

"Sure, Ben." Guido nodded. His connection with Mario Barone went back to their childhood days. Even though Mario was now the head of the powerful Television Labor Union, he still kept in touch with his old friends.

"Mario owes me a favor."

"That's right, Ben." Guido leaned forward. "You want to collect?"

Santini nodded. "Tell him to have his boys strike Empire Cable in the morning. I'll provide the setup and the phony complaints from L.A. Make it clear that I need Courtney shut down for at least a month."

"Got it." Guido nodded. "I'll make the call now. Can you stay overnight?"

"Not this time, Guido. Things are tight at the studio."

"So what time do you have to leave?"

"I'm booked on a flight at midnight."

Guido began to smile. He poured Ben another glass of wine and reached out to clasp his arm. "Good! I'll go tell Maria she has a couple more hours to fatten you up."

Sherrie stood out on the patio of the beach house, letting the night air play over her naked body. She and Tom had just finished making love and now they were watching the lights of a large boat off the coast. At first Sherrie had wanted to dress because the patio was brightly illuminated but Tom had explained that this area was completely hidden from the surrounding houses. The boats were too far out in the ocean to see them and the beach was fenced and private.

"This is heavenly, Tom!" Sherrie leaned against the rail and sighed with contentment. "What kind of boat is that out there? A cruise liner?"

Tom laughed and slipped his arm around Sherrie's waist. "It's almost big enough for one but I think it's a private yacht. Hold on a second and I'll get my binoculars."

In a moment Tom was back. He held the powerful binoculars up to his eyes and looked out at the lights for a few seconds. Then he handed them to Sherrie. "It's definitely a yacht. Take a look, Sherrie, they're having a party."

Sherrie pushed the binoculars back to Tom. "Thanks, but I never use binoculars. I can't adjust them right with my glasses."

"You're not wearing glasses anymore."

Sherrie laughed, and as she held up the binoculars, she made a mental note for Dan. Yet another advantage for the contact-lens wearer. It was easy to use binoculars, or telescopes, or microscopes.

"What do you see?" Tom stepped up close behind her and cradled her breasts in his hands. Sherrie sighed and leaned back against him. The air was chilly and she'd read somewhere that cold had an effect on a man's ardor but that didn't seem to be the case with Tom.

"Why don't you lean over the rail? You can tell me what they're doing out there and I'll just amuse myself while you do."

"Oooh!" Sherrie gave a little gasp of pleasure as Tom eased himself inside her. "There's a whole crowd of people in evening clothes. They're lounging on the deck and waiters in white jackets are bringing them . . . Oh, Tom! I can't talk when you do that!"

"Come on, Sherrie, tell me more. You're the one with the binoculars."

"Well . . . there's a big table with food, all kinds of hors d'oeuvres, and . . . Tom! What are you . . .? Ooooh!"

Sherrie gave a squeal of excitement as Tom reached

down and spread her legs. He dropped to his knees and her whole body shuddered as she felt his warm breath on her body.

"What else is happening? You keep right on talking and I'll make you come."

"Oh!" Sherrie wiggled and spread her legs even farther apart as she felt the heated tip of Tom's exploring tongue. "There's an orchestra and they're . . . they're playing all sorts of instruments and . . . some of the guests are . . . uh, dancing . . . and . . . oh God, Tom!"

Tom chuckled as Sherrie held on to the rail and gasped in wordless delight. He waited until the last delicious tremors had passed to stand up and grin. "What are they doing now, Sherrie?"

Sherrie gave a cry of genuine alarm as she raised the binoculars. "I'll get you for this, Tom. There's a whole bunch of people out there with binoculars and they're all watching us!"

As Tom laughed, Sherrie quickly reversed positions. She drew him deeply into her mouth and teased him with the tip of her tongue.

"Jesus! Let me go, Sherrie. I'll turn out these lights."

"Not a chance." Sherrie giggled as she wrapped her arms around his waist and held on. "Let them watch. It's probably more fun than they've had all night on that fancy boat."

Dan was at loose ends. He'd left Maree and driven straight to the house to deliver Joanna's rhubarb plants but she hadn't been home. The gardener had been working in the yard and Dan had given him the plants and listened to an account of the problems with the sprinkling system. He'd tinkered around for an hour, resetting the clock, but Joanna hadn't come home. Vaguely disappointed, Dan had gone back to the office and worked on a new series idea for the rest of the afternoon. Then, when the rest of his staff had left the office at five, he'd gone back to his apartment alone, determined to catch up on his sleep.

At midnight, Dan woke up. He'd slept for an uninterrupted six hours and he was too restless to go back to bed. He got up, put on the coffee, and then paced the floor of his small living room with its nondescript rented furniture, waiting for it to perk. At times like these, living alone was miserable. He was hungry, a steak would be nice, but he didn't feel like going to a restaurant by himself. He thought of calling Tom but Sherrie was spending the night with him. Even if they were still up, he'd be a fifth wheel. There was always Alice but he couldn't very well expect her to be on call twenty-four hours a day and he didn't feel like listening to all that crap about her lifeguide. The person he really wanted to see was Joanna, but she was probably asleep and he wasn't sure about the etiquette involved in calling an estranged, pregnant wife at midnight. He'd simply have to bite the bullet and go out alone.

Dan pulled on a pair of jeans and a blue denim shirt, slipped his feet into deck shoes, and grabbed his car keys. He'd drive to the Pacific Dining Car, they were open all night, and treat himself to a steak dinner. The downtown restaurant was a haven for people in the industry who'd worked long past the regular dinner hour. It was possible he'd run into someone he knew.

For once, the freeway traffic was light as Dan drove through the Sepulveda Pass and started the steep descent into the city. On the way was an expensive condo complex he'd looked at with Joanna before they'd decided to buy the house in Brentwood. Joanna had done a little research and found that the entire complex was built on the site of an old dump. They had referred to it, from then on, as La Cassa Landfill.

As Dan turned onto Sunset, he realized that he was taking the long way around to get to downtown. It would have been much quicker to take the Hollywood freeway. Alice would say his subconscious was acting up again, choosing to drive past the turnoff to Joanna's house. Dan hesitated at Cliffwood Drive and then turned onto it. He was almost positive that Joanna was asleep but it couldn't hurt to just drive past.

At first the house appeared to be dark inside. Then Dan spotted a dim light from the bedroom. Joanna was watching television. He came very close to pulling up in the driveway and ringing the bell but he hesitated. What would he say when Joanna came to the door? He couldn't use the excuse of being in the neighborhood. His apartment was miles from here. Dan put his foot on the accelerator and pulled away, knowing he'd saved them both from an awkward and embarrassing moment.

An hour later, seated at one of the red leather booths in the front room of the restaurant, Dan was just finishing the best steak in town. The wide front windows looked out onto Sixth Street and he watched the traffic idly as the attentive waiter filled his coffee cup. A limo was pulling into the parking lot and Dan's face lit up in the smile as he recognized the Empire insignia on the door. Tom was driving, wearing the chauffeur's cap, and Sherrie was beside him in the front seat. This was a stroke of luck. He could order more coffee and sit with them while they ate.

Dan watched as Tom and Sherrie got out of the car. Then the back door opened and another couple emerged. Dan's smile turned into a frown as he saw who their passengers were. Stan Lorman and Maree. Stan slipped his arm around Maree's waist as they walked toward the door of the restaurant and Dan's frown was replaced by a look that could only be described as a glower. His anchorman was at it again.

The waiter had already brought the check and Dan quickly slipped cash onto the silver tray. Then he made a hasty exit out the back door. His hands were shaking as he started his station wagon and pulled out of the lot. What was it with Lorman? First Joanna and now Maree. That bastard had no loyalty in him. Poor Joanna was home alone, pregnant with his child, and Stan was out romancing a new woman.

Dan sighed as he drove back over the pass. He was a mass of conflicting emotions. On the one hand, he was relieved that Stan and Joanna were no longer involved. At the same time, he felt sorry for Joanna, having her baby alone. He still loved his wife, that much was clear. But if he went back to her, he'd have to raise a child that wasn't his.

How did adoptive parents handle the problem of raising someone else's child? Dan parked in the lot at the studio, walked to his office, and thought about it. Their situation was completely different. The whole process with filling out forms and being interviewed by social workers was time-consuming and they had plenty of time to back out if they weren't sure. He'd had this baby thrust on him without warning. It was the old one-two punch. One: *I'm pregnant!* Two: *Of course it's your baby!* And he knew that was impossible. At least he thought it was impossible. It was true that he'd never kept those appointments with the fertility expert but his track record spoke for itself. All those years of trying without any results was pretty conclusive, wasn't it?

But what if Joanna was telling the truth? She'd never lied to him before. Of course the whole thing was improbable but that didn't mean it was impossible. What if Joanna's baby was his and he'd left her, alone and pregnant?

Dan's hand shook as he took out his key and unlocked the door. No, he was positive that Joanna's baby had been fathered by Stan Lorman.

So, he'd been justified. Did that make him happy? Dan sighed as he switched on the lights and took out the paperwork he'd been meaning to do for the past six weeks. How would he feel if he resumed his life with Joanna and Stan knocked on the door every Saturday morning to take the baby out to the park? New fathers always passed out cigars, vile tasting things with little ribbons that said *It's a boy!* or *It's a girl!* Would Stan have the nerve to pass them out at Empire Cable?

Dan imagined himself at Empire Cable's annual dinner party, showing a wallet full of baby pictures. Stan might be at the other end of the table, passing around identical pictures. There was no way he could handle such a situation, no way.

_____ **13**

"GOOD MORNING, BOSS. It's nine o'clock."

It seemed as if Dan had just closed his eyes when Alice came into the office. He'd wrestled with the paperwork until dawn and then sacked out on the couch for a nap. With her usual efficiency, Alice opened the drapes and Dan groaned as the bright morning light streamed in. Another beautiful day with puffy white clouds floating in a pure blue sky just like every other beautiful day they'd had this month. No wonder Minnesotans claimed California never had any weather!

"Up and at 'em. It's gorgeous outside! I got here early and jogged around the old mining town. I just love that place, boss. It's really too bad no one's using it anymore. Can't we make a Gold Rush series?"

Dan took one look at Alice, jogging in place in the center of the room, and quickly shut his eyes again. She was dressed in a day-glo purple sweatshirt and yellow shorts. Her kneesocks were orange and her designer jogging shoes were a brilliant kelly green. It was not a sight for first thing in the morning.

"Come on, boss . . . rise and shine! If you're tired in the morning, it means you're not getting enough exercise. My lifeguide says jogging is food for the psyche, and she's right."

Dan groaned again. Alice was always disgustingly cheerful in the mornings. It was a real character flaw. He was about to tell her to stuff it when she jogged out of the room and came back with a freshly perked cup of coffee and a chocolate chip Danish. "What happened last night? I thought you went home to catch up on your sleep."

"I did, until midnight. Then I woke up and came back here to work."

Alice frowned as she noticed Dan's rumpled clothes and the dark circles under his eyes. "My lifeguide says that—"

"Spare me, Alice!" Dan sat up and reached for the coffee. "Can you run to my apartment and get me something fresh to wear? I'll clean up here. And Alice? Pick up a bottle of Courvoisier while you're out. I think I'm going to need it today."

Simon Jacobi threw his empty carton of vitamin C–enriched orange juice in the wastebasket by his desk and checked off another item on his list. It was nine o'clock and government employees were now at their desks, time to make his first call. He wanted to catch Nate Armstrong before he was tied up in morning meetings.

"Nate? Simon Jacobi here. There's a little matter I need to discuss with you. Can you call me back?"

In a few moments, his phone rang. It was Nate, on a private line that didn't go through the federal switchboard.

"Are we clear?" Simon drummed his fingers on the desk and waited for confirmation. "Good. It's a matter of some urgency. The usual fee?"

Simon smiled as Nate agreed and asked how he could be of service. They'd done business before and Nate knew the rules. He was the most reliable contact Simon had at the Federal Communications Commission.

"All you have to do is put a bug up the commission's ass to look for violations at Empire Cable. It should be fairly simple. I'd say community programming would be a good place to start."

Nate asked a question and Simon frowned. "No, don't expect any results. As far as I can tell, Empire's as clean as a whistle. It's just a hassle, that's all, and I want it to last as long as possible."

Simon listened for a moment and then he nodded. "Sure, Nate. I'm always open to suggestions. If I can use it, it'll put an extra twenty percent in your pocket."

Simon drummed his fingers on the desk for a moment as Nate put him on hold. Within seconds, he was back on the line, and when Simon heard what he had to say, a smile spread over his face.

"Great idea, Nate. How long will it take?"

There was a moment of silence while Nate answered and then Simon threw back his head and laughed. It was not a nice laugh. "*That* long? Fantastic! I'll drop the money in the usual place, plus the extra, of course. And you say their broadcast may be interrupted?"

Simon was in a rare mood when he hung up the phone. Euphoria was not his usual state of mind but everything was falling into place with Empire Cable. That extra twenty percent had been well worth it. He took a moment to lean back and stretch.

The second number Simon dialed was posted in government offices all over the country. There had even been a series of commercials on network television urging people to use it. The I.R.S. had done Simon a favor by putting in a hotline for tips on tax offenders.

A woman answered and Simon put on his best tentative but concerned voice.

"I'm not sure I'm doing the right thing but I'm a junior accountant working for a relatively new corporation and I'm disturbed about the tax returns my supervisor filed."

The woman asked a question and Simon paused for a moment as if he were considering what she said. "No, I really can't give you my name. If they ever found out about it, I'd lose my job for sure. I wouldn't have called

177

in the first place, but I have to dig deep to pay my personal taxes and it makes me mad that the corporation I work for is getting away with murder."

Simon smiled as he heard papers rustle on the other end of the line. "Sure, I'll give you the name, as long as they won't know that I turned them in."

There was a moment while the woman explained the system. The corporation would be audited under a routine investigation. The tax hotline would never be mentioned.

"Okay. It's Empire Cable, owned by Dan Courtney. I went over the returns for the past three years and compared them to the books. I was really staggered by the irregularities. You may have to dig a little, but you'll find them."

Simon smiled as the woman took down the information, then stepped in neatly as she asked another question. "Oh, no, I'm not interested in the reward. It's enough to know I've done my duty as an American."

Simon hung up the phone and leaned back in his chair. Two down, one to go. The I.R.S. would chew and worry Empire Cable for months like a dog with a bone, trying to find something. Even if they didn't discover any irregularities, they'd tie up Empire's accounting department until next Christmas.

Simon's third call went smoothly. His contact at the Securities and Exchange Commission, agreed to open an investigation of Empire Cable's stock manipulations. Again, it was nothing more than a hassle, but Simon's man was more interested in the payoff than he was in discovering fraudulent trading.

With a sigh, Simon turned on his answer phone. One task remained. He was due at the Brentwood Country Club in an hour to play tennis, a game he despised and a match he'd set up himself. He'd be playing doubles with a federal congressman, one of Empire Cable's biggest investors, Harold Rubin, and the vice-president of a powerful international bank—the very bank Dan Courtney would approach at ten tomorrow morning, seeking a loan to meet his debentures at Empire Cable. There was a little side bet on the game and Simon's backhand was weak, but right now his odds were a lot better than Dan Courtney's.

"He fixed your sprinklers?" Alice stirred freeze-dried carob into her unflavored yogurt and sprinkled in a generous half cup of wheat germ. Joanna's court case was taking a recess and she'd called to thank Dan.

"Personally, Joanna, I think you ought to start making plans to marry Stan Lorman."

Alice was in the coffee room at the office, fixing a midmorning snack. The blender she'd brought from home was on the counter, along with Tupperware containers of various ingredients from her lifeguide's health store.

"Don't be silly, Joanna. Love isn't the issue here. Lots of women get married to men they don't love." Alice cracked open a fertilized brown egg and added it to the mixture in the blender. Then she dutifully added a chopped banana. She hated bananas unless they were surrounded by ice cream and covered with chocolate syrup, but her lifeguide had recommended she increase her intake of potassium.

"No, it doesn't matter that Stan hasn't asked you. And you don't have to go *through* with it, you know. All you have to do is let Dan think you might do it. Then he'll try to win you back."

Joanna responded and Alice groaned. "Of course he'll try to win you back. My lifeguide assured me it would work. Hold on a second. I've got to get something from the refrigerator."

Alice opened the tiny refrigerator and took out a bottle of sparkling mineral water. She poured three ounces into the blender and recapped the rest, taking time to throw out a soggy tomato and the remains of a petrified tuna on rye.

"I'm back. So what do you think? A little jealousy might do wonders. Hold on and let me mix this up." Alice put the top on the blender and turned it to high. Ten seconds later her quick energy shake was done. She picked up the phone again and swore as she poured the shake into a glass.

"No, not you, Joanna. I just forgot to put in the protein powder, that's all. Hold on, it'll just take a second." Alice took out the three-pound can of protein powder she kept under the sink and wrinkled up her nose as she opened it.

"Joanna? Can protein powder spoil in the heat?" Alice gave another sniff and threw the can in the trash. "You've got a point, Joanna. Maybe I should go down to the commissary for a regular shake. I'm getting pretty sick of all this health food stuff. I wouldn't eat it at all, but my lifeguide . . . oh sure, Joanna. Yes, I'll talk to you later." Alice hung up the phone with a puzzled expression on her face. Every time she mentioned her lifeguide, Joanna cut her off.

Before she had time to reconsider, Alice dialed her lifeguide's number. She needed a few minute's consultation over the phone. Alice knew she wasn't fully enlightened, but it sounded as if Joanna had a deep-seated fear of professional advice. If Joanna was too timid to seek help, Alice would just have to be a good friend and do it for her.

Dan's first stop on his daily tour through his facilities was the brick building that housed his local transmitter. Signals from the local transmitter were beamed to his relay station on Mount Wilson and his affiliates in Southern California picked up the signal directly from there. The dish on Mount Wilson also served as a relay point to Empire Cable's satellite station, which fed Dan's other affiliates across the nation. When he had first started Empire Cable, Dan had decided to go with the best equipment and the newest technology. It had been an expensive proposition but Dan had felt it was worth sticking his neck out to borrow the money. If, as he dreamed, Empire Cable eventually were to go international, he already had the capability to broadcast around the world.

"Hi, Mr. Courtney. Got one for me?"

"Naturally." Dan smiled at his chief engineer, Daryl Plummer. Empire was currently running a movie, *Victory at Sea,* and Daryl's assistant had things well under control. He followed Daryl into his office and waited until the older man had shut the door.

"Okay, Daryl. No fair reading titles. The one I've got is probably right here on your shelves." Dan gestured toward the shelves of video tapes that lined Daryl's walls. Daryl was an old-movie buff and he had all his favorites on half-inch professional cassettes. Every time Dan dropped in to Daryl's office he tried to stump him with a movie quote, as yet unsuccessfully.

"How many titles have you got now, Daryl?"

"Twelve hundred and three as of last night. I just got a clean recording of *Red River.* That's not it, is it?"

"No." Dan took a piece of paper from his pocket and unfolded it. "The subject is men."

"All right. Shoot."

"There are no great men, buster. There are only men."

Daryl threw back his head and laughed. "That's easy. Elaine Stewart in *The Bad and the Beautiful.* It's tape number six hundred seventy-one and it's halfway down the third shelf on your left."

Dan sighed.

"Okay, try this one. The subject is parents. *His mother and father together are like a bad car wreck.*"

"Tape number seventeen, fifth shelf on your right. Chris Sarandon in *Dog Day Afternoon*."

"Damn!" Dan shook his head. "Okay, here's one you'll never get. The subject is . . . winning. Ready?"

Daryl smiled and nodded.

"A wise man lets his opponent win once in a while."

Daryl frowned and looked up at the ceiling. After a long moment he shook his head. "I hate to say it, but I don't recognize that one. Give me the next line."

"Okay." Dan laughed. *"A wise man lets his opponent win once in a while . . . especially if he's playing Dan Courtney!"*

"You made it up?"

"It's the only way I could stump you today, but I'll get you fair and square next time."

Dan left Daryl laughing at his desk and made his way past the projection room to the largest section of the first floor. It was reserved for the "Nite News" team and, even now, six hours before the first newscast was scheduled, personnel were scurrying back and forth carrying bulletins from the major syndicated news services to a small office in the back where the master script for the news was prepared.

"Hi, Mr. Courtney." One of the script girls waved and Dan waved back. He moved past the desks with clicking computer keyboards and went through another door to the studio. Here all was relatively quiet, except for a few workmen running routine maintenance.

Dan stepped onto the stage and checked the new backdrop, a giant painting of the city at night with a blank screen behind the skyline. His technicians would use rear-screen projection to create the lighting for each broadcast, matching the sky to the actual time of day. Dan had wanted something different from the plain cyclorama with the network logo that most news teams used, and he had gotten it at considerable expense. If it worked, it would be magnificent.

"We're ready for you, Dan." Tom's voice came from the control booth. "Hold on a second and I'll join you."

A moment later Tom signaled to the technician and the blank screen behind the view of the city was filled with glorious color. There was daylight for the six o'clock show, gradually fading to blue with streaks of a glorious sunset for the broadcast at seven. Then the twilight deepened into velvety black for the ten o'clock news with a moon rising slowly over the city.

"Very impressive!" Dan beamed at his brother. "Now, let's see your addition."

Tom signaled again and Dan watched as the lights in the tall buildings began to wink on and off. Tom had worked with the artists, making cutouts for some of the larger windows in the tall skyscrapers. With randomly controlled lights behind the cutouts, it looked very realistic.

"It looks great from here. Let's see it on the monitor."

This was the true test. It was possible to have an extremely realistic backdrop that looked like a fake on the monitor. Then they'd be seeing what the viewers at home would see.

"Okay, roll it!" Dan and Tom watched critically as the tape ran and the skyline went through its changes again. Dan gave a satisfied sigh as the lights twinkled realistically and the tape ran out.

"It's a winner, Tom." Dan grinned at his brother. "Let's send a second unit out to film the sky in different types of weather. We'll need rain, fog . . ."

"And smog?"

Dan laughed at Tom's expression. "Los Angeles doesn't have smog. It has *coastal gray,* ask any of the natives. If you're convinced that all the bugs are out, let's go ahead and use it tonight."

"Sounds good." Tom nodded. "Why don't you tell

the news team yourself? We'll have to reposition their desks slightly but that shouldn't throw them. They've been asking when we're going to start with the new backdrop."

"You tell them, Tom, and show them the tape. I've got to get over to stage seven."

Tom shrugged as Dan walked away. Usually Dan wanted to be the one to initiate new procedures but he had delegated all authority for the "Nite News" to Tom. Tom knew it was a tactic to avoid Stan Lorman but Dan's attitude wasn't fair to the rest of the team. People were beginning to talk.

"Did you see Dan?" Alice rushed in, notebook in hand. "I've got a couple of messages for him."

"He went to stage seven."

"Naturally. He doesn't want to bump into Stan Lorman. Somebody ought to talk to him, Tom. My lifeguide says—"

"Forget it, Alice. You'll just end up making him mad. He'll come around but he's stubborn. It's going to take time."

"Maybe not, Tom." Alice glanced at her watch. "Oops, I've got to run. I've got a lunch date in half an hour."

"New boyfriend?"

"No, strictly business. I'm having lunch with Pinky."

Tom shook his head as Alice took off at a dead run. He almost called after her to tell her to be careful but warning Alice not to run off at the mouth was like telling the sun to stop shining.

"Good work, Maree." Dan picked up the telephone and told the projectionist to rewind the tape while Maree leaned back, smiling. They were sitting in the twenty-seat theater that served as Empire Cable's screening room. The large screen that had been used for movies had been replaced by a twenty-four-inch monitor, mounted close to the front row of seats. Most people had consoles or portables, and while a twenty-foot picture might be perfect for moviegoers, it lost something in translation to a regular living-room television set. Dan wanted to see what his viewers saw, and Maree's opening segment of her fashion show had looked damned good.

"What are you working on next, Maree?"

"Accessories." Maree looked a little worried. "You know, belts . . . gloves . . . hats . . . costume jewelries." Dan nodded and waited for Maree to go on. "Your computer peoples told me who watches your television and the women, they come from un-rich monies. They cannot spend for a wardrobe but they can spend for accessories. I will teach how to make new outfits out of old favorites."

"That sounds fine, Maree." Dan smiled at her. "Now that I think about it, Joanna used to have a long black dress she wore with her grandmother's pearls. I thought it looked wonderful but she'd worn it so often, the hem was frayed. We didn't have much money that first year and my boss invited us to a dinner party. I could only come up with thirty dollars."

Maree looked clearly intrigued. "And did she find a new dress with such short monies?"

"She did even better than that. She cut off the bottom of her black dress and raised the hem. Then she went out to Woolworth's—that's a dime store—and bought an extra wide yellow belt and a matching scarf. There was a florist down the street from us and she talked him out of a whole bouquet of little yellow flowers for a dollar. That night she braided them into her hair and everyone wanted to know which designer had done her outfit."

"And how many monies did she pay?"

"Five dollars for everything."

The screen went white just in time for Maree to see

Dan's anguished expression. She was about to ask him if she could help when Tom came rushing into the room.

"We need you, Dan. There's big trouble on stage fourteen. It looks like a full-scale union walkout!"

Maree stayed in her seat as Dan and Tom hurried out. She'd heard about the powerful unions that controlled the television workers. She liked Dan and she was beginning to feel very sorry for him. There was trouble with his marriage and now there was trouble with his business too.

Jerry Niehoff was waiting for Dan at a table in a small, expensive French restaurant a few blocks from the studio. When Dan had met Jerry, he'd been a shop steward but he'd been promoted several times since then. He was currently the secretary of the local and he wielded the power. As in most unions, the president of this local was merely a popular figurehead. Jerry called the shots for the TVLU.

"Jerry." Dan shook the big man's hand. "Thanks for coming over on such short notice. It's good to see you again."

"Sit down, Dan." Jerry motioned to a chair. "Here comes your drink. I figured you could use one."

While the waiter delivered the drinks, Dan studied Jerry closely. He'd put on weight since Dan had worked with him at GRN and the big burly man looked comically out of place perched on a spindly chair at the round pink bistro table.

Dan waited until the waiter had left. "Well?"

"It's not good, Dan. Empire Cable went on the strike list at noon. That's why the walkout."

Dan was puzzled. "But . . . why, Jerry? We signed the latest contract and there haven't been any complaints against us."

"That was true until today. National received a

complaint that you had six nonunion men working for you."

"Nope." Dan shook his head. "They can't get me on that one, Jerry. The business office checks every union card before they hire. There's no way Empire has any nonunion employees in union jobs."

Jerry drew a paper from his pocket. "These men were picked up by your shop steward this morning, working on one of your sets. Every one of them said they'd been hired by you personally. Philip Hickman, Maurice Fernald, David White, Raoul Rodriguez, Wesley Jennings, and Marvin Fruggnucker."

"Marvin Fruggnucker? For Christ sake, Jerry! Don't you think I'd remember if I hired someone named Marvin Fruggnucker? I swear you won't find any of those names on the Empire payroll."

"You're right, Dan. I checked. But these men claim they were paid in cash and they've signed statements to that effect."

"They're a plant, Jerry. I'm being set up."

Jerry nodded. "That's possible, Dan, but you didn't hear it from me. And now Empire's in a shitload of trouble with the union."

"Christ!" Dan shook his head. "I can't afford a shutdown, Jerry. What's the fine? I'll pay the damn thing, whatever it is, and we'll sort it all out later."

"I figured you'd say that, so I called national. The fine won't be set until they run a full investigation."

"How long will that take?"

Jerry sighed. "I don't know, Dan. National's handling it."

"Look, Jerry." Dan grabbed his arm. "There's got to be some way I can stay in business. This strike could break me."

Jerry nodded. "I know all that, Dan, but it's completely out of the local's hands. I shouldn't say this but I think someone at National's got it in for you personally.

They've never taken a hard line like this before. Why don't you get in touch with Mario Barone and see if you can work out something? And don't mention I suggested it."

"Thanks for the advice, Jerry." Dan tried to smile. "Can I buy you lunch?"

"No, thanks." Jerry stood up and patted Dan on the shoulder. "Off the record, my boys are real upset about this strike. You've always treated them well and they like you. Now I've got to run before somebody spots me. I could get in hot water for just talking to you."

Dan stared at Jerry's retreating back until he was out the door. Then he pushed his drink aside and got to his feet. The alcohol might lift his spirits but he needed a clear head for his call to Mario Barone.

Dan drove back to the lot and parked in his space. He'd grab a quick sandwich at the commissary, lock himself in the office, and try to think of a bargaining chip to use with the union boss. He was just pushing open the door to the commissary when Pinky Calvert came barreling out. Today she was wearing a voluminous floor-length caftan that fluttered when she moved her arms. She looked a lot like a fat flamingo, flapping its wings.

"Dan, darling! Just the man I wanted to see!"

"Uh . . . Hi, Pinky. How are you?"

"Marvelous, darling. The question is, how are *you?* I just heard the news and I'm simply devastated!"

Dan took a second before he answered. Was Pinky referring to the strike or to something else? He decided to play it safe.

"I'm fine, Pinky."

Pinky reached out to pat his arm. "I'm so relieved, darling. I was really a bit worried about you. But I suppose you've known for a while and you've had time to get used to it."

Dan's patience snapped. Pinky wanted to play guessing games and he had much more important things to do.

"Pinky? What the hell are you talking about?"

Pinky's caftan fluttered a bit but she stood her ground. "You *know* what I'm referring to, darling. The whole studio's buzzing about it."

"About *what,* Pinky."

"Joanna and Stan's wedding, of course. Do you think your divorce will go through in time? Of course Stan could always adopt later but that's such a bother and . . . Did I say something wrong, Dan?"

Dan felt as if he'd been slammed in the head with a brick. All he could do was shake his head and turn to walk away.

"Dan? Dan, darling!" Pinky chased after him, surprisingly agile in her high-heeled sandals. "Are you going to give Joanna away at the wedding? I understand that's the newest custom and it *would* be good publicity for . . ."

Dan walked quickly past the security office but Pinky kept up his rapid pace.

"Dan? Could you give my viewers a quote? You know . . . something to show that there's no hard feelings between the two of you?"

That was the final straw. Dan stopped so suddenly, Pinky almost tripped.

"You want a quote, Pinky? I'll give you a quote. Tell your fucking viewers, *No comment!* That's all. *No comment!* And if you don't stop following me, I'll give you a pink slip to match the rest of you!"

14

JOANNA TOOK ANOTHER sip of water and sat up straight in her chair as she waited for Judge Franklyn to finish reading the documents she had secured for her client from the city assessor's office. Joanna's client, an eighty-year-old widow named Emily Nordhoff, had been charged with removing a huge dead ponderosa pine at the edge of her property after the city had listed it as a fire hazard. The bill would come to well over five hundred dollars. Joanna had claimed that the tree was not on her client's property. What had started as a routine dispute over property lines had turned into much more when Mrs. Nordhoff's neighbor had produced documents from the same assessor's office showing that his property line also fell short of the ponderosa pine in question.

"Do you think I'll have to pay to have that tree removed, Joanna?" Mrs. Nordhoff, a tiny, birdlike woman with white hair and quick mannerisms had dressed in her best for this court appearance. She had on what she called her "church dress," a navy-blue shirtwaist with a white collar and cuffs. Her only jewelry was a needlepoint broach, which, she'd proudly told Joanna, she'd made herself. Joanna could see she was nervous and turned to reassure her.

"Don't worry, Mrs. Nordhoff. We have proof that the tree isn't on your property."

Mrs. Nordhoff had wanted to pay for Joanna's legal services, but Joanna knew that her client had very little to spare from her monthly social security benefits.

Finally, they had come to an agreement that delighted Joanna and satisfied her client's sense of pride. It was very close to the old barter system. Emily Nordhoff, a skilled seamstress, had agreed to make a layette for the baby from material that Joanna had provided.

"I hope he doesn't make Mr. Sesnon pay, either. He's on disability, you know."

"Mrs. Courtney?" The bailiff tapped Joanna on the arm. "Judge Franklyn would like to see you in chambers."

Joanna stood up and gave Mrs. Nordhoff her brightest smile. "Now you sit right here and don't worry. Everything will work out just fine."

Mrs. Nordhoff still looked worried but she smiled back. "Have a little more water, dear. You look peaked."

Joanna took another sip of water and got up to follow the bailiff. It was true she didn't feel well today. Perhaps it was the heat in the old courtroom or the fact that she hadn't gotten much sleep last night. Whatever the reason, she felt weak-kneed as she walked down the long corridor and into Judge Franklyn's chambers.

"Joanna? Are you all right?" Judge Franklyn, a round-faced man in his early fifties, motioned to the bailiff and they helped Joanna to a chair.

"Thank you, Judge Franklyn. I'm fine . . . just fine."

"Did you have breakfast?"

"Uh . . . no. I didn't feel much like eating this morning."

"That's the trouble, then." Judge Franklyn pushed a Tupperware container across the desk toward her. "Here. My wife baked some cinnamon rolls this morning. Take one."

Joanna wasn't about to refuse a direct order from the judge and the rolls looked delicious. She took one.

"Nellie bakes the best rolls in California."

Joanna took a bite and smiled. "I agree with your decision, Judge Franklyn."

"That's one out of two, then." Judge Franklyn laughed. "You didn't like the one I handed down last week denying your client that rent control appeal. Now what about this tree, Joanna? It looks as if the original error occurred in the 1893 surveyor's report. Somehow it failed to account for that three-foot strip of land running between lots seventeen and eighteen of tract number 30437. My initial inclination would be to divide up the strip and charge Mrs. Nordhoff and Mr. Sesnon jointly with the expense of the tree removal."

"Yes, Your Honor. You said your *initial* inclination?"

Judge Franklyn nodded. "You managed to work in the words 'economic hardship' in your brief. Is your client unable to pay for the tree removal?"

"Yes, Your Honor. She lives entirely on a small social security benefit. And even though Mr. Sesnon is not my client, I know that his income is also barely above the poverty level."

"Hmmm. So who would you charge with the expense?"

"Why not the city, Judge Franklyn? Statue 509, Section 4 of the code states that land not included in the official assayer's report should belong to the municipality."

"That section refers to easements, Joanna."

"True, Your Honor. But this land is not claimed by either of the two adjacent landowners. It rightfully belongs to the city and the city must be charged with either selling it or maintaining it."

Judge Franklyn laughed. "You must be feeling better, Joanna. You're as hardheaded as usual. All right. The city of Los Angeles will pick up the tab this time and we'll list it officially as an easement. Are there more trees on this strip?"

"No, Your Honor. The rest is grass and Mr. Sesnon's grandson keeps it mowed. I'm sure there won't be any future disputes."

"Take another roll for the trip home, Joanna." Judge Franklyn stood up and Joanna got quickly to her feet. "By the way, are you going to have that baby soon? Or is this just a ploy for the sympathy of the court?"

Joanna laughed as Judge Franklyn opened the door for her. "It's no ploy, Your Honor. Although, on days like today, I almost wish it were."

"Nellie said the same thing when we had ours, but it's all worth it in the long run. A baby in the house brings happiness."

Joanna sighed as she walked down the corridor and back into the courtroom. She could use a little happiness in her house.

Tom walked across the lot and sidestepped a group of women dressed in spangled tights, carrying gold spears. It was difficult to tell which show they were with. As far as Tom knew no one was filming an African three-ring circus.

As he crossed the street, Tom noticed that a red light was flashing outside Dan's office and the area was barricaded. Tri-City studios was filming something set on the eastern seacoast. The whole street had been faced to look like a town in New England and a fake widow's walk had been built on the top of the building.

Tom went around to the side and entered the building through the rear door. Here, at least, everything was normal. He rushed up the stairs and was slightly out of breath when he arrived at Dan's office. Alice had sent him an urgent message to come over right away.

"Hi, Tom. Glad you're here. I'll be with you in just a second." Alice turned to the phones and pushed several buttons in quick succession.

"Mary? Something came up. Can I call you back?

"Yes, Mr. Chambers, we received your shipment. The accounting department has the bill and they should be sending you a check by the end of the week.

"Transportation? Hi, Bill. Alice, in Dan Courtney's office. We need a messenger right away for a delivery to Santa Monica."

Tom waited until Alice had pressed the buttons on her phone, putting all six lines on hold.

"How do you keep them all straight, Alice?"

"Just a knack, I guess. We've got another problem, Tom, and Dan's not here. That's why I called."

Tom leaned against the desk and waited until Alice plucked a message from the tip of Jumbo's right tusk.

"A Mr. Crowell called from the F.C.C. and he's coming out tonight to run a test on our transmitter. Some computer firm across the street claims we're knocking their computers off line."

Tom nodded.

"Okay, Alice, I'll check it out with Daryl Plummer. Do you know when Dan'll be back?"

"Haven't the foggiest." Alice waved her hand. "I don't even know where he went."

"That's not like Dan."

"I know." Alice sighed. "He hasn't been himself all day but I can't say I blame him with this union thing on top of all his problems with Joanna. My lifeguide says that—"

"See you later, Alice." Tom headed out of the office, leaving Alice staring after him with her mouth open. Perhaps her lifeguide had been right, after all. Something in the working environment at Empire Cable made people resistant to hearing professional advice.

It was close to three in the afternoon when Joanna got home from the courthouse, and she barely had time to change into her maternity jeans and a sweatshirt before the phone rang.

"Joanna, it's Pinky! Why didn't you tell me yesterday, darling? I'm just so thrilled about the news!"

Joanna winced and held the phone an inch from her ear. Pinky's voice was loud and excited. "What news, Pinky?"

"About you and Stan, of course! I think it's marvelous and I'm devoting a whole show to—"

"Pinky!" Joanna interrupted. "I don't have the slightest idea what you're talking about."

"Now don't play coy with me, Joanna. I've known you for too many years. I have it from a very reliable source that you and Stan are planning the biggest wedding of the year!"

Joanna sat down hard in the chair by the phone. "Hold on a second, Pinky. Do I detect the fine touch of Alice Dolinski in that source you mentioned?"

"Well . . . you've got to promise not to take it out on poor Alice but yes, she told me and I'm simply thrilled. When's the wedding, darling? Before the blessed event, I hope."

"No, Pinky. Not before, not after. No wedding."

"But I don't understand! Alice said that—"

"Alice is not living in the real world, Pinky. She has been severely deluded by a woman she calls her lifeguide. If you want a hot story for your show, I suggest you call Alice's lifeguide and ask her for her credentials!"

There was silence for a moment and then Pinky spoke again. "No wedding?"

"No wedding, Pinky."

"Not even an engagement?"

"Not even that."

"Well . . ." Pinky sighed deeply. "In that case I owe you an apology. And I guess I'd better call Dan to apologize too."

"Dan? Oh, Pinky! You didn't!"

There was another silence and Pinky's voice was very small when she came back on the line.

"I'm afraid I did. I ran into him on the lot and asked for his reaction."

"What did he say?"

"Well . . . he said several unprintable things and he threatened to fire me but it all boiled down to 'No comment.'"

15

ALICE CAME IN with her usual smile but she quickly sobered when she saw Dan's face.

"Anything I can do?"

"Yes. Place a call to this number in Chicago. I need to talk to Mr. Mario Barone. And then call a staff meeting right away."

Alice left the office quickly before Dan could think of anything else. She still had to tell him about the call from the F.C.C. but now wasn't the time to mention it.

Five minutes later, Dan was still on hold at union headquarters while someone tried to locate Mario Barone. This was rapidly turning into the worst day of his life. He shuddered to think what else could happen before business hours were over at five. He'd already gone down to bookkeeping and told them to start the paperwork to fire Stan Lorman. He'd be damned if he'd support the man Joanna was going to marry.

"I can put you through to Mr. Barone now, sir."

There was a series of clicks and a loud voice came on the line. "You got a lot of nerve calling me personally, Courtney! I'm a busy man."

Dan tried his best not to react to the belligerence in the union president's voice. Nothing would be solved by getting into a shouting match over the phone and a great deal could be lost. It was important to keep communications open.

"I called to save you some time, Mr. Barone. I'm sure you don't want a strike any more than I do. So if you'll just levy a fine for the alleged infractions, I'll pay it."

"I can't do that, Courtney. Not until we send out a team of investigators."

"When will that be?"

"Well, now . . . my boys are very busy this month, but since you're so cooperative, we can probably get to you in three or four weeks."

Dan almost groaned out loud. They couldn't manage without union workers for one week, much less a month. "Can't we work out some sort of interim arrangement, Mr. Barone? Your union's asking for a wage increase effective in the next calendar year. If you send them back to work by tomorrow, I'll pay that increase immediately. Plus the fine when you finish your investigation."

Mario Barone whistled. "You're running scared, right, Courtney?"

"That's right, Mr. Barone, but don't forget this deal is to your advantage too. I can't stay in business without your union men and there'll be no money to pay the fine if I go under before you finish your investigation."

There was a pause while the union president thought it over. His voice was regretful when he came back on the line.

"Sorry, Courtney. You've got a point but there's more here at stake than money. You hired nonunion workers and if TVLU lets you get away with it, other companies'll try the same thing. We're just gonna have to make an example out of you."

Dan drew a deep breath. "Okay, Mr. Barone, let's talk about those nonunion workers. I didn't hire them and neither did anyone else on the Empire staff. Someone set me up. I don't know who but I'm going to find out."

There was a long moment of silence, and when the

union president spoke again, his voice was tight. "Something like that might be difficult to prove."

"I'm sure it will be but I have the resources. It would help if your men came back in, tomorrow. That way I wouldn't have to bother."

"I resent that implication, Courtney. My union's lilywhite. And to prove it, if you can finger the rat who hired those nonunion workers, we'll help you prosecute!"

"But you won't tell your men to come back to work?"

There was another long pause. "Can't do it, Courtney. The complaints against you have already been filed. But keep me posted. And be careful with that investigation of yours. You may have some dangerous enemies."

Dan hung up the phone and took a deep breath. The first thing to do was put his investigative reporters to work. Stan had some excellent contacts and . . .

"Damn!" Dan thumped his fist down so hard his coffee cup rattled. He'd just fired Stan Lorman.

"Boss?" Alice's voice crackled from the intercom on his desk. "We're all in the conference room, waiting for you."

"I'm on my way." Dan stood up and walked toward the door. Why had he called this staff meeting? Oh, yes . . . to ask everyone to work a double shift, filling in for the union workers until the strike was settled—which wouldn't be soon, because now that he'd fired Stan, there was no one to investigate those nonunion workers. Empire Cable was going to go right down the tubes and he really didn't give a damn because Joanna had agreed to marry Stan and that meant she didn't love him anymore and he might as well . . .

Dan's jumbled thoughts carried him across the floor to the conference room. He pulled open the door and was greeted by nine sober faces at the table. Dan knew he had to pull himself together somehow or he wouldn't be able to hold a simple staff meeting.

"Okay, let's get started." Dan sat down at the head of the table. Then, for the life of him, he couldn't think of what to say. After a moment of tense silence, Alice prompted him.

"We all know about the union walkout, boss. Did you have any luck talking to Mr. Barone?"

"No."

Alice frowned. Dan looked like the pictures she'd seen of shell-shocked veterans. "Well . . ." She stepped in again. "Since we can't shoot anything new without union workers, the best we can do is to stay on the air with what we've got in the can."

"How many hours of programming do we have?" Barry Snyder, Dan's in-house director, asked the question in everyone's mind.

"Dan?" Tom prompted, but his brother looked dazed.

"I can answer that." Alice flipped a page in her notebook. "We've got a total of sixty-two hours plus the bottle shows like the 'Nite News' and Maree's fashion thing. How about our late-night movies, Daryl?"

Daryl Plummer, the chief engineer, took out a thick folder. "Seventy-two hours. And I can put together another twelve or so with Tom's help."

"Sure." Tom nodded. "What have you got in mind, Daryl?"

"We can fill up a week's worth of two-hour blocks with a series of cuts from the movies we've already shown. Famous fight scenes, famous love scenes, that type of thing."

"That's good, Daryl!" Sherrie spoke up for the first time. "I'll help with that."

Tom grinned. "You can do more than help. We'll use you for the host. Barry can shoot some inserts with you saying things like, 'Now, boys . . . there's no need to fight over me,' and 'What a kiss! My lips are still numb.' "

"That's ridiculous, Tom." Sherrie laughed, although she looked very pleased. "You need a gorgeous starlet for a part like that."

Barry gave her an appraising look. In her pale blue knitted dress and her upswept hairdo, Sherrie looked the part.

"You can do it, Sherrie. Your image has really changed since you ditched your glasses and started wearing dresses instead of jeans. Don't you think so, Dan?"

"Hmm?" Dan looked startled. "Oh . . . sure, Barry. Whatever you think is best."

There was another moment of silence as everyone stared at Dan. It was clear he wasn't paying any attention to their plans to keep Empire running. Finally Alice took over again.

"Okay, let's recap. We can get through two weeks with what we've got in the can. Then we'll start rerunning things. We've had requests for all those shows we did in our first year and that'll buy us another couple of weeks. If we all work double shifts and fill in where we're needed, we might be able to hold on for a month or more. Does that sound about right, Dan?"

Dan nodded but he didn't even bother to look up. Alice sighed and went on.

"I've prepared a list of critical union jobs. Daryl's already agreed to work a double shift to transfer our feature film to tape."

Tom turned to look at the chief engineer. "That's great, Daryl, but do you know how to operate a telecine?"

"Nope." Daryl shook his head. "I figured you'd give me a crash course."

"We can all help," Sherrie offered. "Once everything's rolling, it's just a matter of monitoring to make sure nothing goes wrong. Maybe we could hire—"

"No outside hiring." Alice's voice was sharp. "We've got enough problems with the union already. We're all supervisory personnel so we can fill in under their rules, but hiring scabs is just asking for trouble. Now, who can do lighting? It's a big job since we lost all our grips."

"Barry and I can do it." Mike Evans, the line producer, spoke up. "Between the two of us we can handle anything that's done live."

Alice jotted their names down on her list and frowned. "Okay, that brings us down to the biggie. Transportation. We can rent a truck but we need someone who's licensed to drive a sixteen-wheeler."

"How about you, Dan?" Tom made another effort to draw him into the plans. "You still have your license, don't you?"

"What? Oh, yeah. It's around somewhere."

Just then the door to the conference room opened and Maree rushed in. "I am sorry to be late. The market had many people but I have brought the eggs you asked."

"Oh, Maree!" Alice looked ready to sink through the floor. "I forgot you don't speak English."

"But I do, Alice." Maree pulled a crumpled memo out of her purse. "It says, right here . . ."

"Not now, Maree!" Alice gave her a warning glance as Dan looked up. "Just a little joke, boss. Nothing important. Let's get back to the list we were making. . . ."

"Give me that memo, Maree." Dan roused himself from his lethargy with a snap and held out his hand. Alice winced as he read the memo aloud. *"Emergency staff meeting immediately about TVLU strike. Bring eggshells."*

"Uh, boss . . . I'm really sorry about this. I hope

you don't think I . . ." Alice stopped abruptly as Dan threw back his head and started to laugh. He laughed even harder when Maree said she still didn't understand why Alice needed eggshells.

"It's like this, Maree." Dan finally stopped laughing long enough to attempt an explanation. "Alice was warning you to walk on eggshells because she knew I was in a bad mood. It's an American idiom that means to be careful what you say."

Maree nodded gravely. "To walk on eggshells. I will remember that. But we do not need to take so much care now that you are laughing, no?"

Dan nodded. "That's right, Maree. And I apologize for sitting here like a lump while the rest of you tried to figure a way out of this mess. Give me that list, Alice, and stop licking the feathers off your chin."

Maree looked confused and Dan stopped her before she could ask. "Another American idiom, Maree. Alice'll explain later. Now . . . who can go out on location with 'Nite News' to run the field generator?"

Ben Santini sat at his antique marble-topped desk in his executive office at NNT, his fingers drumming out a rhythm of exasperation. Mario Barone had just called him personally to deliver an ultimatum. The union would continue to strike Empire Cable, but if Courtney managed to finger Santini for the setup, he was on his own. Santini was almost positive that Courtney couldn't prove anything but almost positive wasn't good enough.

The frown lines between his bushy eyebrows grew dangerously deep as Santini considered his alternatives. It would be a simple matter to hit Courtney and take him out of the picture for good but that led to all sorts of complications. It would be better to scare him off. Everyone knew that tempers flared during a union strike and sometimes people got hurt. If he arranged a little accident to show Courtney that he was playing a dangerous game, he'd back off in a hurry.

Santini picked up his private line and dialed a number that wasn't listed in his rolladex. When the phone was answered, there was no need to identify himself.

"I need a meeting. The regular place."

The voice on the other end of the line sounded nervous. "Give me an hour. I'm right in the middle of—"

"Now!" Santini's voice was threatening. Before the voice could reply, he slammed down the phone so hard that the receiver cracked. Then he stalked out of the office and past his private secretary, who was caught red-handed, doing her nails.

"Get me a new phone!" He looked back at the door. "I'll be out for the rest of the day!"

His secretary, a pretty little redhead who hadn't been hired for her secretarial skills, jumped to her feet. "But . . . Mr. Santini. You have a meeting with—"

"Cancel it!"

"Yes, sir. Right away, sir." The secretary sank back down in her chair. Her knees were shaking and she shuddered as the door to the corridor closed behind her boss. The expression on Mr. Santini's face had been murderous and her fingers trembled as she dialed the number of the personnel office. Thank goodness she'd stockpiled five days of sick leave!

When the staff meeting broke up, Alice cornered Dan. "Boss? I have to talk to you in your office for a minute." She waited until he had poured himself a fresh cup of coffee. "Sit down, boss. You're not going to like this."

"It can't be any worse than what's already happened to me today." Dan sighed and sat down. "What is it, Alice?"

"Uh . . . Mr. Doric's secretary called from the bank. You had an appointment at four-thirty this afternoon?" Dan nodded and Alice took a deep breath. "Well . . . it's canceled. Mr. Doric's secretary said . . ."

Dan moaned like an animal in pain and Alice stopped in midsentence.

"Are you sure you want me to go on, boss?"

Dan motioned her on and Alice took a deep breath. "Well . . . she said that Mr. Doric can't see you until next week, something about a mixup in scheduling. She promised to call tomorrow to reschedule but she couldn't give me a time until she talked to Mr. Doric and he was gone for the day. Then, about an hour ago, an agent from the I.R.S. . . ."

Alice looked alarmed as Dan gave another groan. "Are you sure you're all right, boss?"

"Hunky-dory, Alice. Please go on."

"Well . . . as I started to say, an agent from the Internal Revenue Service called. They want to audit your corporate tax returns for the past three years."

"Oh God!" Dan buried his face in his hands. "Better get the bookkeeping department right on it. They'll want to see everything."

"I did that already. And Mr. Askos called, three times. He said it was urgent and he left his personal number. Do you want to call him back now?"

Dan shook his head. USAT was probably sweetening their job offer and he didn't feel like dealing with it now.

"And one other thing." Alice looked down at the message pad in her hand. "A Mr. Crowell from the F.C.C. called. He's had a complaint on our transmitter. Something about our signal interfering with a computer firm across the street. He's coming out tonight to run a test and he warned me that we may have to interrupt our scheduled broadcast."

Dan was silent and Alice began to get worried. No groans, no sighs, just silence.

"Boss?" Alice waited until Dan looked up. "Why don't you let me do a bio-rhythm chart on you. I think you must be in a down cycle."

"Not now, Alice." Dan shook his head. "Any more bad news?"

"Not exactly. Joanna called but she wouldn't leave a message. She sounded upset."

"Oh, Christ! Is it time for . . ."

"No, I asked her that first thing. She just said she needed to talk to you personally about something very important. Do you want me to get her on the line?"

Dan shook his head. Joanna probably wanted to speed up their divorce so she could marry Stan before the baby was born. There was no way he wanted to deal with that now.

"I'll call her later. Leave me alone for a while, Alice. No calls. No visitors. I need to think."

Waiting till Alice left, Dan opened the liquor cabinet. It was made out of a crocodile's jaw, another inheritance from the previous tenant.

His hand shook slightly as he poured a generous shot of Courvoisier into a paper cup with the orange and yellow Tri-City studios logo on the side and drank it down neat. Thinking over the day, Dan poured himself another shot. If any other bad news was coming in today, he was going to be well anesthetized.

"Dan?" Tom knocked softly on his brother's door. Alice had said that Dan was locked in his office contemplating the universe and that didn't sound good. Ordinarily, Tom wouldn't have disturbed Dan in such a state but he wanted to talk to him about the F.C.C. inspection.

There was no answer and Tom knocked a little

louder. "Dan!" Tom resorted to banging on the door, and at last it opened. He gave a little sigh as he saw Dan's red-eyed and rumpled appearance. Tom could see an empty bottle of Courvoisier on his desk. For a man who didn't drink much, Dan was giving a convincing performance as a drunk.

"Jesus, Dan! I haven't seen you look this bad since the night of the senior prom."

"If you came here to talk about my drinking, turn right around."

"No, that's not why I came."

Tom stepped in the room before Dan could close the door. At least Dan wasn't slurring his words. Perhaps there hadn't been that much in the bottle. "We've got to talk about this F.C.C. thing, Dan. I smell a rat."

"A rat? What do you mean?"

Tom was glad to see Dan begin to perk up. "I don't believe our transmitter knocked anybody's computer off-line, Dan. I checked with an expert at one of the big computer companies and he said it was impossible."

Dan thought for a minute and then he got to his feet.

"Pour me a cup of coffee, Tom, and I'll wash up. Then let's take a walk around the block and see if we can find the computer firm that registered the complaint."

"Great!" Tom drew a breath of relief. "Let's take Daryl Plummer along. He knows that transmitter inside and out."

After a quick trip around the block, the three men had spotted only one computer firm. They walked in the front door of American Financial Services, a squat pink stucco building directly across from the studio gate, and found themselves in a small storefront reception room.

"Is anyone here?"

Dan frowned as he looked at the unimposing room.

An orange plastic sofa sat against one wall, its left front leg propped up with a brick. Several computer printouts were tacked to a bulletin board over the sofa and the only other furniture was an old gray-metal receptionist's desk with a telephone console on top.

"Here's a sign." Tom walked over to the desk and read the hand-lettered sign that was taped on its surface. "It says, RING BELL FOR USER-FRIENDLY HELP."

Dan reached out and depressed the red button on top of the desk. After a moment, a thin, balding man in a white shirt, dark blue trousers, and a heavy gray wool sweater with elbow patches came out of the back room. He was slightly stoop-shouldered and appeared to be in his fifties. With his horn-rim glasses and unfashionably wide knit tie, he looked like a retired schoolteacher. "Yes? What can I do for you gentlemen?"

"I rent space from Tri-City studios across the street." Dan smiled and held out his hand. "Dan Courtney, head of Empire Cable. This is my brother, Tom, and my chief engineer, Daryl Plummer."

"Jeffrey Goldberg."

The man shook each of their hands in turn. Then he looked at Dan questioningly.

"I got a call from the F.C.C. this afternoon and they said that my transmitter was interfering with a computer firm across the street. You seem to be the only one."

"That's true, but I'm not having any problems with interference."

"Perhaps one of your employees made the complaint."

Jeffrey Goldberg laughed. "Impossible. I'm the owner and only employee of American Financial Services."

Daryl pulled out the copy he'd made of the transmitter specs and handed it to Jeffrey. "Would you mind taking a look at these? I'd like to know if there's anything that could possibly cause trouble for your computers."

"Computer. I only have one, a cranky old mainframe I call Betsy. She's not as fast as the new models but she's never let me down. Old Betsy and I run an information bank for loan institutions. She can spit out all the billings for Southern California in an hour and you don't need much faster than that. Just hold on a minute, now."

Jeffrey pulled open a drawer and took out a pair of small square reading glasses. He took off his horn-rims, folded them neatly, and perched the reading glasses on the bridge of his nose. Then he spread out the pages on the top of the desk and studied them carefully. Dan, Tom, and Daryl watched anxiously as he went over the specs, stopping every so often to make calculations on a notepad. For approximately five minutes, the only sound in the room was the rustling of the paper, the scratching of his pencil on the pad, and the little comments he made to himself.

"What do you think, Mr. Goldberg?"

Jeffrey Goldberg looked up, startled. "Oh! I'm sorry, gentlemen, I got so interested in these papers I almost forgot you were waiting. The answer is no, Mr. Courtney, nothing you're running at Empire Cable could possibly interfere with Betsy."

"Are you sure?"

"Positive!" Jeffrey Goldberg looked up at the three men and suddenly remembered his manners. "Would you care for a cup of coffee? I have a pot in the back and while we're there, I'll show you around. Betsy and I go for weeks at a time without seeing anyone and I guess I'm not used to visitors."

"I'd like to see Betsy." Daryl spoke up. "I don't think I've ever seen a mainframe before."

The moment the three men stepped into the back room, they knew why Jeffrey Goldberg had been wearing a wool sweater. It was barely fifty degrees inside.

"Betsy runs better when it's cold." Jeffrey Goldberg led them over to a coffeepot near the door and poured three cups for his visitors. Pitch black, it had obviously been perking for hours.

"I hope it's not too strong."

"No, it's fine." Dan managed to swallow a bit of the bitter, steaming brew as Jeffrey showed them around his inner sanctum. The room reminded Dan of a remodeled bunker. The walls were made of concrete blocks, painted a high-gloss white. Black metal shelves lined two walls, stacked high with file boxes. The floor was linoleum. Jeffrey explained that rugs often caused problems with static electricity. A temporary partition had been built against the back wall and Dan noticed that it contained a metal bunk and a small closet. A small hotplate sat on the counter in the bathroom and several cans of soup and stew were on the shelf next to the towels. All in all, the work space was spartan and completely self-contained. It was clear that Jeffrey spent most of his time here, waiting for important computer printouts.

As the men were examining the high-speed printer against the fall wall, it activated. Jeffrey switched on another bank of lights so they could see the printout.

"Loan docs for First Western Bank and Trust. They used to type their own but my service is much faster. The bulk of the material is held in Betsy's memory and all I have to do is enter the rate, the name, and the address. All the rest is boilerplate."

Dan looked up at the banks of lights that illuminated the room and realized that there were no windows to the outside. He wondered if Jeffrey Goldberg had trouble telling if it was night or day, or whether it really mattered to him.

"I see the keyboard and the printer but where's your

computer?" Dan looked in vain for a huge console with flashing lights and ringing bells.

"Right this way." Jeffrey led them over to a metal box, the size of a small office desk, and stood by it proudly.

"That's Betsy?" Daryl was incredulous. "Somehow I thought a mainframe computer would be much bigger."

Jeffrey Goldberg laughed. "You must have seen pictures of the old models like Univac. With microchips there's no need for anything that big, and Betsy has another advantage over those behemoths of the fifties. She has over a thousand times their capacity."

Tom looked puzzled. "I thought you said Betsy was old."

"She was built three years ago and that makes her an old lady in the computer business."

"This is the shielding?"

Dan pointed to the metal around the computer and Jeffrey nodded.

"It's over an inch thick. Without all that metal, Betsy could fit in a briefcase."

"And that's why my transmitter doesn't affect her?"

"No." Jeffrey smiled. "I could run Betsy without any shielding at all and your transmitter still wouldn't bother her. It's like trying to add apples and oranges. The signals you transmit aren't the same as mine."

Dan gave a deep sigh of relief.

"I'd better call the F.C.C. and tell Mr. Crowell. It sounds as if they won't have to interrupt our broadcast after all."

"Phillip Crowell?"

"Yes. Do you know him?"

"Very well. He was one of my students. Phil Crowell majored in computer science at M.I.T. He knows your transmitter couldn't possibly interfere with my computer."

"But he said there was a complaint."

Jeffrey Goldberg frowned. "Then he's selling you a bill of goods, Mr. Courtney. Someone is trying to make trouble for you and Phil is the type to play along if there's money involved."

16

"AND YOU HAVE no record of a complaint from American Financial Services?"

Dan gave a tired smile as he listened to the voice on the other end of the phone. After being rerouted through several extensions, he had finally managed to contact Phillip Crowell's supervisor.

"So there's no need to test our transmitter at this time?" Dan's smile widened as he listened to the supervisor apologize for any inconvenience.

"Thank you very much, sir. I appreciate the fact that you looked into this matter directly."

Dan hung up the phone and leaned back in his chair. Jeffrey Goldberg had been right. The whole problem with the F.C.C. had been a hassle, pure and simple. Now all he had to do was figure out who was responsible.

It wasn't beneath Ralph Barton to put a bug in the F.C.C.'s ear to check Empire Cable's transmitter, but there was no way Dan could prove it. And all three network presidents were upset over Empire's ratings.

Dan groaned and looked around for the aspirin bottle. His head was splitting and the aspirin was just out of reach on the file cabinet. He was gathering the energy to rise to his feet when Alice buzzed him on the intercom.

"Hamilton Peters on line three, boss."

Dan sighed. There was no way he could refuse to take a call from his chairman of the board. Ham Peters had inherited a thriving auto-parts business from his

father in the fifties and now Peters Auto Parts stores
had over two thousand locations and a gross revenue of
several million dollars a year. Three years ago, when
Dan had started Empire Cable, Ham's accountants had
advised diversifying and Ham had invested heavily in
the fledgling cable service. Over the past thirty-six
months, Hamilton Peters had brought in other investors and Dan owed at least eighty percent of his capital
to Ham and his friends.

"Hello, Ham." Dan picked up the phone. "Did you
see your new ad on Empire?"

"I watched it for the first time last night. Hell of an
idea, Courtney. Everybody's talking about that kid
with the soap-box derby car."

"That was my brother's idea, Ham."

"Well, tell him he's a fucking genius. Three of my
stores have already called in and they say all their
customers are talking about that spot."

Dan scribbled a memo for Tom as Ham raved on
about the commercial, in which a cute little towheaded
girl pushes her broken-down racer into a Peters Auto
Parts store and the employees help her fix it in time to
win the derby.

"I just wanted to make sure you were coming to the
bash, tonight." Ham chuckled. "It'll be the same as last
year."

Dan winced as he glanced down at the date book
Alice kept for him. He'd forgotten all about Ham's
yearly barbecue. "No problem, Ham. I'll be there with
bells on. Eight o'clock, right?"

"Right. I've invited two potential investors but they
want to ask you some questions before they turn over
their money. Come a little early and I'll fill you in."

Dan said his good-byes and hurried across the room
to the aspirin bottle. He slugged down the pills, washed
his face with cold water, and made a quick call to the
commissary for a tray of sandwiches. Ham Peters threw

the wildest barbecues in town and it would be financial
suicide to arrive tired and bleary-eyed, especially to
meet two new investors. Ham's friends might be able to
provide the cash he needed to tide him over until the
bank loan came through, but there was no way they'd
climb on a sinking ship.

Dan took the exit for Meadowlark Lane and zipped
off the busy Simi Valley freeway. Hamilton Peters lived
on his father's ranch in Granada Hills, a three-mile
tract of land that he'd insisted on keeping intact despite
rising property values and constant offers from devel-
opers.

"Good evening, Mr. Courtney." A guard at the
entrance to Ham's ranch eyed the Empire limo appreciatively as he checked Dan's name off a list and pressed
the button that opened the gate. Dan drove through,
smiling slightly. Ham had pretensions of being a Texas
cowboy. The elaborate security gate had been specially
designed to look like an ordinary rail fence and a sign
hung above it, naming Ham's property, the Bar Room
Ranch. Ham's father had named it the Bar None Ranch
but Ham had changed it after last year's barbecue when
he'd overheard a guest's comment.

The ranch house itself had been remodeled several
times in the years that Ham had owned it. Currently, it
sprawled over the crest of the hill and down four levels
to a spectacular swimming pool and forest area.

The driveway extended for a mile and Dan drove
carefully. He had to stop several times to avoid the
tame deer that Ham kept on the property. Ham had
decided to make this a wildlife preserve and he employed a staff of ten groundskeepers to take care of the
animals and the land. It didn't seem to bother Ham at
all when a curious raccoon wandered up to the swimming pool or a skittish mule deer trampled the flowers
in his front yard.

Dan parked and rang the front bell, which played "Deep in the Heart of Texas." A moment later a girl in nothing but a fringed cowgirl miniskirt opened the door.

"You must be Mr. Courtney." The cowgirl gave him a radiant smile. "Mr. Peters said you might arrive early. He's waiting for you in the den."

Dan tried to keep his eyes on the cowgirl's face as she led him to the den but it was difficult. Ham's hostesses always looked like Playboy Bunnies. The only thing this one was missing was the powderpuff tail. She rapped lightly on the door to the den and stood aside for Dan to enter.

"Ah, Dan!" Ham Peters rose from his leather armchair. Even though the air outside was in the low eighties, he had been sitting in front of a roaring fire. Dan stepped into the room and realized the air conditioning was turned up high. Only Ham would think to refrigerate a room just so he could enjoy a fire.

"I'll get Mr. Courtney a drink, Shirl." Ham turned to the girl with a smile. "That will be all for now . . . unless Mr. Courtney wants you for something else?" Ham turned to Dan with a question in his eyes and Dan shook his head.

"No . . . thank you, Shirl."

"Thank *you*, Mr. Courtney!"

Dan waited until the girl had left the room before he laughed. "Where do you get them, Ham?"

Ham grinned as he poured out a tumbler of Glenmorangie, Dan's favorite unblended Scotch whiskey. "Things are rough now that Heffner closed his L.A. club. I figure the least I can do is give the girls a little work now and then."

"Then they *are* Bunnies!"

"Naw, just kidding." Ham handed Dan his drink and waved him to a chair. "Every girl here is an employee from my Culver City store."

"They're your employees?" Dan took a big gulp of his drink. "Tell me, Ham, aren't you a little nervous about one of them filing a sexual harassment suit?"

Ham threw back his head and laughed. "Don't be naive, Dan. These girls sign up months in advance to work one of my parties. They get to eat expensive food, drink good booze, and meet the real shakers and movers of the business world. It's a golden opportunity to meet Mr. Right, a small-town girl's dream come true in the glorious tradition of the American way! Dan? Good buddy? Why are you looking around like that?"

"Oh, I'm just waiting for the flags to unfurl from the ceiling and the band to start playing 'The Stars and Stripes Forever.'"

Ham laughed so hard he had to wipe his eyes. When he had finally stopped chortling, he shook his head. "That's what I like about you, good buddy. You cut through the bullshit. Actually I'm paying the girls three hundred apiece for the night and they don't have to sleep with the guests if they don't want to. That's more money than most of them make in a week at the store."

"How about the two investors you have lined up, Ham? What should I know about them?"

"Oh, them." Ham shrugged casually. "One's Joseph Springer of Springer Furniture. He's a tall wimpy-looking guy with one of those thin mustaches, like the French diplomats used to wear. And the other's Earl Pemberton."

"Earl the Pearl?"

"Right, the costume jewelry manufacturer. Always wears a bunch of gold chains around his neck, except they're real gold, not the fake stuff he sells. I'll introduce you, but don't plan on anything coming through right away. You see, they were with me when I ran into that guy from the S.E.C. this afternoon."

"What guy from the S.E.C.?"

Dan put down his drink. Ham looked serious and this

217

was the first time he'd ever seen the florid-faced businessman without a ready smile.

"I was at the club with Joe and Earl, having a few drinks, when this buddy of mine from the S.E.C. came over and told me that they're investigating Empire Cable's stock negotiations. There's no problem, is there?"

Dan's palms began to sweat and he was glad he'd put down the glass. Another problem, and if the S.E.C. was involved, it was a big one. Somehow he managed to keep the panic off his face.

"It's routine, Ham. The computer kicks out a name and they investigate. It's one way of justifying their budget to the taxpayers."

Ham nodded but Dan could tell he wasn't entirely convinced. "And how about the TVLU strike? Any chance of settling it fast?"

"I've already agreed to pay the fine." Dan kept the smile on his face. What he'd said was perfectly true. He just hadn't mentioned the amount of time it would take for the union to finish their investigation and assess the fine.

"That's smart. It doesn't pay to fuck around with the union. I hate to tell you, but you got another problem, old buddy. I guess I really shouldn't mention it until the stockholders' meeting tomorrow but forewarned is forearmed, right?"

Dan nodded. Just what he needed. Another problem.

"We got a buy-out offer for Empire today from an outfit called Amalgamated Electronics, seventy cents on the dollar. According to our bylaws, I'll have to introduce it for a vote tomorrow."

Dan nodded again. He didn't trust himself to speak.

"Well, I checked it out to see if it was legitimate and it is. They're a brand-new corporation but they've got money behind them. And they stipulated that they won't buy unless they get a majority so they can put in their own man as president. Naturally, I'll vote against it but I can't predict what the rest of the boys'll do."

"Thanks, Ham." Dan forced a smile. "I appreciate your faith in me."

Ham sat forward a little, not through yet. "I tell you, good buddy, I laughed myself sick when I got that ridiculous offer but . . . well . . . with the strike plus that pending S.E.C. investigation, some of our stockholders might get a little antsy. There aren't any more problems at Empire that I don't know about, are there?"

"No, no problems."

"That's good!" Ham sighed and took a sip of his drink. "Now how about those debentures I'm holding, Dan? My accountants tell me they've got less than a week to run. Are you going to ask to renew?"

Dan felt his stomach turn cold. Of course he'd been planning on asking to renew but now wasn't the time to mention it. He shrugged casually. "I don't know, Ham. The ratings are looking so good, we might not need to go for an extension."

"That's good, old buddy." Ham smiled in relief. "I wouldn't want to let you down but things are a little tight now and . . . well . . . my accountants figure maybe we'd better wait until the S.E.C. boys give you a clean bill of health. Appearances and all. That won't cause any problems for you, will it?"

"No, not at all." Dan picked up his drink and took a big gulp. This conversation wasn't going at all the way he'd planned it.

"Well . . ." Ham stood up. "Let's go enjoy the party."

"Great, Ham." Dan kept a smile on his face, even though he felt like screaming in frustration. The union was striking, the I.R.S. was auditing, the S.E.C. was investigating, the investors he'd planned to woo tonight were running scared, his stockholders had received a buy-out offer, Ham wasn't going to give him an extension on the debentures he held, and Joanna was going to marry Stan. And Ham had told him to enjoy the party?

The moment Dan stepped into the crowded room, Jack Decker hailed him from a seat at the bar. He swallowed his distaste for the rotund manufacturer who always reminded him of the drunk on "The Jackie Gleason Show" and slid onto the next bar stool.

"How's it hanging, old buddy?" Jack clamped his arm around Dan's shoulder and breathed into his face. The smell of stale booze was strong but Dan managed to keep a pleasant expression on his face. Jack was a sloppy drunk but he was also one of Dan's biggest backers.

"Just fine, Jack. How have you been?"

"Not so hot, old buddy. Not so hot. Seems to me I hold some paper that's due real soon. I don't have to lose any sleep over it, do I?"

Dan laughed heartily, took a big sip of the Glenmorangie the bartender set down in front of him, and lied through his teeth. "No problem, Jack. If you saw the ratings yesterday, you'd know you backed a winner."

Jack laughed but his eyes narrowed. He had the uncanny ability to sober at a moment's notice when matters of money were involved. Dan had seen him negotiate a contract after hours of heavy drinking, and when it came time to sign on the dotted line, Jack always got exactly what he wanted.

"That's what I told my financial adviser when he called me today. He heard from an I.R.S. buddy that Empire Cable is facing a total audit. That'd make an extension on your notes a little chancy, wouldn't you say?"

Before Dan could think of an appropriate reply, a young blond cowgirl twirling a lasso captured Jack's attention.

"Why don't ya rope me, honey? I'm fit to be tied." The cowgirl threw out a loop and Jack caught it, laughing. Then he slid off the stool and went after her, reeling her in as he went. He didn't even look back at Dan, who was sitting at the bar, shaken.

Dan fumbled in his pocket and took out a cigarette. He was not a habitual smoker but he needed something to calm him. He had known he couldn't keep the I.R.S. audit a secret for long, but he'd been hoping that the news wouldn't come out just yet. While he was still fumbling for matches, a hand with a lighter appeared in front of his face.

"Courtney! Good to see you here!"

Dan turned and put on a smile. The hand holding the lighter belonged to Malcolm Appleton, one of Los Angeles' biggest investment counselors. Malcolm had expressed interest in Empire Cable at the last party but he hadn't been ready to invest at that time. Dan knew that if he could talk him into making a commitment tonight, other backers would line up in droves. Malcolm bragged that he'd never made a bad investment and he'd become somewhat of a legend in the financial world.

"Nice job in the ratings. Congratulations."

"Thank you, Malcolm."

"And Ham tells me you've settled that little problem with the union?"

"I'm paying the fine." Dan nodded.

"A word to the wise, Courtney." Malcolm leaned over and lowered his voice. "My friends tell me the F.C.C. is on your back."

Dan nodded. This he could handle. "That was true four hours ago, but it's not true now. It was a mix-up over an erroneous complaint."

"Hmmm."

Malcolm motioned for the bartender, who poured him what looked like a tall glass of whiskey. Dan knew it was iced tea but that was Malcolm's carefully kept secret. He was a sober alcoholic and Ham always made sure there was iced tea in a cut-glass decanter behind the bar for him.

"Look, Courtney. My little girl runs in some pretty high government circles and she says you're in trouble. Maybe you cleared up that transmitter thing but that's only one out of three. How about the I.R.S. and the S.E.C.? You'd better clean up your act over there."

"There's nothing to clean up, Malcolm. We've followed S.E.C. regulations to the letter and all our tax papers are in order."

Malcolm shook his head, sadly. "I don't doubt that for a minute, Courtney, but following regulations doesn't count when it comes to the government. You can be as innocent as a lamb but they'll still wreck your business before they're through with you. And if you fight and prove that they're wrong, they'll send you a nice little letter of apology suitable for hanging on the wall in the office you used to have."

It was two minutes past eleven and the "Nite News" was over. Piles of paper littered the V-shaped table, a throwback to the days of "rip and read," when newscasters read the news as it was rushed to them from the Teletype. Dan's surveys had shown that viewers still liked to see paper in a newscaster's hands even though the script for the "Nite News" was actually typed into the Empire computer and projected on a state-of-the-art teleprompter. Since the teleprompter technician was out on strike, Tom had operated the large-screen projection device, matching its speed to the news team's delivery.

Now Tom was perched on the edge of the wide,

V-shaped table flanked by Alice on one side and Sherrie on the other. Maree sat in the anchorman's chair, recently vacated by Stan Lorman.

"Nice job, Tom." Barry Snyder, the director, clapped him on the shoulder. "Which job are you going to try next?"

Tom grinned. "Minicam operator. As soon as Stan gets back, we're all going out on location to shoot another segment for Maree's impressions of Los Angeles."

In less than five minutes Stan came back waving an envelope. His face was a mask of anger.

"What the hell is this supposed to mean? I just found it in my mailbox."

"It's a two-week termination notice." Alice peered over his shoulder.

Maree looked up at him anxiously. "No, Stan. This cannot be. It must be a misfire."

"That's mistake, Maree," Alice corrected her, "and you're right. Dan needs every one of us to keep Empire running and he knows we can't do the 'Nite News' without you."

"This is no mistake." Stan's voice was hard. "Dan signed it, himself. And he can forget this two-week bullshit. I'm walking now!"

"Don't do that, Stan." Tom reached out to take his arm. "At least you owe Dan the chance to explain."

"I owe him?" Stan glared at Tom. "Your brother's an asshole. He's been treating me like shit, he's accused me of knocking up Joanna, and now he's fired me for no reason. The only thing I owe him is a good punch in the chops!"

Maree looked puzzled and Sherrie explained quickly, before she could ask. "That's slang for hitting someone in the face. But Stan . . . this doesn't make sense. We all know you and Dan don't get along, but why would he fire you now? Something must have set him off."

"Oh, oh." Alice's face turned pale. "Does anyone know if Dan talked to Pinky Calvert this afternoon?"

"Does she wear red hair? And a pink dress?" Maree went on when they nodded. "I saw Dan talk with this woman when I return from lunch. There was much anger on his face."

Alice groaned. *"That's* what set him off. Pinky must have told him that Stan and Joanna were getting married."

"You will marry with Dan's wife?" Maree was clearly astonished. "Then you will get the punch in the steak . . . from me!"

"Punch in the *chops,"* Stan corrected automatically. "And I'm not going to marry Joanna. She's my lawyer, that's all. Where the hell did Pinky Calvert ever get a stupid idea like that?"

"From me." Alice's voice was very small. "I really apologize, Stan, but I was sure Dan and Joanna would get back together if he thought she was going to marry somebody else."

"Jesus, Alice!" Stan glared at her. "You know about the trouble I've had with Dan. Why the hell did you pick *me?"*

"I didn't . . . not exactly. I told my lifeguide all about it and she suggested you."

Maree looked thoroughly confused. "Alice? What is this lifeguide?"

"You don't want to know." Stan grabbed her hand and pulled her to her feet. "Come on, all of you. We've got to find Dan and clear this up right away."

17

JOANNA SAT AT the kitchen table in her most comfortable jeans and a red cotton maternity sweater and stared down at her cold bowl of soup. She had absolutely no appetite even though it was almost midnight and she'd eaten nothing but the roll from Judge Franklyn this morning.

The congealed yellow liquid with its smattering of fat pale noodles made her shudder and Joanna got up and dumped it down the garbage disposal. She'd cooked her favorite, chicken noodle, but after one small spoonful she had given up, propped her elbows on the table, and nibbled on a soda cracker.

The thought of sitting down on the hard wooden kitchen chair again made Joanna's back twinge. She had awakened this morning with lower back pain and it had gotten worse throughout the day. Dr. Whitney had told her to take aspirin for minor aches and pains but Joanna had resisted drugs of any sort throughout her pregnancy and she wasn't about to give in now. Perhaps her back would feel better if she moved around a little.

She walked through the doorway into the living room and stared at her favorite overstuffed leather chair. It would be nice to stretch out and start the murder mystery she'd bought last week but she had almost gotten stuck in that very chair this afternoon and she wasn't willing to do that again.

Joanna found that with each day that passed, it was more difficult to do those everyday things most people took for granted. It was hard to drive her car with the steering wheel rubbing against her stomach, but if she put the seat back, she had to stretch to reach the brake. Revolving doors were tricky, and the booths in the courthouse coffee shop made no provisions for pregnant ladies. Even the simple task of putting on panty hose had become a balancing act of major proportions.

The air in the room seemed stifling but the thermostat on the living-room wall read a mere sixty-five degrees. Joanna shoved it down even further and paced restlessly across the Persian carpet. Why hadn't Dan called her back? She'd left a message with Alice and another on his answerphone at the apartment. She *had* to tell him that Pinky's gossip wasn't true.

The strap on her sandal gave a loud snap and Joanna tried to look down to assess the damage but all she could see was her protruding stomach. Her feet were so swollen she was wearing her oldest pair of stretched out drugstore thongs and now one of them had finally given up the ghost. Joanna kicked them off and let them lie where they landed, not daring to bend over to pick them up. She had stopped at a shoe store this morning and bought a pair of extra-wide tennis shoes with velcro fasteners that were wonderfully comfortable but she couldn't put them on by herself. She wasn't able to lift her feet up far enough to see the fasteners and it was impossible to bend over and reach around her stomach to put them on. She told herself that this was only another temporary inconvenience but tears came to her eyes anyway. Other mothers-to-be had husbands to help, loving husbands who rubbed their backs and put on their shoes and drove the family car.

As Joanna paced, barefoot, she caught sight of herself in the gold-framed mirror over the fireplace. The man who had said that women were never more beautiful than when they were pregnant must have been legally blind.

A strand of hair fell out of her silver clasp and Joanna

226

reached up with both hands to tuck it back. She felt hot and sticky and she longed to sink down into a warm scented bubble bath but Dr. Whitney had advised against bathing now unless she had help. It was too easy to fall getting in or out of a tub. Showers were permitted, of course, but it was impossible to stretch out in a shower and read a good book.

The more Joanna paced, the more tired she became. She was about to take a chance and lower herself into her favorite chair when the telephone rang. Luckily, there was a living-room extension and she managed to regain her balance and pick it up on the fourth ring. It just *had* to be Dan!

"Mrs. Courtney?" The voice was vaguely familiar. "This is George Askos. I hope you remember me. We met at a convention last year."

"Of course." Joanna frowned slightly. She knew that George was one of Dan's competitors.

"Is Dan there?"

"No, George, he's not here. Did you try the office?"

There was a long silence and then George spoke again. "Three times, but he hasn't returned my calls. It's very important that I reach him tonight . . . about the union walkout at Empire today."

"The TVLU?" As Joanna asked, she felt a cold chill of foreboding. The TVLU had a reputation for violent strikes.

"Yes." George sounded grim. "I've come up with a way to stop it, but I have to talk to Dan."

"Do you think Dan could be in any danger?"

"He could be if I don't talk to him tonight."

"Come straight here, George." Joanna's voice was shaking as she gave him directions. "I'll locate Dan."

The moment George hung up, Joanna dialed Dan's apartment and got the answering machine again. Beginning to panic, she tried to get through to Alice. And

Tom. And Sherrie. Finally, in desperation, she called Pinky Calvert, rousing her from a sound sleep.

"I have to find Dan, Pinky. Do you know where he is?"

"Joanna?" Pinky sounded very sleepy. "You're not in labor, are you?"

"No, but I've got to find Dan. It's critical."

There was a pause, and when Pinky spoke again, her voice was suddenly alert. "Do I sense a story in the making, darling?"

"You might. But first I have to find Dan."

"And if I help you, you'll give me an exclusive?"

Joanna tried hard to control the exasperation in her voice. "Yes. Now where is he?"

"Try Hamilton Peters's ranch, darling. You know, the annual barbecue? And don't forget that you promised me . . ."

Joanna hung up and re-dialed quickly. Hamilton Peters's line was busy. It was still busy when she saw George's headlights turn into the driveway. Before he had time to get out of the car, Joanna had grabbed her purse, locked up the house, and opened the passenger's door. She was carrying her new shoes in her hand. It was embarrassing, but George would just have to help her put them on. The Bar Room Ranch was just over the pass and they could be there in less than an hour.

Dan sat by the side of the pool, watching Ham's cowgirls do a badly choreographed nude water ballet, when he spotted a familiar face in the crowd. It was Keith Doric, the loan officer who had canceled his appointment.

"Keith? Wait up." Dan waved and began to make his way through the crowd. He wanted to find out the real reason Keith had canceled his loan appointment. Keith looked as if he wished he could hide but Dan saw him square his shoulders and he'd even managed to put a smile on his face by the time Dan got to his side.

"Dan. Good to see you again." Keith looked anything but glad, but he held out his hand and Dan shook it.

"I need to talk to you, Keith. Privately."

"Uh . . . sure, Dan. Let's walk over to the barbecue pit."

Keith glanced at Dan nervously as they walked across the slate patio and headed toward the fire of the barbecue pit, their way illuminated by rustic lanterns at the side of the path. As they passed a lantern Dan noticed that Keith looked extremely uncomfortable. Dan let him stew for several more moments and then he gave him a smile.

"Relax, Keith. I'm not going to jump all over you. I know that canceled appointment wasn't your fault."

"Uh . . . I'm not sure what you mean, Dan. I told your assistant it was a matter of scheduling."

"I would have done the same thing in your position. There are times when it's rough being a company man."

Keith didn't say anything but he looked less nervous and Dan followed it up quickly. "If you want to hold on to your job, you stall. Right, Keith?"

This time Keith nodded and Dan rushed on. "I know I've got enemies out there who'd like to see me fail. And tightening the purse strings is one way to force me out. I don't suppose you know who's behind the bank thing, do you, Keith?"

Keith took out his handkerchief and wiped his face. He was sweating all out of proportion to the coolness of the evening.

"I know, Dan, but it's my neck if I say anything out of line. I just want you to know that I disapprove of the way the bank's acted toward you. You've been a valued customer at First World and you've always made your loan payments on time. It used to be that loyalty counted for something in the banking business, but now it counts for shit!"

Dan raised his eyebrows. Keith wasn't the type to use any kind of profanity. He was really upset by this whole thing and that just might work in Dan's advantage.

By this time they had reached the barbecue pit and both men stared down at the suckling pig roasting over the coals. Dan gave a short laugh.

"That's how I feel, Keith. I'm as helpless as that skewered pig. I know somebody's trying to sabotage Empire Cable but nobody will tell me a damn thing."

Keith looked down at the pig for a long moment, then cleared his throat. "Okay, Dan. But if you quote me, I'll deny it."

"Fair enough. Who got to you at the bank, Keith?"

"It's not who got to me, Dan. It's who got to Bowers."

Dan sat down on the bench by the barbecue pit. So the orders had come down from Ian Bowers himself, the vice-president of First World.

"I explained how stalling your loan would put you in danger of defaulting on your debentures, but Mr. Bowers said that couldn't be helped. I managed to look at his appointment book. Mr. Bowers played tennis this morning with Simon Jacobi."

Dan was glad he was sitting down. He'd heard of Simon Jacobi before in connection with several major company takeovers. It was rumored that Jacobi worked for a fee, a huge one, and no one could ever pin anything on him. Simon Jacobi was invincible.

Dan stared down into the barbecue pit where the coals glowed and hissed as the suckling pig turned rhythmically on its spit. It was a scene straight out of Dante's *Inferno* and Dan couldn't help but think that he'd have to sell his soul to the devil to work his way out of this one.

Stan pulled up to the gate at the Bar Room Ranch and stopped at the guardhouse. Tom was in the front seat beside him while Alice, Sherrie, and Maree rode in the back.

"Is Dan Courtney still here? I need to see him right away. My name's Stan Lorman."

The guard, who had been warned about party crashers, frowned slightly. "I'm sorry, Mr. Lorman, but I can't let you in unless your name's on the guest list."

"Oh, for Christ sake!" Tom leaned over to speak to the guard. "Look . . . I'm Tom Courtney. Can you tell me if my brother's still here?"

The guard consulted his list. "Mr. Dan Courtney checked in at seven-forty-five and he hasn't driven out yet. I'm really sorry about this, but I have strict orders."

Stan nodded. "Okay. We don't want to get you in any trouble. Can you call the house and get him on the phone for us?"

"Sure." The guard picked up the phone and pushed a button while they waited anxiously.

"It's busy." He announced. "Do you want me to keep trying?"

Alice, who was watching the exit road, shook her head. "Don't bother . . . here comes Dan now."

The Empire limousine pulled up to the other side of the guardhouse and Stan honked his horn to get Dan's attention.

"Dan! I need to talk to you!"

Dan looked over at Stan's car and frowned. "I don't have anything to say to you, Lorman." He rolled up his window, stepped on the gas, and the limo pulled away.

"Follow him." Alice nudged Stan. "He probably thinks you want to argue about that pink slip."

The guard opened the gate but it took several seconds to turn around on the narrow road. Even though Stan broke the speed limit on the winding road, the Empire limo's taillights had disappeared as they took a hard right turn on Balboa Avenue.

"Faster, Stan." Alice urged. "We can catch him on the freeway."

Stan pulled onto the now-deserted 118 freeway and got in the fast lane. There was no sight of the limo.

Sherrie sighed. "He must be going like a bat out of hell. That means fast, Maree . . . very fast. Keep after him, Stan."

"Take the Simi to the Golden State to the Hollywood." Alice advised. "I think he's going back to his apartment."

They saw the limo ahead in the distance as they got on the Hollywood freeway interchange. Just then a truck passed them on the right, so fast that Stan's car rocked.

"Jesus!" Tom glanced over at Stan's speedometer. "He's really highballing it."

Stan swerved over another lane as a horn beeped behind him. It was a second truck, going even faster than the first. On its tail was a third speeding truck.

"Another two bats, going highball." Maree clutched the back of the seat.

Before anyone could correct her, Sherrie grabbed Tom's shoulder. "They're flanking the limo. Get out the minicam, Tom. I think they're trying to run Dan off the road!"

Dan saw the three sets of lights approaching fast in his rearview mirror. He slowed, but the moment he saw that they weren't the highway patrol, he stepped on the gas again. All he wanted to do was get back to his apartment and crawl into bed. Ham had called the board meeting for ten in the morning and he had to be on his toes to convince the board to reject the takeover offer from Amalgamated Electronics. From the snatches of conversation he'd overheard at Ham's party, Dan knew that most of his investors wanted to sell. He'd have to come up with a miracle to keep them from deserting his sinking ship.

The trucks were right on his tail and Dan pulled over into the slow lane to let them by. The lead truck pulled out to pass him and Dan breathed a sigh of relief. When the truck had cleared Dan's limo, the driver cut back into Dan's lane again.

Dan swore and slowed slightly but the truck slowed too. What was going on?

Before he could react, the second truck pulled up to pace him on the left. And the third driver moved up behind him in the slow lane to box the limo in. Dan began to feel like the filling in a sandwich. There was nowhere to go except onto the shoulder and it was too narrow to accommodate the wide limo.

Dan tried to jockey for position, first slowing down and then speeding up, but the trucks did the same. As he approached another curve, bordering a steep embankment, the truck on his left began to inch into Dan's lane, forcing him over to the very edge of the shoulder. There was no doubt in Dan's mind now. They were trying to force him off the road!

There was only one thing to do. Dan knew every inch of this freeway, he'd driven it so often. Less than a mile ahead was the Conoga Road exit. It was a steeply banked curve with posted signs that advised motorists not to exceed a speed of forty-five. Dan glanced down at his speedometer and shivered. The trucks were out to get him and it would be suicide to stay on the freeway. He'd have to chance the Conoga off-ramp at seventy miles an hour.

Without any warning, Dan pumped his brake lights.

The trucker behind him hit his air brakes, giving Dan just enough room to career off the freeway onto the exit. The guard rails clicked past the fender of the limo, much too close for comfort and Dan hit his brakes for real this time in a desperate attempt to slow the heavy car. By steering out of the resulting skid, he miraculously managed to get around the first tight curve before the hurtling limo squealed out of control and crashed through the guard rail.

George slowed his car as the traffic ahead of them began to brake. "There must be an accident up ahead."

"I can't see anything." Joanna leaned forward. "It must be on the southbound. Yes . . . there's a wrecker and an ambulance."

George nodded. "It doesn't seem to matter which side of the freeway the trouble's on, people still slow down to look."

"Oh, God!" Joanna gasped as they crawled past the Conoga exit. "Take the next exit and turn around! That tow truck was hauling the Empire limo!"

Twenty minutes later, Joanna rushed into the emergency room of North Hollywood Community Hospital while George parked the car. She found Stan sitting in a row of mustard-yellow plastic chairs, looking glum.

"Joanna! What are you—"

"Where's Dan?" Joanna interrupted. Just then Maree came in with two cups of coffee.

"Here is your coffees . . . I think."

"Joanna, meet Maree Dubois. Maree, this is Dan's wife, Joanna."

"I am pleased to acquaint you." Maree extended her hand. "Your husband, he is behind the doctor's curtain. The nurse tells me he has many bruises but she is certain there are no brokens."

"Thank God!" Joanna sank down in a chair. Her face was very white. "I've got to see him right away!"

"I will take you but first you will drink this cup, yes?" Maree handed it to her. "I think it is coffee but there are much buttons on the machine."

Stan picked up his cup and sniffed. "It looks like ink and it smells like ashes. That's hospital coffee, Maree."

Joanna shuddered but she drank the contents of the cup obediently. After a moment, a little color began to come back into her cheeks.

"That is better." Maree pronounced. "Now come and I will show you the room for your husband. It is where the pictures are taken."

"That's X-ray, Maree." Stan called out to correct her as they went through the door.

Joanna was sitting on a stool in the examination room when the nurse came to get her. Dan would have to remain under observation for a few hours to make sure there was no concussion but then he could leave. Joanna pushed open the door to his room and blinked away tears as she saw him. He was propped up in bed with a wide white bandage around his forehead. His left arm was wrapped in a sling.

"Oh, darling! I was so scared!" Joanna hurried across the room to the bed. Then she stood there, uncertain, until he reached for her hand.

"Stan told me everything in the ambulance on the way to the hospital." Dan pulled her down to sit on the bed and put his good arm around her. "I've been such a fool! I know what I've put you through and I wish I could take it all back. I love you, Joanna. I've never stopped loving you. Can you forgive me?"

Joanna gave him a radiant smile through her tears. "Oh yes, darling! But it was my fault too. I should never have been so stubborn about—"

Dan cut off her sentence by kissing her. Many long moments passed before he spoke again.

"I'm going to lose Empire but somehow it doesn't matter as much as I thought it would, now that I've got you back."

"Lose Empire?" Joanna looked up at him in dismay. "Oh no, Dan! We've got to talk to George Askos the minute they let you out of here."

"George?"

Joanna nodded. "He knows who's behind this whole plot to put you out of business. And he can prove it."

"But why would George want to help me? We're competitors."

"I know that, but between the two of you, you can knock out Barton and Santini. Then, while the other two networks are regrouping, you and George can make a killing in the ratings."

Dan shook his head. "I don't understand. How are we going to knock out GRN and NNT?"

"I'll let him tell you." Joanna smiled. "Now I want you to close your eyes and rest like the doctor said . . . right after you give me another kiss."

It was almost six in the morning before the hospital released Dan. A half hour later, they all took the largest booth in the back room of Coco's, an all-night coffee shop, for a strategy session. Joanna knew she'd never been happier as Dan sat next to her, his good arm around her shoulders. A pot of coffee sat on the table and Dan was speaking.

"Okay, George. You told Joanna that you've got the goods on Barton and Jacobi. And you say you can prove that Santini set me up for the union strike?"

"That's right." George nodded. "And Tom was right behind you when Santini's men forced you off the freeway. He taped the whole thing on the minicam."

Dan turned to Joanna. "You're the expert, honey. Do we have enough to prosecute?"

Joanna shook her head. She hated to dash his hopes but she had to be truthful. "I don't think so, Dan. Part of the evidence was obtained illegally and we don't dare use it. The phone taps aren't admissible without a previous court order and neither is the tape recording that George's private detective made of Santini and his brother in Chicago. Even if George takes the stand to testify, it's a weak case."

Dan nodded. "I was afraid of that. We're right back where we started."

"Wrong." Tom shook his head. "Now we know who's behind this whole thing. Our proof's no good in court but it's got to be good somewhere. Santini answers to someone and so does Barton. Maybe we could go to them."

"And beat them at their own game!" Sherrie began to smile. "I see what you mean, Tom. Santini's powerful but there's got to be someone who can knock him down."

"There is." Dan leaned forward. "We'll make a deal with Mario Barone. We'll give him the tape recording and the footage Tom shot of the accident if he calls off the strike and takes care of Santini for us."

George began to smile. "Good idea. Mario Barone won't stick his neck out for someone who almost got his union into trouble. He'll make Santini shut up and take a long vacation."

Maree gasped. "A vacation? Bad mens like this Santini should not take vacations. Instead, he should be locked up in the jar!"

"Locked up in the what?" George was puzzled.

"The jar." Maree looked very serious. "It is an American idiom for prison."

"Locked up in the *jug*, Maree." Joanna corrected her. "I wish we had enough evidence to do that but we don't. In America, a man is innocent until he's proven guilty."

Maree sighed. "America is very different. In France we do things the reverse and it saves much troubles. What will happen to this Santimi, Joanna?"

"He'll jump on a plane and head for some foreign country that doesn't have an extradition treaty with us. Then he'll live in luxury until Barone lets him come back."

"That is not fair!" Maree looked outraged.

"True"—Joanna nodded—"but at least he'll be off our backs."

Maree frowned and Joanna hurried to explain. "That's an expression that means he won't be able to cause any more problems for us, Maree."

"Okay." Dan brought them back to the problem at hand. "Let's decide what to do about Jacobi. Any suggestions?"

"Yes." Stan spoke up. "George has proof that he bribed a S.E.C. official. That's a federal offense, isn't it, Joanna?"

Joanna nodded. "Jacobi will be easy. All we have to do is turn our evidence over to the F.B.I. and they'll handle it."

Dan leaned back and shaded his eyes. It was seven in the morning and the sun was streaming through the plate-glass window. "The only one left is Ralph Barton. We can't actually prove anything, can we, George?"

"No, but I don't think we have to. Barton's board gave him an ultimatum. If he doesn't put you out of business, he'll be replaced. And the minute your union strike is settled and the F.B.I. nabs Jacobi, Ralph's board will know he's failed. Personally, I wouldn't give a plug nickel . . ." George caught Maree's expression and reworded his sentence. "Uh . . . personally, I wouldn't want to bet on Ralph's chances of hanging on to his job."

Dan frowned. "If I stay in business, Barton gets fired. Is that what you're telling me, George?"

"That's right. It's as simple as that."

"Then we're in big trouble. I've got a stockholders meeting in less than three hours to vote on a takeover offer from Amalgamated Electronics. They're going to sell me out, George, and nothing I can say will stop them."

George frowned. "What's Amalgamated offering?"

"Seventy cents on the dollar."

"Robbery!" George thumped his fist on the table. "And if Amalgamated buys, you'll be replaced as president?"

"Naturally. I've been told that Amalgamated is grooming someone for the spot."

George looked thoughtful. "Could you get your stockholders to sell out to you if you offered them seventy-five?"

"Of course. Their only concern is bailing out fast for the highest price they can get."

"Then you'll buy your own stock back. There's no problem."

"Only one, George. I don't have that kind of money and no bank'll loan it to me."

George stood up and grabbed his car keys. "My father taught me that it's not good business to borrow from a bank. They just loan you the money they borrowed from someone else. Why pay them to be a middleman when you can go directly to the source? Come with me."

Dan shrugged. "Why not? I don't have anything to lose. But we'll have to stop by the office to pick up a balance sheet and the current profit and loss statement."

"It's not necessary. Only banks need paperwork. Come on, Dan. We're wasting time."

Dan gave Joanna a quick kiss and got to his feet. "Alice? If I'm late getting back, stall the meeting. I don't care what kind of tricks you have to pull but don't let them vote until I get there!"

18

IT WAS TEN o'clock and the last of Empire Cable's stockholders were taking their seats. Ham Peters, the chairman of the board, glanced at his watch and leaned close to Tom, seated on his left. "Where's Dan?"

"He's running a little late but he'll be here."

"Good. I wanted to tell him I'm renewing those debentures."

"He'll appreciate that, Ham."

"Hell, Tom. What're friends for?" Ham leaned closer and lowered his voice. "Your brother's still got big trouble. I did everything I could to sway the boys but they're going to vote to sell out to Amalgamated."

"He figured that, Ham. That's why he's late. He's working on something."

"It'll take a fucking miracle. I'd help if I could, but I don't know how."

Tom stared hard at Hamilton Peters and made a decision. "There's one thing you can do, Ham. Stall that vote for as long as you can. We're all going to try to buy Dan some time."

Ham nodded. When several stockholders urged him to start the meeting, he picked up the gavel and pounded it on the table.

"Sammy? Pass that jug of coffee over here, will you?"

Ham took his time about pouring himself another cup. Then he looked around the table with a sheepish smile. "Can you boys be patient awhile longer so I can slurp down this coffee? I can't quite figure out why, but I've got a real fuzzy head this morning."

There was a resounding laugh from the men around the table. Most of the Empire stockholders had been at Ham's barbecue.

Tom gave Ham a grateful smile, and Ham took as long to drink his coffee as was humanly possible, but eventually it was gone. He was about to pound his gavel on the table for order when there was a knock at the board-room door.

"Excuse me, gentlemens?" Maree appeared in the doorway, wearing one of her most fashionable outfits. "The meeting has not started yet, no?"

Ham looked surprised but he shook his head.

"No, little lady. Are you a new stockholder?"

"Oh, no! I do not have that much monies." Several of the stockholders laughed appreciatively and Maree gave them a brilliant smile. "I am here to introduce myself to these gentlemens as the newest member of the Empire Cable staff."

There was a buzz of conversation as several men recognized Maree from covers of *Elle* and *Vogue*. Maree took her time, shaking each board member's hand and repeating their names. Finally she had made her way around the table, and the stockholders didn't seem to mind the delay at all.

"I would be pleasured to tell you about the new fashion series Dan Courtney is planning. Will you indulge me?" There were murmurs of general approval and Maree went on to speak before anyone could object. Tom glanced at his watch when she finished. Twenty minutes, even better than he'd expected.

". . . and I invite all of you gentlemens to join me on the set. After this important meeting, of course."

"Why not now?" Larry Tyler, one of the youngest stockholders spoke up. He had been eyeing Maree's low-cut neckline with obvious interest. "The meeting hasn't even started yet."

"*After* the meeting!" Harold Rubin, Larry's father-in-law, objected. "Start this meeting, Ham, or I'll take over as majority stockholder. It's past ten-thirty."

Ham nodded and banged the gavel on the table. He knew Harold was hot to sell out.

"This meeting is called to order. Will the secretary read the minutes of the last meeting?"

Alice opened her mouth to read but she hadn't even finished the first sentence before Harold jumped in. "I move the minutes be approved as they stand."

Ham rolled his eyes heavenward. There would be no stalling with the reading of the minutes if Harold's motion passed.

"Is there a second?"

Larry Tyler winced as his father-in-law poked him, but he opened his mouth obediently. "I second the motion."

Ham banged his gavel again.

"Motion has been made and seconded that the minutes of the previous meeting be approved as they stand. All in favor?"

There was a loud chorus of ayes. Most of Empire's stockholders had other dealings with Harold Rubin and they weren't about to antagonize him.

"Opposed?"

There was silence. Tom didn't even bother to vote.

"The first item on the agenda is a buy-out offer Empire Cable received yesterday from Amalgamated Electronics. Alice? Could you run off copies of this for everyone?"

"Objection!" Harold spoke up again. "Just read us the offer. We don't need copies."

Tom glanced at his watch as Ham began to read the offer as slowly as possible. It was ten-forty. There would be discussion after Ham finished, but that wouldn't take long.

"The floor is open for discussion." Ham waited, his hand on his gavel. Harold Rubin raised his hand. "The chair recognizes Harold Rubin."

Tom sat uncomfortably as Harold briefly summarized Empire's financial status, including the outstanding debentures, the heavy expenses for the expansion, and the negative cash flow. Somehow, Harold had found out about every single problem Empire Cable was facing, including the I.R.S. audits, the S.E.C. probe, and the F.C.C. investigation. He'd probably been coached by Ralph Barton.

". . . and to make matters worse . . ." Tom could see Harold was cranking himself up for a final blow. "Dan Courtney, the president of Empire Cable, didn't even bother to come here today! I can only assume he's too embarrassed to show his face since he assured us all that the union strike would be settled."

Tom leaned over and whispered in Ham's ear. Ham raised his eyebrows in a question and Tom nodded emphatically.

Ham banged his gavel on the table. "Point of clarification, Harold. Do you know for a fact that the TVLU strike against Empire Cable is still in effect?"

"Of course it is!" Harold's face turned red. "We all saw the picket line when we came through the gate."

"The chair has received information that the strike has been settled and demands verification. This meeting is in recess until such verification is provided."

"But, Ham . . ."

Ham banged his gavel on the table again, cutting off Harold in midsentence. "Come on, Harold. We'll check it out together."

It was a good ten minutes before they were back. Ham was smiling as he banged the gavel on the table for order.

"The chair has determined that the strike has been settled. You still have the floor, Harold."

Harold was glowering. "Strike or no strike, the fact remains we have no choice. Empire Cable is financially unhealthy. I intend to sell out to Amalgamated and be thankful that I got something back for my unwise investment."

Tom glanced at his watch. Ten fifty-five. He had to speak up now, before someone called for a vote.

"The chair recognizes Mr. Tom Courtney."

"Objection!" Harold leaped to his feet. "While it is true that Tom Courtney is a stockholder, his shares also bear the names of Mrs. Joanna Courtney and Mr. Dan Courtney. Without their signed agreement giving him permission to speak, Tom Courtney cannot be recognized at this meeting."

"That's ridiculous, Harold!" Ham stepped out of his board chairman's role long enough to glare at him. "Tom's authority to speak has never been questioned before."

"I'm questioning it now. If you check the facts, you'll find I'm well within my rights. A stockholder has no authority to speak without the permission of his co-stockholders!"

Ham rapped his gavel on the table for order. Several men were speaking at once and they stopped. That gave Tom just the opportunity he needed. "Harold could be right, you know." Everyone at the table turned to look in astonishment, but he went on. "I think we should check the bylaws. I'd sure hate to risk a breach of procedure."

Ham banged his gavel again before anyone else could speak. "Point taken, Tom. I guess we'll just have to take a recess while I look it up. Get me a copy of the bylaws, will you, Alice?"

Harold's face turned red. "There's no need to check. I know I'm right!"

Tom patted his pocket containing the paper Joanna and Dan had signed and smiled his best friendly smile. "Maybe you're right, Harold. But I don't think anyone on this board is foolish enough to accept that point without verification. The issues today are critical and a breach of procedure might render any vote we make invalid."

Tom could pick out several voices among the general murmur at the table.

"Good point, Tom!"

"Well taken!"

"Let's look it up before we vote!"

Ham picked up his gavel and banged it on the table again. "Will someone make a motion to check the bylaws to learn Tom Courtney's standing?"

The motion was made and seconded immediately. Ham was smiling as he went on. "Motion was made and seconded to check the bylaws to learn Tom Courtney's standing. All in favor?"

There was a loud chorus of ayes.

"Opposed?"

Harold was the only dissenter and Tom turned to give him a cheerful grin. Harold had been hoisted on his own petard.

Alice came back with a copy of the bylaws and set it down in front of Ham. The leather-bound book was at least an inch thick with tons of legal boilerplate inside. It was the best stall in the world.

19

GEORGE AND DAN had stepped onto the deck of the *Odyssey* an hour ago. Now they were seated in Anatole Askos's wood-paneled office and George was explaining their proposition.

Dan was impressed by the opulent yacht but he was even more fascinated by the Greek tycoon's office. It was a huge room, at least twenty by forty feet, equipped with state-of-the-art communications equipment. Paper rolled noiselessly from a console in the corner giving the latest quotations on major stocks. Dan knew that Anatole Askos had made his fortune in exports but he had his fingers in many pies now. There was even a tie-line to world market prices on numerous commodities.

"Your reasoning is faultless, son." Anatole Askos leaned back in his chair and looked pleased when George had finished his explanation. "Let me repeat it once more, for clarification. Together, you and Mr. Courtney have gathered enough information to get rid of Ben Santini. That is good. And if Empire stays in business, Ralph Barton will lose his spot. Then you, George, will have the opportunity to move up in the ratings. And you, Mr. Courtney, will also rise. Is that correct?"

"That's right, Father."

"But this only works if I loan Mr. Courtney the money to buy out his stockholders. And my guarantee is based on the gain in ratings and subsequent advertising price that Empire Cable will show during the reorganization of GRN and NNT."

Both Dan and George nodded.

"What proof can you give me that Empire will capture more of the market than it has in the past?"

Dan sighed. "None, Mr. Askos. I'm afraid it's pure speculation based on the two-point-seven share we got when we aired our new programming."

"And you have no tangible assets to secure this loan you ask me to make?"

"No assets, Mr. Askos. I rent my facilities and it's only fair to tell you that my credit line is already overextended."

"Then you are a hungry man, Mr. Courtney?"

Dan nodded. "I guess you could say that."

"Excellent!" Anatole Askos smiled. "You have your loan. I have learned never to lend money to a well-fed man. A man who is hungry has much more at stake. Did you bring ouzo, George? We will celebrate with a toast."

George walked over to the bar and took the bottle they had brought from the freezer. He poured three glasses, added the required drops of water to make the liquid cloud, and served it. Anatole Askos raised his glass ceremoniously in the traditional Greek toast.

"*Yassou!*"

Dan and George repeated the toast and drank. Dan's eyes watered as the fiery liquid burned its way down his throat.

Anatole Askos laughed. "We must teach this man to drink like a Greek. And now that the formalities are over, there is only one more question I must ask before I arrange your loan."

Dan held his breath. He hoped Mr. Askos wasn't going to ask him for a written account of his ledgers.

"You boys were in such a hurry, you forgot to tell me how much money you need."

Ham was still struggling through the bylaws when Dan came into the board room, followed by Joanna. She had just finished drawing up the necessary papers.

"Dan, old buddy!" Ham sounded very relieved. "We had a question about the bylaws but it's not important now that both of you are here."

"Here's another item for the agenda, Ham." Dan handed over the papers.

Ham looked down to scan them and a huge smile spread across his face. "You can back this up with hard cash?"

Dan pulled the cashier's check from his pocket and Ham whistled. Then he hurried to the head of the table and banged the gavel down hard.

"Meeting's in session again, boys. Somebody get Sammy away from that window in the hallway. He's been watching those starlets for an hour now, and it's gonna raise his blood pressure."

"Mr. Chairman?" Harold Rubin stood up. "I believe I still have the floor."

"You gave it up when we recessed." Ham pushed Harold down, none too gently.

"But, Mr. Chairman! I demand . . ."

"Shut up, Harold! You've caused enough trouble." Ham used the tone he'd perfected with recalcitrant workers. "Before we vote on the Amalgamated proposal, we have to give equal time to a second proposal. Dan Courtney has just offered to buy our stock, providing he can get a majority."

"He can't do that!" Harold jumped to his feet. "We all know he's broke!"

"That's twice, Harold."

This time Ham's voice was low but Harold was wise

enough to recognize the inherent threat. He sat down quickly and Ham gave him an approving nod. "Dan's just handed me a certified check that proves he has the necessary resources. He's offering seventy-five cents. Any discussion from the floor?"

The room was so silent, Dan could hear his heart beating. His stockholders were stunned. Finally, Harold recovered enough to get out his calculator.

"If there's no discussion, let's put it to the vote. Stand up, Harold. I'm gonna let you make the motion that we go for the highest offer."

It was one in the afternoon and the entire Empire staff was sitting in the executive dining room at the studio. It hadn't taken long for the stockholders to vote to sell out to Dan.

"I feel positively sinful!" Joanna giggled, watching the waiter fill her glass. "Champagne at one in the afternoon on a workday?"

Dan bent over to kiss her. "You deserve it, honey. Putting Pinky Calvert on the air with those thinly disguised rumors was a touch of genius. I'll bet the board at GRN is ditching Barton right now."

Maree nodded. "I will bet a plug nickel on that, also."

While Alice and Sherrie attempted to explain what a plug nickel was to Maree, Joanna took a sip of her champagne. Her back was killing her and she wanted to go home and crawl into bed but she didn't want to put a damper on their celebration by mentioning it. Instead, she studied the menu and listened while everyone else ordered.

"I will have the combination Mexican plate." Maree smiled at the waiter. "It is much hot, yes?"

Joanna's mouth watered. It sounded delicious. She had just decided to have that too, when Tom and Stan both ordered the prime ribs. A good slice of beef, blood-rare would be wonderful. Perhaps she should switch.

"The seafood salad for me." Sherrie ordered next. "Could you put the dressing on the side?"

Joanna almost smacked her lips as she considered shrimp and crab and avocados. Then Dan ordered veal oscar and that struck her fancy until Alice gave her predictable order for the health-food salad with poppy-seed-and-honey dressing. Even though she'd never particularly cared for alfalfa sprouts, Joanna was seriously considering ordering it when the waiter turned to her.

"I'm having trouble making up my mind. Everything sounds so delicious."

"Why don't you have the chicken breast in wine sauce?" Dan suggested. "That's one of your favorites."

"Yes, I'll have that." Joanna agreed quickly. "And could I have a small order of the health-food salad on the side?"

Dan turned to her with a puzzled expression. "I didn't know you liked sprouts and sunflower seeds?"

"I don't. For some reason it just sounds delicious right now."

The executive dining room was known for its fast service. Joanna was just getting ready to taste her scrumptious-looking chicken when her fork clattered to the tabletop.

"Honey! Are you all right?" Dan put his arm around her.

"I . . . I'm fine. I think."

"She's awfully white." Alice stared at her. "Maybe you'd better take her home, Dan."

Sherrie nodded. "That's a good idea. She's been up all night and in her condition . . ."

Joanna glanced at her watch. What she'd thought

251

were hunger pains had now turned into regular occurrences, five minutes apart.

"Come on, honey. I'll get you home right away." Dan got to his feet. "All this is my fault."

"I'm glad you finally realize that!" Joanna gave him a big smile. "But don't take me home, Dan. I think we'd better go straight to the hospital."

Moments later, the waiter began to clear Empire Cable's hastily vacated table. He'd always figured that television people were weird but this proved it. They'd barely tasted their entrées and the second bottle of expensive champagne Mr. Courtney had ordered was untouched. At least he could take it to the kitchen and share it with the other waiters. Mr. Courtney had been in such a rush to leave, he probably hadn't left a tip.

The waiter wore a puzzled expression as he picked up the partially full wineglasses and dumped them. It wasn't that unusual to see one executive rush off after lunch but this was the first time he'd seen a table of seven run out the door like demons were chasing them. He picked up Mr. Courtney's plate and found the tab under it, properly signed. There was a figure written in the space for gratuity, and his eyes widened. A hundred dollars? It had to be a mistake.

It wasn't until he took the tab up to the register that the waiter noticed the note scrawled across the back. It said, *No mistake. Go out and celebrate on me. I've saved the Empire and I'm having a baby!*

It was one-fifteen and Simon Jacobi was in the Rose Room at Leila Pritchard's house. He had arranged to use the room all afternoon and he was sleeping peacefully after an hour in bed with Violet and Keith. He groaned when someone shook his arm. "Not now. Let me sleep."

Simon rolled over but the hand was persistent. After a few moments he opened his eyes, mad as hell. "Dammit! I told you . . ."

Leila Pritchard had wheeled her chair close to the bed and was peering down at him. "There's someone here to see you, Mr. Jacobi."

Simon was so surprised, he didn't even notice that Leila Pritchard had used his real name. He was even more astonished when the two men at her side flashed badges.

"Agents Pelton and Welles of the F.B.I., Mr. Jacobi. Come with us, please. We have some questions."

At the Los Angeles offices of *Daily Variety*, a nationally distributed paper specializing in show business news, a pretty secretary, dressed in jeans and a very tight satin top, whistled loudly as she hung up the phone. Her coworker, a middle-aged woman with frizzy brown hair and an ever-present pencil behind her ear, looked up. "What is it this time, Margie?"

"You're not going to believe it! Remember the flash we just got about Ben Santini's retirement? Well . . . Ralph Barton's just been voted out as president of GRN!"

Doris, the older secretary, laughed. Margie was always joking about hot news flashes. "I won't bite on that one. I know you're kidding."

"No. Honest, Doris, I'm not! I listened on the line just now, when Leroy called in his story. Ralph Barton got the ax five minutes ago. We've never had two network presidents go out in one day before. Askos is the only one left."

"Not quite." Doris shook her head. "Dan Courtney's still head of Empire Cable."

"He'll be gone soon. Didn't you hear? Everybody's investigating him."

"Like who?"

"There's the S.E.C."

"That's been dropped."

"How about the I.R.S.?"

"They just gave Empire Cable a clean bill of health."

"There's another one of those groups with three initials but I can't think of it right now."

"The F.C.C. They dropped their investigation too."

"But how about the stockholders, Doris? They met this morning to vote on a motion to sell Empire."

"Courtney'll hang on to Empire somehow." Doris sounded confident. "Remember what happened in *Mr. Smith Goes to Washington* and *It's a Wonderful Life*? Dan Courtney's the James Stewart of the eighties. And no one in his right mind would cast their vote against Jimmy!"

———— Epilogue

DANIELLE COURTNEY WAS one month old and Dan and Joanna had invited their friends to a party to celebrate. Empire Cable was on its feet once again and it was doing even better than Dan had hoped in the ratings. It looked as if Empire might take over third place but they didn't have to feel sorry for George Askos at USAT. George's network had moved up to second place and was now threatening the faltering GRN.

Dan smiled at Maree and Stan. Maree's fashion show was an unqualified hit and she and Stan were an item.

Munching on a canape, Alice took up a position by the new member of the Courtney family. The guest of honor was in a pink-ribboned bassinet in the center of the family room, just waking up from her nap.

"I think I saw her hand move, Joanna." Alice peered into the bassinet. "Yes, there it goes again. She has your long narrow fingers, Joanna."

"The shade of her hairs is beautiful, no?" Maree pulled Stan closer to the bassinet. "Do you not think Danielle has Dan's hair?"

"Maybe"—Stan nodded—"but definitely Joanna's nose. It's pure Scandinavian."

"I think her nose is a little shorter than Joanna's." Sherrie spoke up. "It's more like Tom's. Don't you think the baby has Tom's nose, Joanna?"

"Not really." Joanna smiled at her brother-in-law. "I think the baby has Tom's *commercial*."

Tom burst into laughter and everyone joined in. Without realizing it, they had been doing a parody of Tom's baby commercial.

There was a soft little gurgle from the bassinet and Danielle opened her eyes. Dan scooped her up and cuddled her while Alice looked on enviously.

"Oh, good! She's awake. Can I hold her Dan . . . please?"

"Well, I'm not sure." Dan gave Alice a teasing grin. "What would your lifeguide say?"

"Oh her!" Alice shrugged. "I'm not seeing her anymore."

"Because of the bad advice she gave you about Joanna and me?"

"Well . . . not exactly." Alice looked very uncomfortable. "My lifeguide is . . . uh . . . unavailable right now."

Stan jumped in. He sensed a good story in the making. "Unavailable, Alice? What exactly does that mean?"

"Oh, you really don't want to know. Come on, Dan, please let me hold Danielle."

"Not until you tell us why your lifeguide is unavailable."

"Well . . . they came and got her last week. She's locked up."

Sherrie looked shocked. "Your lifeguide is in jail?"

"It's not exactly jail." Alice sighed again and caved in. "Well . . . it turned out that my lifeguide wasn't a psychiatrist at all. She was an escapee from a mental hospital in Northern California. And now, while you're all busy laughing at my expense, can I please hold the baby?"